Rachel Wells is a mother, writer and cat lover. She lives in Devon with her family and her pets and believes in the magic of animals. Rachel grew up in Devon but lived in London in her twenties working in marketing and living in a tiny flat with an elderly rescued cat, Albert. After having a child she moved back to Devon and decided to take the plunge and juggle motherhood with writing.

She has always wanted to write and found her voice in her first novel, *Alfie the Doorstep Cat*, which became a *Sunday Times* bestseller, as did her second and third books, *A Cat Called Alfie* and *Alfie & George*. *Alfie the Holiday Cat* is her fourth book.

RACHEL WELLS

ALFIE
The Holiday Cat

avon.

This novel is entirely a work of fiction.
The names, characters and incidents portrayed in it are
the work of the author's imagination. Any resemblance to
actual persons, living or dead, events or localities is
entirely coincidental.

AVON

A division of HarperCollins*Publishers*
1 London Bridge Street
London SE1 9GF
www.harpercollins.co.uk

A Hardback Original 2017
1

A catalogue record for this book is
available from the British Library

ISBN 978-0-00-825332-5

Typeset in Bembo by Palimpsest Book Production Ltd, Falkirk, Stirlingshire

Printed and bound by CPI Group (UK) Ltd, Croydon CR0 4YY

MIX
Paper from
responsible sources
FSC™ C007454

Acknowledgements

I am so grateful to have been able to write a fourth Alfie book - Alfie is such a huge part of my life that I can't imagine it without him, so thanks again to everyone who reads the books, and enjoys Alfie and George's journey. We wouldn't be able to do this without you, so a huge cheer for you all.

On a serious note, we were all devastated by the Grenfell Tower fire and the lives affected by it. A wonderful auction was set up by *Authors for Grenfell Tower* and we offered a chance to bid on your cat being a character in the new book. Thank you again to everyone who put in bids for this wonderful cause, I was so thrilled and wish you could all have won, but my heartfelt thanks and congratulations go to Faye Talbott and her amazingly special cat Lily. Lily makes her debut in this book . . . I hope the fame doesn't go to her paws!

Thanks as always to the wonderful team at my publishers, Avon, and especially my lovely editors Helen Huthwaite and Victoria Oundjian - always a pleasure! Also, a very special thank you to Rhian, for a very supportive and clever copy edit. And of course my agents Diane Banks Associates for all your continued hard work on my and Alfie's behalf!

Again, it has been a joy to bring Alfie to life once again, so a massive thanks to anyone who has made this possible and I hope you enjoy reading Alfie's next adventures as much as I did writing them.

For Tammy

Prologue

I was dreaming about pilchards when I felt a tail tickling my fur. I opened one eye to see George, my kitten, hopping around my bed excitedly. I opened the other eye.

'Wake up, Dad, it's Christmas,' he purred in my ear. I raised my whiskers. It felt far too early to be awake.

'Wake up, everyone!' Summer's voice shouted, shattering any peace and quiet. 'It's *Chrissssmass*.' She had joined George and they were both jumping around, making me feel quite dizzy.

'Meow,' I replied. I saw shadowy darkness poking through the landing window, but I knew no one would be getting back to sleep. When Summer made up her mind, no one stood a chance, and George was turning out to be the same way. The door opened and Claire, wrapping her dressing gown around her, emerged with a sleepy, tousled Jonathan on her heels.

'Goodness, it's only five,' Claire complained.

'But Santa's been, I know he has,' Summer shouted. 'So, it must be Christmas time right now!' She stamped her little foot. George tried to stamp his paw but he hadn't mastered that.

'Where's Toby?' Jonathan said, picking Summer up and

1

giving her a hug. 'Happy Christmas, my little princess.' She snuggled into him.

'Meow,' I replied. He was still in bed. Toby was the only sensible member of the family, it seemed.

It was George's first Christmas ever and Toby's first with us, which meant it was one of the most special Christmases ever in Edgar Road. We had all been full of excitement and expectation, although Summer had been the most excited, with George a close second. Toby had been a little hesitant. Claire and Jonathan said it was because he hadn't had a good life up until now. Toby had been adopted by us. He was five years old and, although Claire and Jonathan hadn't shared details of his life so far, I knew he had been taken away from his parents and had lived in foster care before he came to us. That meant he had had more than one home up until now. Claire said to him, to Summer, and to me and George that we were his forever family and he had a forever home with us now. I understood that better than most. I had had a life before here too, although that did seem so long ago now.

When I first came to live on Edgar Road, I had also had a home before. My home had been happy, full of love, but my old owner died leaving me homeless. Instead of being put in a shelter I had taken matters into my own paws and I'd taken a treacherous journey to Edgar Road where I learnt many things along the way, and then I became, as I am today, a doorstep cat. This means I have more than one home and more than one family to love me and love in return. It so happens that I mainly live with Claire and Jonathan now

– this is my forever home too. But they used to live separately, and I lived with them both until I brought them together and they got married. I also have two other houses I visit and we're all great friends, more like family even. Claire and Jonathan, with Summer and Toby; Polly and Matt who have two children, Henry and Martha; and Tomasz and Franceska, my Polish family who have two sons, Aleksy and little Tomasz. They are my families, and since George came to live with us as a tiny kitten – I adopted him – they are his families too.

But back to Toby; he had obviously had a traumatic beginning in life and although he was loved and safe now, it was a big adjustment for him. When he first came to live with us he cried every night. Claire would go and cuddle him, Jonathan would read him stories and in the end George took to sleeping in his bed, right beside him. He does that every night now. Toby sleeps really well with George beside him, it's the only way he will sleep I think. I worried at first that Summer might mind, she is a madam and she thinks that George is her kitten, but actually she's been very lovely about sharing. Although she tried to demand a goldfish, which is a terrible idea. A fish where two cats live, whoever heard of such a thing?

So Toby and George have a very special bond, which I like to think is down to me a bit. They were both the newest members of the family, which helped to bind them, but of course we all love them both very much. It is clear, though, that George has been instrumental in helping Toby to feel at home – he's a chip off the old block it seems – and now he's settled in it feels as if Toby has always been with us.

Before Christmas, when Claire and Jonathan tried to get him to write to Santa and ask for presents, he was reluctant. In the end Jonathan got a catalogue with lots of toys in it and they went through it together; it was a slow process as Toby didn't want to ask for anything. And this is the heart-breaking part: he told George, when they were in bed one night, that it was because he thought if he asked for things he might get sent away. When George told me this I felt my heart shatter, and trying to convey that to the humans wasn't easy but in the end they seemed to get it. I did have to work quite hard, and George shredded the catalogue in the process, but I think they began to understand.

Jonathan and Claire sat Toby down and told him he was their son now and that nothing he could do would change that. They also showed him Summer's list – although she couldn't yet write, she managed to draw pages of toys she wanted (it was pretty much an entire toyshop), and in the end they managed to coax a letter to Santa out of Toby. Jonathan explained that Santa would bring him a special present but Mummy and Daddy would buy him some as well. This seemed like an alien concept for Toby but he seemed to understand a little.

Claire went to Toby's room, where he was waking up, rubbing sleep from his eyes.

'Is it Christmas?' he asked.

'It is, darling,' Claire replied. 'Now shall we go and see if Santa's been?' She kissed him and engulfed him in a hug.

'But what if he hasn't?' Toby asked.

'I know he has, and do you know how I know that?' Claire asked. Toby shook his head. 'Because I have it on good

4

authority that you were on his good boy list,' she said gently. She was such a good parent, to all of us.

'Really?'

She nodded, then picked him up and carried him downstairs.

Summer had already bounded ahead with Jonathan trying to hold her back as she rushed to open the living room door. George had almost flown down after them and I trotted behind Claire and Toby.

I was trying and failing to restrain George. The run-up to Christmas was exhausting for parents, I had heard that before, but this year I experienced it first-hand. George, as well as being full of excitement, loved the shiny baubles on the Christmas tree. He liked to look at his reflection in them – no idea where he gets his vanity from – trying to use his paw to get them off the tree, and on occasion he succeeded. He had been told off many times by Claire, Jonathan and me for playing with them, and there had been breakages. He also liked to try to hide under the tree, jumping out to surprise us, which had meant that the tree had been relieved of a few of its branches and quite a lot of pine needles. (By the way, having to get the pine needles out of George's fur had been pretty much a festive full-time job.) Jonathan moaned about the mess, Claire complained about the broken baubles, and I had possibly lost enough of my lives with the shock of having him jump out at me on numerous occasions. There was nothing we could do to stop it, however, except keep a close eye on him, keep the living room door closed and Claire had moved his favourite mirrored baubles higher up the tree.

Jonathan stood at the door. We all crowded around.

'I should check that Santa really has been,' he said. He opened the door a crack and George skirted through – honestly there was no keeping him back once he saw the tree. I noticed that Jonathan switched the Christmas tree lights on before fully opening the door and, as they winked and twinkled, we all made our way into the living room where a mountain of presents waited.

Before the children could dive in we all stopped.

'George!' Claire shouted. George, it seemed, had spotted the mirrored baubles straight away and launched himself at the tree, jumping about half way up. It seemed to play out in slow motion as he yowled, having not thought it out, and ended up clinging to some of the branches. He had got his paw tangled in the lights and the bauble that he had been after fell to the floor with a thump, eliciting another cry. As the tree began to lean to the left, it looked as if it might fall. I didn't know what to do as I stared on in horror.

'Yowl!' George shouted.

'Daddy, do something,' Summer cried. Jonathan sprang into action, grabbing the tree and pushing it back upright. Claire batted her way through the piles of presents to secure it again, emerging looking a little dishevelled with pine needles in her hair. And as I meowed anxiously for George to let go, he did, managing to disentangle his paws from the lights and falling into Toby's arms. Toby appeared surprised as he caught him, and then as George nuzzled him to say thank you he smiled.

'Oh George,' he said.

We'd been hearing that a lot since the kitten had become part of the family.

I looked at Jonathan. I was ready for him unleash his anger, using words unsuitable for children or cats, but instead he grinned.

'It wouldn't be Christmas without a near disaster,' he said. 'Nice catch Tobe.' Claire hugged him. Relief flooded me, from my paws to the tips of my whiskers.

'Right, kids, presents.'

Summer instantly dived into her pile. Toby hung back a bit, but Jonathan took his hand.

'Shall we go and see what Santa got you?' he asked. Toby nodded. Shock graced his face, as if he'd never seen anything like it before. He probably hadn't. Neither had George, who was now playing with the wrapping paper that Summer discarded as if it was the best present in the world and as if he hadn't just nearly ruined our beautiful tree. I turned my head to Claire. She had tears in her eyes as she pulled out her phone and took pictures of the children, my kitten and Jonathan by the Christmas tree. I felt emotional as well as I went and rubbed against her legs.

'Oh, Alfie, this is the best Christmas ever,' Claire said as she picked me up. I blinked at her and purred my agreement.

'I really need coffee,' Jonathan said, as the children took a break from present-opening.

'Mummy, Daddy, I love Peppa Pig,' Summer announced as she played with her Peppa Pig playhouse. Toby was playing with a remote control car, exclaiming that it was the best present in the whole world. Jonathan went and put his arm around Claire.

'This is such a whirl, I'm exhausted. But I'll make us coffee and then I'll give you your gift.' He kissed her.

'What about George and Alfie? Can we give them their presents first?' Claire said.

'Oh yes, come on, boys, we've got a special Christmas breakfast for you.'

I really hoped it was pilchards.

As George and I tucked into our pilchards – they were big juicy ones from the fishmonger – we enjoyed a bit of peace and quiet.

'This Christmas business is quite overwhelming,' George said. 'All that stuff everywhere. Although I really like the paper and the boxes.'

'I know, and we are the lucky ones, George, look at us, fish for breakfast, a stocking full of toys and cat treats for us to enjoy later, a loving family and not to mention that after a big lunch we will get some yummy turkey. Honestly, you will see what a lucky kitten you are this Christmas.'

'Of course I'm lucky, I've got you.' George nuzzled me and I grinned. I was the lucky one actually.

I had an idea. 'George, would you like to give me a Christmas present?' I asked.

'Course I would. Dad,' he replied, sweetly.

'Please, no more climbing the Christmas tree.' I had my paws crossed.

'Oh, I can do that. I promise I won't climb it ever again. It was too scary when I thought I might fall down.'

Breakfast was a distant but lovely memory by the time we went outside for a breath of air and also in the hope that we would see Tiger, my cat girlfriend, who George thought of as his mum. It was becoming parents to George that had brought us together, and we were very happy in our roles and our relationship. I had been madly in love once, with a cat called Snowball who lived next door. At that time Tiger and I were only friends. But when Snowball moved away, leaving me heartbroken, Tiger did all she could to help me and when George was adopted as my kitten, she took on a motherly role, which made me see her in a different light. I was an older and, I liked to think, wiser cat by then, and so a relationship with Tiger was what I needed. We had been friends for a long time, she kept my paws firmly on the ground and I made her more adventurous. We complemented each other and being parents to George, who liked to get himself into scrapes, was definitely a bonding experience. He kept us both on our paws.

The cold nipped at us as soon as we entered the garden, but we kept going. The sky was thick and grey, it was early still. I could tell that it was going to be a crisp winter's day, there was a little frost sticking on the grass, which made walking quite uncomfortable, cold and wet. We didn't hang around, as we ran to Tiger's.

We lurked at her back door, under a bush, out of sight of her humans in case they came out. They didn't mind George but they didn't like me being around. I couldn't think why; most people seemed to think I was quite a charming cat. Before long I heard the clang of the cat flap and Tiger emerged.

'Tiger mum!' George bounded up to her and they nose-kissed. It always melted my heart to see the love between them, I was a softy when it came to those I loved, humans and cats alike.

'Happy Christmas,' I said, trying to keep my emotions in check.

'To you both too,' Tiger replied. 'Gosh, you are early though, I had barely woken up. Anyway, George, how is your first Christmas so far?' she asked with a swish of her tail.

'Well, Santa brought me wrapping paper and we got pilchards for breakfast so so far it's the best day ever!' George's enthusiasm was so refreshing; I know it taught me a lot. I loved the way that he made me see things through his eyes, as if I was seeing them for the first time. That was the joy of kittens and children if you paid enough attention to them.

'And he jumped on the Christmas tree and nearly sent it flying,' I added. George conveniently left that out.

'Oh, George,' Tiger said, but she didn't sound cross, she was amused. I was the disciplinarian in this parenting duo.

'How is your day so far, Tiger?' I asked.

'It's barely started! But you know, my family have a very quiet Christmas. We haven't exchanged gifts yet, although I get one of those cat stockings every year so, surprise! Thankfully they are cooking a proper Christmas dinner but really Christmas is for the kids, isn't it?' She nuzzled George.

'It is, you should see Toby, he's so happy now. I think he was so scared by the whole thing, I don't think he'd had very good Christmases before, which is really upsetting, but he's playing with his toys and he's having a lovely time now.'

George was playing with a leaf which was wet as the frost had melted and drops kept falling onto his head. We laughed as he tried to brush the water away, indignantly, with his paws.

'And Summer?'

10

'Summer is Summer. She's obsessed with this pig called Peppa, and she's got toys, games and all sorts. She's still our little ray of sunshine. They're all happy, which makes me happy.' I snuggled into Tiger and grinned. Life was good right now, and Christmas was just the icing on the (fish) cake. I was always conscious of the fact that me and all my families had been through tough and challenging times, so when things were good I had learnt to appreciate them. I was an optimistic cat but even I knew the good times didn't always last. In fact they rarely did.

'Well, long may it last,' Tiger said, echoing my thoughts. 'Are you seeing your other families today?' I swished my tail; I had told Tiger, but she had a terrible memory.

I had three families altogether. Claire and Jonathan's was my main home, but also on Edgar Road lived Polly and Matt, Henry and Martha. Franceska, big Tomasz, Aleksy and little Tomasz (who now insisted on being called Tommy) lived a few streets away but I had met them on Edgar Road when I first moved here and they moved from Poland. Aleksy, being the oldest of the children, was my first child friend – he and I are still best friends actually.

'Well Polly and Matt have gone to Manchester to spend Christmas with their parents and Tomasz and Franceska have gone to Poland. It's very exciting for them; their first Christmas back there since they moved to England. I miss them but they'll all be back before New Year. We're all going to be together on New Year's Eve in fact.'

'Does that mean you get turkey again?' Tiger's eyes were wide with envy.

'I hope so!' I grinned. I hadn't thought of that.

'And have you heard from Tasha?'

'We Skyped her yesterday.' I was a cat of the computer age after all. Although it was Claire who'd actually called her on the computer, I'd sat on her lap so I could see her and Elijah.

Tasha was Claire's best friend and one of mine. Her son Elijah was almost the same age as Summer. She had gone through a bad break-up with Elijah's dad and lived on Edgar Road for a while, becoming another family for us. Then Claire did something called match-making with a friend of Jonathan's called Max, which worked out a bit too well as she moved to somewhere called Dubai with him. He got a very good job there and she said she and Elijah needed a fresh start. I was happy for her, but sad for me. We missed them very much – Claire and me especially – so every week she calls them on the computer and we chat. They are all very happy, so although I miss them, I am pleased at the same time.

Saying goodbye is a fact of life. I have had to do so more than your average cat, so I should know. It doesn't get any easier but you learn to accept that it's necessary sometimes, I guess. It always hurts but there is nothing to be done. Life is like that, it moves all the time, it rarely stands still and so we have to move along with it. I am trying to teach George that, but it's not an easy lesson to learn.

'Right, well I better get this little one inside. Fancy a stroll later?' I asked Tiger as I tried to get George's attention. He was chasing his tail and totally ignoring me.

'Yes, call round after lunch and we can go and see if anyone else is hanging out.'

'You're on.' I nuzzled her goodbye and finally managed to get George to stand still long enough to tell him we were going home.

I was exhausted as I lay curled up on the armchair, resting. Claire and Jonathan were clearing up, and then I expected they would snuggle up on the sofa to watch a film or something. The children were in bed, exhausted after a day when their excitement levels knew no bounds and George was the same. He was sleeping with Toby, of course. I checked on them earlier and he was lying next to Toby on the pillow – they looked so cute together, I felt choked with emotion again. I looked in on Summer who was clutching one of her new toys to her as she slept. She looked angelic.

I was so full of lovely food, so I felt sleepy too. This really had been the best Christmas I'd ever had. I gave a thought for all of those I loved in my life: Margaret my first owner, Agnes my sister cat, all my cat friends, Snowball of course, and I also gave thanks for all I had now. I was the luckiest cat in London if not the world.

'So, what's this last surprise?' I heard Jonathan ask. I opened one eye and saw that he and Claire had entered the room. Intrigued, I woke up properly, stretched out and went to join them on the sofa.

'Here,' Claire said, handing him a photograph. I peered at it over his shoulder. It was a picture of a house, a shabby-looking house. It was quite big though, I thought as I looked at the windows. In front of a large wooden front door stretched a lawn, which was overgrown, and the house was cream with peeling paint.

'Please don't tell me you've bought a house?' Jonathan said, holding the picture, blinking at it in confusion.

'No, of course not. I've been desperate to tell you but I got the idea that today, Christmas Day, would be the best time to surprise you.'

'Surprise me with what exactly?' Jonathan was suspicious but then I couldn't blame him. Claire tended to spring things on him. And when he objected she would normally wear him down. It was the same with the adoption. She wanted to adopt so badly but Jonathan was reluctant, but she persuaded him, and of course he's delighted she did as he loves having Toby, but you get the idea.

'So you know we went to the funeral of my Great Aunt Claire, the woman I'm named after?'

'Yes, Claire, that was about three months ago.'

'I know, but it takes time, you know probate, but recently her estate was sorted out and it turns out she left me this cottage in Devon.'

'She left that to you? A house?' Jonathan looked again at the photo.

'I had no idea she still owned it.' Claire's eyes gleamed with excitement. 'You see we used to go there when I was a child for holidays but when Aunt Claire got dementia she went into a home, and I assumed that the house had been sold. But no, it was there, empty all this time. She probably forgot she owned it.'

'How can someone forget they own a house?' Jonathan frowned. I guess it was a big thing to forget.

'Well she did have dementia remember, and her accountant

14

took over her affairs, or whatever you call them . . . Anyway Dad told me that she wanted me to have the house because I loved it so much when I was young. It's called Seabreeze Cottage and it's right opposite the beach.' Claire had a wistful look. 'I remember the best holidays there as a child, spending days on the beach, playing on that lawn, eating jam sandwiches in the big old kitchen . . .'

'So why didn't you tell me?' Jonathan narrowed his eyes.

'Jon, we've been given a house, it doesn't happen every day!' Claire pushed and I knew there was a but.

'But?' he echoed my thoughts.

'OK, so the reason I didn't tell you was that we don't know what state it is in. Mum and Dad went down there for me and they said it's been neglected and is in need of a bit of work. They took these photos.'

'So how much work are we talking?' Jonathan flicked through the photos.

'We don't know exactly yet. When all the paperwork is done, I can get quotes, we can even go there, but at the moment I'm not sure if I'm honest.' She chewed her lip as she did when she was nervous. I went and sat on her lap.

'And what do you want to do?' he asked.

'Well, obviously it depends on the cost and everything, but ideally I want to keep it. I just felt as if I'd been taken back to my wonderful holidays as a child and I want that for Summer and Toby, more than anything. Imagine, Jon, week-ends away, summer holidays by the sea, it would be wonderful for us all.'

'Darling,' Jonathan turned to his wife, 'I know this cottage means a lot to you and it would be lovely for us to have a house by the sea but you know how feasible it is. You're not working at the moment and yes I have a good job but with the kids' education, and everything . . . My guess is that the kind of money we probably need to put into this cottage might be a step too far for us right now.'

'I know and I thought you'd say that. I just dreamt of my children having holidays like I did as a child.' She looked wistful. Jonathan softened and put his arm around her.

'If there was any way . . . Listen, honey, has it been valued?' I saw tears in Claire's eyes. Christmas wasn't ending quite as planned after all.

'Jonathan, I'm not sure I could bring myself to sell it. It feels like selling my childhood.' Claire was nothing if not dramatic. I think she got it from me . . . or vice versa.

'Well, listen, let's have a think, find out what exactly is involved, but you know unless we get a large mortgage, one which would make me feel very uncomfortable, I don't know how we can do it.'

'Oh, we'll find a way. I'm sure.' Claire didn't appear as confident as she sounded but as they settled down to watch a film I could almost see her mind whirring. I looked at the picture again. A cottage by the sea. I had been to the seaside once, it hadn't exactly gone according to plan but I did have a lovely time. I could picture us all, sitting on the lawn, George chasing butterflies, Toby and Summer playing, Claire lounging in a deckchair with a book, and Jonathan lying on a picnic blanket. It was like a perfect idea, and one which suddenly I wanted for us more than anything. I looked at Claire, who still seemed to be deep in thought, as was Jonathan, and I said a silent prayer that they would find a way to make this work.

After all I quite fancied being Alfie the holiday cat.

Chapter One

'I'm going to miss you all,' Jonathan said, in a moment of tenderness as he kissed Claire.

'We'll miss you, but be honest, you'll love the peace and quiet, and then when you come down for the weekends you'll be flavour of the month with the kids.'

'And with my wife?'

'Of course.' She smiled and snuggled into him. I purred from my place on the armchair. It was summer now and a lot had changed since Christmas. An awful lot.

Claire had got her way. Sort of. As if there had been any doubt. She had been very clever about it, though even I, cat of many successful plans, was impressed with this one.

Seabreeze Cottage was going to be our holiday home for now. And now the summer holidays were upon us, we were all decamping to Lynstow and Seabreeze Cottage for the school break. And I mean *all*. It was beyond exciting.

After Christmas, unbeknown to Jonathan, Claire had persuaded her parents to take a friend of theirs to Seabreeze, and do what they called a survey. It turned out that they needed to do some work on the roof, but otherwise the house was structurally sound. However, the interior needed a lot doing to it, new heating and hot water system, and all sorts of modernisation. There was also a big attic which could be converted, so Claire had got together a rough idea of how much the work would cost and then had presented this to Jonathan, who just couldn't see how they could afford it unless he sold some vital organs, whatever that meant.

Claire was despondent but over drinks just after New Year, the women from my other families, Polly and Franceska, had a brainwave. Or actually Polly did.

'Hey, Claire, this sounds fantastic. What's the village called again?'

'Lynstow in North Devon. It's on the estuary, perfect for sailing, windsurfing or paddleboarding. The village itself has three pubs, a lovely village shop and a café. It's changed a lot since I was last there, which was over twenty years ago, but Mum and Dad said it was still charming.' Claire sounded wistful again, I knew she was thinking of the childhood summers she had spent in Lynstow and I knew how much she wanted it for her children. To be honest, the way she spoke about it, I was desperate to go there too. And I'm a cat, who certainly wouldn't be doing any sailing or anything to do with water, actually. But I am a romantic and I was definitely caught up in the romance of it all.

Polly asked to see the details, and Claire pulled out her folder with the pictures and the details from the builder in it – she was nothing if not organised. Polly sipped her wine and looked over it, then passed it to Franceska.

'It is so pretty, my boys would love it here,' Franceska said.

'I agree,' Polly said. I could almost see her thoughts racing. 'And I can see the potential. This could be such a beautiful house with a bit of love. And of course I could manage this project easily.'

'That's what I keep saying to Jonathan. If we did the work it would be worth so much more money, not that I want to sell it ever. As I said, I would love it for Toby and Sum, and you guys could join us for holidays – it's got five bedrooms at the moment, but the attic is huge and ripe for conversion. There's only one bathroom but the builder said that it would be easy to put in one en suite and one in the attic, and three bathrooms would be plenty. I mean it's a big house. When I was little I thought it was enormous, because it was so much bigger than Mum and Dad's house. I thought it was the biggest house ever.'

I rubbed against Claire, I didn't want her to be sad, because I knew how much she wanted this. But I also understood Jonathan. They couldn't just magic up money, that was a human problem I had learnt about in my life. Thankfully not something us cats needed to concern ourselves with.

The women lapsed into silence as they all sipped wine and Franceska nibbled an olive.

'This might sound crazy but here's an idea,' Polly started. Claire looked at her hopefully. 'Of course we all live in London, and we all want our children to see there are beaches and countryside out there, but it's expensive going away, even in the UK. We went to the Lake District last holidays, and the cottage we rented cost more than a five-star hotel in Spain.'

'I agree, Polly, but I don't understand what your point is?' Franceska interjected.

'Oh yeah, sorry it's the wine. So here's my mad idea. How about we pool our resources? I can help re-design the place as you know and I am also used to dealing with contractors. As I'm freelance now I can devote time to it and Franceska, your restaurants are doing really well, so I thought, mad I know, but if we all chip in maybe we can restore Seabreeze and use it for our holidays. Like a sort of joint holiday home.'

I was amazed when I heard this. A holiday cottage for us all – I assumed she was including me and George of course – and I meowed loudly to show I for one thought it a very good idea.

'Alfie approves,' Claire laughed. 'And now I think of it, imagine if our families shared the cottage?'

'But it is your cottage, Claire, and there is an issue of ownership if we get involved, no?' Franceska said sensibly.

Oh, I hadn't thought about that. After all I'm a cat, not a solicitor.

'I have thought of that,' Polly said. She seemed to have done a lot of thinking in a very short space of time. 'We get it valued now, then whatever we each put in gives us a share but not the main share, which stays with Claire. I was thinking that one day it will go to her children and, well, in our ideal world our children will carry on like we are, the best of friends, but anyway we can get it all done properly and above board. I know it's unorthodox but it could work, we could make it work. And of course it would have to be done legally, that would be the only way the men would agree to it.'

'Ah the men.' Claire looked a bit perplexed.

'Firstly, in my wildest dreams I didn't think we would have a holiday house.' Franceska suddenly sprung to life. 'I didn't think we would have all this but for the boys it will be so amazing. It would be like a timeshare for us, we could all use it together or at other times and if we need to make money we could always rent it out. We need to show it to the men as a business proposition. An investment for all of us and our futures and our children's futures. Right, how much money are we talking?' Franceska was now caught up with enthusiasm.

And just like that my three favourite women formulated a plan.

I felt proud of them, it was as if they had learnt their planning skills from me – and OK, some of my plans do go a little awry but they always end up successful. Anyway, they weren't going to leave anything to chance so they cooked a fantastic dinner – Franceska was the best cook so she took charge of food. The children were all asleep; they were having a sleepover here which I was excited about, as was George, who was asleep with Toby and Henry, who was sharing his room. Aleksy wasn't asleep; I had been to see him and he was playing on a computer thingy, but that was our secret. So, after the food and quite a lot of beer and wine, the women swooped in with what they called their presentation, which Claire was in charge of. It was funny how formidable they all looked, standing there in a row, with the men almost quaking with fear. As well they should – they didn't stand a chance.

'But you mean we would all own the house?' Jonathan scratched his head as they finished talking.

'Yes, but obviously to different degrees. The input from us would give us a share but a minor one, and we'd do it all legally. So for example if we wanted to sell or get our money out we couldn't just do that,' Polly expanded on the legal side, which I couldn't concentrate on; I was eyeing up the left-overs and wondering how long I'd have to wait before they would remember to give me some.

'So we all go there for holidays?' Tomasz asked, his eyes narrowed.

'We could do! Imagine, Tomasz, the children get to see the sea and the countryside when they're not at school. And we thought that we could all go this summer, us women and the kids, and then when you could get time off work you join us, that way we can supervise the work and the kids will love it, it'll be an adventure.'

'But hang on, it sounds as if the house is going to be a building site this summer, will that be safe for the children?' Matt asked.

'It'll be safe but obviously a bit chaotic,' Polly said. 'Listen, I'll manage the restoration and I'll do it so there'll be minimal disruption. The children will be out all day when the builders are in, there's so much to do: the beach, trips to the countryside, the older ones can learn to surf or paddleboard. Honestly, I'll make sure the house is safe.' Polly gave Matt's shoulder a squeeze.

'And if you all agree, we can get essential work done before the summer,' Claire chipped in.

'You've thought this all through, haven't you?' Matt said, shaking his head.

'If you mean have we anticipated all of your objections, then yes,' Polly replied with a wry smile.

'Look, between the three of us we can afford to get the cottage looking amazing again,' Claire started. 'We've done the figures and, worst-case scenario, we will have added value and can sell it for a profit for everyone. Best-case scenario, we enjoy it with our families, together at times, on our own at others, but we will have a holiday home and the children will get to enjoy beach life the way I did growing up.'

'But it was valued for more than I expected,' Jonathan said. 'So I still think the sensible option is to sell.'

'This way, though, Jonathan, we can do it up and sell it for even more if we decide to,' Polly persisted. 'But we all think that this summer, when we get the work done, we'll all fall in love with it and won't want to let it go.'

'Just look at the figures, I promise they make sense.' The men all studied the spreadsheet that Claire thrust at them.

'But are you sure it's habitable for the children?' Matt reiterated, looking worried. And for cats, I wondered.

'Well, not exactly, but the summer holidays aren't for two months so we thought we could all take it in turns to go down before, just the adults, and each time we could do what is needed to make it habitable. We can buy beds, appliances, make sure the water and heating works, we'll get it ready for the summer and also get some alone time.' Polly raised her eyebrows at her husband.

He shrugged, defeated. Honestly, these women had thought of everything and my whiskers stood up with pride.

'We can do this!' Claire added with a smile.

'You make it sound like a fantastic idea,' Tomasz said. 'And now I take more time from work I can come and join you more I guess.' He looked at the other men for reassurance.

'I can arrange to work from home on a Friday and come down for weekends,' Matt said.

'Hold on, how do we even get there?' Jonathan asked.

'Ah, well we'll be taking the cars but there's also the trains. The station is only a forty-minute drive away, direct from London, so really there's no problem.'

'Have I been stitched up again?' Jonathan asked. I jumped onto his lap and yelped. Of course he had. Everyone laughed.

'Well the house will be quiet, no Claire, no children, just me, Alfie and George this summer.' I suddenly looked up.

'Oh no, darling, Alfie and George will be coming with us. It's their holiday cottage too.'

I purred with delight. Yay! We were going on holiday.

'Claire, you do know it's strange the way you take Alfie and now George everywhere with you, as if they were dogs?'

I yelped. How dare he compare me to a dog?

'They're part of the family and, anyway, Alfie came on holiday with us before, didn't he?'

I put my head down, as a bolt of sadness hit me. We went on holiday with Snowball, my then girlfriend, before her family moved her away, leaving my heart broken. It was all OK now but I still remember my last holiday with a pang. Actually, perhaps this was going to give me new holiday memories, which would mean the old ones would properly fade away. It was about time, after all.

'Well yes, but you know, George hasn't been away from here before,' Tomasz pointed out.

'Yes but Alfie will take care of him and anyway how will Toby sleep without George next to him,' Claire said, indicating any debate was over.

As I finally got my left-overs they discussed the finer details. Everyone, even Jonathan, seemed a little swept away with excitement now. I certainly was, my fur was tingling with the thought of the adventures that awaited us. We were all going to decamp to Seabreeze Cottage for the summer, and we would all spend a lovely, perfect, English summer by the sea. Yes the men had been ambushed, but really it was all for the best.

'I'm not sure Seabreeze or Lynstow know what's going to be hitting them,' Matt said.

'Edgar Road decamps to Devon,' Polly laughed.

'And you know, it will be so great for the children,' Franceska reiterated.

'Meow!' I clambered up her, nudging her with my nose.

'And the cats of course,' Claire finished.

Chapter
Two

Chapter Two

'As you're all off tomorrow, today I'm going to take you and the kids out for lunch and then I thought we'd go to the dinosaur museum,' Jonathan announced proudly.

'Yay!' Toby said.

'Will Peppa Pig be there?' Summer asked.

'Can I go too?' George asked me. I told him no.

'I'm not sure Peppa will be there but there will be lots of dinosaurs to see, darling,' Jonathan said.

'Sounds good to me. I'm nearly all organised anyway.' Claire grinned. Truth be told she had been pretty much packed for weeks. Claire was nothing if not well organised. She had made lists and more lists and, well, possibly even more lists before we headed off to Devon for the summer. I was glad at times like this that I was a cat. All I had to do was to make sure that George and I were clean and ready to go.

As everyone left, I ate some biscuits, had a drink of water and then cleaned myself.

'George, you might want to give yourself a quick groom,' I suggested.

'Why, Dad?'

'Because we are going out to enjoy our last day. With the rest of the neighbourhood cats,' I told him.

'Goody!' He started licking his fur. We had a group of friendly cats on Edgar Road. As well as Tiger, there were Rocky, Elvis and Nellie who all lived on our street and we often hung out together. They were a good bunch who always helped whenever we were in trouble – like last year when George was catnapped by a woman who snatched quite a few cats in the area and they all rallied to help us. Other cats had come and gone but we were the core Edgar Road cat gang and they were all incredibly important to me.

While Jonathan had a day planned for the rest of the family, Tiger had planned something for George and I. She told me because she didn't trust surprises; they normally went wrong. I couldn't argue with her, they did tend to, in our world anyway. She told me to bring George to the recreational grass at the end of our road. It was a small patch, tucked away from the street and where us cats converged regularly without being bothered by humans. Or dogs for that matter.

We made our way to the end of the street and found all our Edgar Road cat friends waiting for us. It was like a party. A leaving party, I guessed.

'You're all here,' George exclaimed excitedly, bounding from cat to cat.

'Of course we are,' Rocky said, gruffly.

'We wouldn't miss a party,' Nellie added, nestling into George. If Tiger was George's mum then Nellie was like his favourite aunt.

'Although I nearly didn't make it, I was eating one minute, then the next I fell asleep. Must be old age.' Elvis wasn't a young tom, and I could sympathise with him. Sometimes I found myself drifting off to sleep these days. I wasn't as young as George, but then I wasn't ready for old age yet – there were lives in this old cat yet!

'Well I'm glad you did make it,' I said warmly. Tiger looked very pleased with herself.

'We have been friends for a long time now,' she said. 'Since Alfie moved here really, and it's just amazing to see that we've all remained friends.' It was true we had.

'It'll be strange without you guys this summer,' Elvis mused.

Just then there was a rustle in the bushes and my friend Dustbin, who lived with Franceska and Tomasz, or more accurately in their yard, appeared. He was a feral cat who worked for the restaurant in return for food, a job which suited him perfectly. When I first met him I was a little intimidated by this wild cat, but he had a heart of gold.

'Wow, Dustbin, you've come!' I was touched. He lived a few streets away and was always busy keeping the rodents under control. Not my kettle of fish, or rats more accurately, but Dustbin loved his work.

'Wouldn't miss it, Alfie,' said Dustbin. 'Seeing you and the boy off. It's going to be strange not having you popping round.'

George and I stayed with Franceska's family quite often, which meant we got to spend time with Dustbin. He was a truly good friend.

'It won't be the same without the lad,' Rocky said, sounding emotional.

'Um, you do know we're going away for a few weeks, not forever,' I said, wondering why everyone was so emotional.

'We know that,' Nellie said. 'But you know how much we see of each other. It will be strange not to see George. And you too, Alfie,' she added as an afterthought. Despite the fact that some said I was quite a vain cat, I was used to playing second fiddle to George.

'We'll be back here before you know it, and then we can tell you all about our summer.' I tried to lift everyone's spirits.

'Yes, we're going to the seaside,' George explained.

'I know and not many cats are lucky enough to go to the seaside,' Rocky said.

'I am so very lucky,' George said. 'But now I want to play hide and seek.' He ran off before anyone could answer. The rest of us cats looked at each other, indulgently. There were only two bushes but we always had to pretend it took us ages to find him. That was what you did with kittens.

We spent a lovely afternoon, seeking with George, playing with leaves and sunbathing. When it was time to go, I knew I would miss each and every one of my friends, but then I also knew we were going to have such a great time on holiday that time would fly by. We would be back before we all knew it.

I still felt a bit emotional as I sat on my back step with Tiger that evening. George had gone to bed with Toby, and Tiger and I were going to say our last goodbye. According to Claire, we were going to be gone for about six weeks. I didn't know exactly how long that was but it sounded like a fair amount of time. I had been away before but not for this long and we were leaving the others behind. I kind of understood now that being left was the hard part, although of course we were coming back.

'Don't you go going off with any of those seaside cats,' Tiger said, not meeting my eyes.

'Don't be silly,' I replied. 'I have all I need back here. Yes, we are going to have a lovely holiday but you know my job will be looking after George. Goodness knows what mischief he could get up to, not to mention the humans.'

'Of course. I know it's supposed to be a holiday but I've got a feeling you'll have your paws full. Look after our kitten, won't you?' her voice urgent.

'Oh, Tiger, I know you'll miss him, but I promise I won't let him out of my sight.' Just thinking about that made me feel tired. Hopefully it would be a bit relaxing as well. What was I thinking? Looking after George was the least relaxing thing ever. But I wouldn't change it for the world.

'I know you'll take care of him, but take care of yourself too.'

'I'll miss you, Tiger, and I will really look forward to seeing you when we get back.' I wasn't sure how to express myself, but I was trying.

'Good, and make sure you do miss me. Alfie, I love you more than all the cat food in the world.'

'And I love you more than pilchards.' I nuzzled into her neck. We stayed there for what seemed like ages in comfortable silence. That was what I liked about my relationship with Tiger; we knew each other so well, nothing needed saying, and that was how I liked it.

A shadow loomed over us and I looked up to see Salmon. He used to be my nemesis, but since George went missing in the summer we had called a truce. It had been the worst time of my life not knowing where my kitten was and all our cat friends had rallied to help, as had Salmon. He was very fond of George, if not so much me.

'Salmon,' I said. Tiger scowled; she still wasn't his biggest fan. To be honest he was a bit of a busybody, like his owners who ran the neighbourhood watch and lived opposite us. They made everything that was going on in Edgar Road their business.

'I was going to say goodbye to the lad but I'm guessing he's in bed?' he said, sounding gruff. He didn't really know how to be friendly, but it wasn't his fault.

'He is, Salmon,' I said, kindly. 'But I'll tell him you came by. Are you alright?'

'Yes, just so you know I'll look after things while you're away. I mean, you know, keep an eye on things.'

'What things?' Tiger asked.

'I'll make sure everything is OK, Alfie,' Salmon said. He raised his tail. 'My owners are going to see yours to say the same. Anyway, have a good trip and hope the lad enjoys himself.'

I raised my whiskers at him and then he left.

'You could be friendlier,' I said to Tiger.

'And you could be less so,' Tiger retorted. 'Anyway, I better get back, supper will be waiting. Bye, Alfie.'

She sounded sad but I didn't prolong the farewell, I understood how she felt, and I knew that by snapping at me, it would make it easier for her. I hated goodbyes too, even temporary ones.

When I let myself back in through the cat flap, Claire and Jonathan were on the sofa together. The doorbell interrupted them. I went to wait by the door, having been warned that it was Vic and Heather Goodwin, Salmon's owners.

'Oh God, we don't even get five minutes' peace,' Jonathan muttered as he opened the door.

Before he could say anything, Vic and Heather were inside the house, a skill they seemed to have. Without being asked they made their way to the living room.

'Well this is a surprise,' Claire said, standing up. I went to join her, as did Jonathan. Vic and Heather always made us feel guilty for some reason, as if we had done something wrong. That was always how it was with them. And Claire and Jonathan didn't invite them to sit down – they weren't being rude but they'd done that once before and Vic and Heather had stayed for hours; we all thought they were never going to leave and Jonathan said if they'd stayed any longer they would have claimed squatters' rights! It was always better not to be too welcoming – we'd learnt the hard way.

'Well, dear,' Heather said. They were both wearing matching blue shirts today; they were always coordinated. 'We wanted to reassure you that, although you are going away, your house is in safe hands.' She grinned, slightly menacingly, I thought.

'Well yes, it's in my hands,' Jonathan replied, tetchily.

'Oh we know,' Vic laughed, 'that you'll be here some of the time, but with your big important job and then when you are going to stay with the family . . . Where is it you're going again?'

'North Devon,' Claire stuttered, terrified; I wondered if they were going to ask for the address.

'Perhaps we should have the information – you know, for emergencies,' Heather said.

'What emergencies? I am going to be here most of the time, you know,' Jonathan reiterated.

'I'll give you my mobile number,' Claire said, reluctantly. 'Just for emergencies and of course Jonathan and I are very grateful that you'll be keeping an eye on the house while we're away, thank you.'

'Um, yes, but when I'm here, you'll know because there will be lights on, so you don't need to worry,' Jonathan said. He grimaced. I could imagine that was because Vic and Heather's binoculars would be trained on the house from across the road. Not that he had anything to hide, but I had learnt through the years that humans liked privacy rather than being stared at by neighbours.

'Of course, we just want to make sure that your house is safe when it's empty. Imagine if you came back from your holiday and found it burgled.'

'It's unlikely,' Jonathan said. We had alarms on the house, it was very safe apparently.

'It's more than unlikely with us on the case, you see. Now we really ought to get moving, we need to go and see Matt and Polly to give them the same reassurance.' Vic smiled. 'Oh but, Claire, if you could just scribble your number down?' he added.

Once Claire had given them her number, and they left, Jonathan turned to her.

'They'll be calling you whenever anything, I mean anything, happens,' he teased.

'Well at least I know you'll behave yourself. Being watched all the time.' Claire giggled, I purred.

'I hadn't thought of that, although of course I'll behave myself. I'm looking forward to some peace and quiet, but I will miss you all,' he quickly added.

I knew what he meant. Our house could be chaos and sometimes Jonathan said going to work was his way of relaxing. I would miss him though, I was used to him always being there and he had very good taste in cat food and cashmere jumpers, which I would 'accidentally' use to sleep on.

'Shall we warn Matt and Polly?' Claire asked.

'No, why let them escape the fun of the Goodwins? I think we should have a last drink and then go to bed. You've got a long drive tomorrow.'

'I'm so excited to see the cottage again. It'll be beautiful when we've finished.'

'I know, darling.' Jonathan put his arm around her. 'It could be amazing but please, let's just all keep our heads out of the clouds. You, Polly and Franceska are all in love with the idea of having this holiday cottage – and I do understand – but if it gets too expensive . . . And of course the school holiday is just under six weeks, we don't know how much you'll be able to get done.'

'I know, darling, but it won't. It's all going to be perfect, I just know it is. Our families will have this wonderful second home and our holidays will be so good for the kids, it's just like a dream come true.' Claire had that faraway look in her eyes, which meant she was already at Seabreeze Cottage. 'Great Aunt Claire would love that we've filled it with children and cats too.'

When Claire made up her mind, it was impossible to argue, and Jonathan seemed to agree with me as, shaking his head, he went to put the kettle on.

Chapter
Three

Car journeys are not on my list of favourite things. Being hustled into a pet carrier usually heralds destinations you certainly don't want to visit – like the vet. But to go on holiday, it was necessary. Claire had got a carrier that was big enough for both of us, plus some snacks if we got hungry on the way. George was so excited, he wouldn't keep still, which made the journey a little bit annoying as he kept falling into me. I was battered and bruised in no time.

'George, just settle down,' I chastised, not that it did me any good.

We left London in the first week of the school holidays. We were in Claire's car with Toby and Summer, driving in convoy with Polly and her children, and Franceska and hers. All three cars were packed up with our belongings too. Jonathan had huffed and puffed a lot when Claire barked instructions at him as he squashed everything in the boot. George and I were on the front seat next to Claire but we were too low down to see anything from the carrier. I thought I would try to sleep as much as I could, it seemed a good opportunity to rest, but George had other ideas.

'Are we nearly there yet?' he asked for the millionth time.

'Yes,' I said, with no idea if that was true but I'd heard Claire saying the same to Summer and Toby, so I guessed it was an appropriate parental response.

'Tell me about the seaside?' George asked as he finally sat down.

'Well I only went there once and that was a different seaside I think. But there were big birds, seagulls, which you need to watch out for as they're not very friendly. And of course we keep away from the water at all costs.' As I repeatedly warned George about the perils of the seaside that I knew about, I hoped there weren't any others. But I knew I wouldn't let George out of my sight. I had done so once and it had all gone horribly wrong, with him being catnapped, and he could be a bit of a pawful. Also, the fear of not knowing where my boy was had been unlike anything I have ever experienced.

'I will do, Dad. But what can we do there?' he asked. I actually didn't know.

'We'll do what we do at home, look after our humans and enjoy ourselves in any way we can,' I replied vaguely. Sea air would do us good, I knew that much. Well, that was what everyone said.

The journey seemed to go on forever, I was beginning to feel impatient. We stopped a few times so the children could eat, and when we did, we were allowed out of the cat carrier, although not out of the car, so we could move around a bit.

I had to be careful, because I had an old injury from when I was hurt in Edgar Road, saving Claire from a horrible man, which bothered me at times, and as I'd been sitting for so long, my bad leg was stiff. I was fine, although I had to be careful, but it was a stark reminder that people weren't always good. I snuck a glance at George and hoped he would never encounter anyone like that. But then, I smiled. George was standing on his hind legs looking out of the car window, paws against it, as people stopped and took photos of him.

'Get down, before you fall,' I chastised him. He loved attention. By the time Claire got back to the car with Summer and Toby, he'd acquired quite a crowd.

'Oh gosh,' Claire said. 'I better get them back in the pet carrier.'

'Lovely kitten,' someone said to her and she smiled and thanked them. She strapped Summer and Toby into their car seats and then I ushered George into our carrier and we settled down again.

'Not far now,' Claire said, as she started to drive off. But, of course, we had heard that before.

It felt like we had been in that pet carrier forever when we finally stopped. I couldn't see anything at first, but then Claire lifted the carrier out of the car and put us on the ground and I saw that we were on a lawn. It was still light outside too, although the sun was dulling.

'Can I let them out?' I heard Aleksy's voice.

'Yes, but make sure they don't run off,' Claire warned. Aleksy opened the door. George sprang out, but Aleksy scooped him up. I walked out behind him, sniffing the air. Yes, it did smell different to that in London, and I looked around. Wow, I could already see that it was pretty lovely here.

Claire had parked her car next to Franceska's at the edge of the lawn, where there was a kind of parking area. Then there was a fence, not too high, but with a gate which we had walked through. The lawn in front of the house was bigger than it looked in the photos, and as it was enclosed, it would be our playground. The cottage was detached and there were lush bushes surrounding the garden. The lawn looked neat and tidy, and the grass felt warm under paw. I turned and looked away from the house.

'Wow,' George said, joining me. We sat side by side for a moment taking in the view. There was a road, but on the other side of it was a sandy beach, which stretched to the water, glimmering in the sun. It was beautiful. Toby and Summer were jumping up and down.

'Can we go to the beach now?' Toby asked.

'Well, darling, I've got to get unpacked and it's nearly teatime,' Claire said. 'And we need to wait for Polly to arrive too.'

'I tell you what, Claire, I take the children over, they've been cooped up in the car for so long and then you have some time to get organised,' Franceska offered.

'Yes!' Toby grinned.

'Come on, Tobe,' Tommy said, taking hold of his hand, and they all headed off towards the beach.

Claire had her arms full as she stood next to us on the lawn watching them run off.

'Right guys, come inside and I'll get you fed,' she said. I purred. 'I know, it's so beautiful here, isn't it? I can smell my childhood,' she said, before heading into the house.

Claire opened the door and George and I ran between her legs to explore. On first glance the house was a bit of a shock, compared to what we were used to at home. The carpet was shabby and almost threadbare. As we made our way through the entrance hall, I noticed the walls were all peeling. With George following me, the first room I came to was large and square with two big windows overlooking the lawn; I guessed this was the living room. As George jumped on the windowsill, I padded around. It had two big old sofas and two floral armchairs in it – I knew from the humans' conversation that they had got them from a charity shop, just until they furnished it properly. There was an open fire on one side, and an old coffee table. It was a nice room, or it would be. I was happy to see there was also a television in the corner. I wasn't sure how the children would have lived without that. I left the room and went to the next room, which was smaller, with two small sofas in it and a fire. Again the walls were peeling, and the carpet was thin. It had a window to the back of the house, where I could see a courtyard. I guessed the lawn at the front was the main garden, and that was enormous. Anyway, the empty room held little interest so I went back to the hall and saw George there.

'What do you think?' I asked.

'It's a bit empty,' George said. It wasn't but I knew what he meant – it was un-lived in.

'We'll soon make it our home,' I told him. There was another smaller room at the front of the house, on the other side to the front door, again it was empty, and next to that was a large kitchen. A massive table dominated the room, and although you could tell it was old fashioned – there were no fixed cupboards like we had at home – the kitchen felt a bit like the life of the house already. Claire was boiling a kettle and she was arranging cupboards. I was about to go upstairs to continue my tour of the house when a noise from the front interrupted me.

'We're here,' I heard Polly call out.

'In the kitchen,' Claire replied. Henry and Martha ran in first, and made a fuss of both me and George.

'Hi, love,' Polly said, as she appeared. 'Thank goodness we're finally here.'

'Bit of a drive, wasn't it?'

'Well the traffic wasn't great, but then it is the start of the summer holiday.'

'Cuppa?' Claire asked.

'Love one. Where is everyone else?'

'Frankie's taken the kids to the beach, they were stir crazy after being in the car for so long.'

'Can we go? Please?' Henry asked.

Polly groaned.

'OK, come on then.'

'I'll put the tea on hold.' Claire grinned. 'But how about some food for you two?' She looked at me.

'Meow!' Yes please.

I forgot about the tour of the upstairs, as we settled down to eat. The cottage had a nice feel about it, I decided. The rooms were big and, despite being old and a bit run-down, it was very light. I don't know why but I thought that cottages were meant to be small and gloomy. Well that was what Jonathan said, until he'd visited of course. Seabreeze felt a bit like its name. It was big, it was bright, and when the work was done I knew it would be lovely. It was definitely a bit shabby now but I felt excited about the summer, not only were we going to have a lovely holiday but Seabreeze would be transformed into a dream house, I just knew it.

him to the big living room where he curled up on the windowsill. The sun was setting but it was a warm spot. I went back to the downstairs rooms and wondered what the two empty rooms would be used for. The back door, which I was delighted to see had a cat flap in it, was right next to the wall where the utility room was. I decided not to go through it yet, because although he was asleep I didn't want to leave George alone in the house. Instead I headed upstairs.

The stairs were uncarpeted and at the top was a big open landing. I decided which way to go and found myself nudging the door of the furthest room. It was a medium-sized room in which they had put two sets of bunk beds. I guessed this was for the four boys. The window looked out onto the sea, and I thought how lucky the boys would be to wake up to that. I also guessed it was going to be George's room as he'd have to sleep with Toby. Luckily, if he did have to sleep in the top bunk, George wasn't afraid of heights. I was a bit, but that's a whole other story. I made my way to the room directly opposite which was a smaller room. There were two beds, both with pink covers. For Martha and Summer. They had got the short straw as the view out back was of other houses and fields, but then there were only two of them. Next to those rooms at the back of the house was a big bathroom. In it was an old fashioned bathtub, with a shower hose, a toilet and a sink. Again, it had all seen better days. I went to the rooms on the other side of the landing, and at the front was the biggest bedroom. It had a lovely view out over the front, and it also had a sink and a toilet in a small room off it. I knew this was what they called the master bedroom and Franceska and Polly insisted it was Claire's room. There were two other small rooms behind it, which Polly and Franceska were staying in. All beds had been set up, and although it was going to be a bit of a squeeze, it was big enough for all of us. Just. I saw there was a staircase leading up to a door and I had heard them talk of an attic room, but I couldn't get through the closed door to explore that.

I tried to quell the feeling of disappointment. Yes the location was spectacular but the house really did need a great deal of work. I tried to imagine how it could be but being a cat it was too hard. I just had to put faith in Polly that it would be like home when finished and of course the beach looked lovely, I couldn't wait to go and explore that, having no real experience of sand. I went to find my kitten. It was time to try to enjoy the holiday.

I walked back into the kitchen and smelt something funny. There was no sign of George, or of my humans as I went to investigate. I nosed around the utility room but couldn't see anything. However, the smell was distinctive; it was the smell of cat, but not George or me. I wondered if some of the local cats had been round when the house was empty. I shook my fur, maybe I was just imagining things. There was no sign of any cat, just the smell. I reluctantly left my investigations to go and get George.

'Meow!' I said loudly. He needed to wake up or I'd never get him to sleep tonight.

'Yelp!' George jumped and fell off the windowsill, landing on his tail.

'Sorry,' I said, trying not to laugh. 'I just wanted to wake you.'

'What's up?' George asked, licking his fur.

'Nothing, I thought we could go out for a quick explore before the others came back.' I was itching to get another sniff of that sea air.

'OK, but can we go to the beach like the children?' George asked.

'No, not tonight, I don't want Claire to worry if she comes home and we're not here, but soon, I promise.'

For now we contented ourselves with jumping out of the cat flap, and making our way round to the front of the house. As we sat on the edge of the lawn staring at the sun setting into the water, I was mesmerised. Yellow sand seemed to sparkle, as the water rolled softly, filling the air with a salty aroma. It was intoxicating. The bright orange sun looked as if it was floating on the water, and the sky was alive with colours of orange, yellow and the electric blue of the beckoning night sky. The smell here was different to that in Edgar Road. It smelt of salt, and sun and combined a heady aroma which made me want to sit there and sniff the air; which was what I did.

I understood why this meant so much to Claire. It was the most beautiful view I'd ever seen and I was so glad, so thankful, as George sat next to me, that I got to share it with my kitten. And it hit me, that we were really on holiday, our first holiday together.

Chapter
Four

I was woken by George tickling my head with his tail yet again. I had opted to sleep on Claire's bed, which was pretty comfortable, and also, I liked being near her when it was the two of us. I guess I felt that, without Jonathan around, I was her protector, the way I was when we first met. Claire was my first human on Edgar Road. She moved there after getting divorced and she was very sad when I first met her. I was lonely, she was lonely, it was as if we were meant to be together. She cried a lot and I comforted her, which in turn comforted me. We have an unshakeable bond and I love all my humans, I really do, but Claire will always have an extra special place in my heart. In a way it was meeting her that led me to meeting my other families, and then in turn I led Claire to them too.

It took me a moment to remember where I was, before I realised that we were by the sea. On our holiday, in our home which, if all went to plan, would be our holiday home. I leapt up excitedly. Claire opened her eyes.

'Hey, boys, are the children awake?' she asked, just as Toby and Summer came running in.

'Mummy, Mummy,' Summer shrieked, jumping on Claire and as Claire laughed, Toby climbed next to her and hugged her.

'Did you sleep well, Tobes?' she asked, stroking his hair.

'I did, Mummy, George kept me warm,' he said and I looked at George, proudly. I saw the sun streaming in through a small gap in the curtains and I couldn't wait to see the sea again.

'Right then, who wants some breakfast?' Claire said, moving the covers and getting up.

'Me, me, me,' Summer chanted, jumping on the bed, sending me up and down with her.

'Meow,' George said loudly. Claire laughed.

'Right, children and cats, let's get you fed.'

It was so nice, us all being together, I thought; the kitchen was full of chatter and laughter. Yes, I missed the men but I could see this house, or cottage, or whatever it was supposed to be called, working already. Franceska was making a cooked breakfast, Claire was making coffee and Polly was organising the children around the table.

'Mum, can I help?' Aleksy said, as he joined his mum by the stove, which worked but had definitely seen better days. It looked a bit like the stove that my first owner Margaret had and I knew that that was very old.

'Yes, darling, you can be in charge of toast.' Luckily we had a new toaster.

'And I'll help you, Aleksy,' Tommy said. Everyone was getting on harmoniously. It seemed that Lynstow, Seabreeze Cottage and the sea air were having a magical effect on us already. The children generally got on well but they also bickered a fair bit too. But not today.

'Toby, do you want to play snap?' Henry asked. Toby and Henry were of similar age, and Henry had been so sensitive in befriending Toby that he had made me proud. They were great friends, although it was more like Henry was his protector, because Toby needed it. Toby had made great progress since being with us, but he was still scarred and vulnerable and we all had to be mindful of that.

But all my children were wonderful and I had done a good job with them, if I did say so myself. Aleksy, who was the oldest at nearly eleven, looked after them all and Tommy who was a bit younger, but actually almost as big, did too. In fact, all my children looked after each other. The older boys definitely looked out for the younger ones, and Summer and Martha as the youngest were taken care of by all. Honestly, no one would ever hurt those girls! Jonathan joked that if they ever dared get a boyfriend, the other boys would definitely scare them off! But it filled my heart to see how our families had grown and bonded, and really the idea of us all being together like this for our holidays was a dream come true.

'What are the plans for today?' Aleksy asked, as he spooned up a forkful of beans. I was sitting on his lap, hidden from view because the humans didn't like us being so close to food, but anyway, apart from the egg, I wasn't that keen on his breakfast anyway. George was sitting at Summer's feet. She used to throw her yoghurt and George developed quite a taste for it. Although she didn't really do that any more, he still lived in hope.

'Well I thought we would all go to the beach. We'll take a blanket for us adults and you children can take buckets and spades and just enjoy the sand.'

'Can we go in the water?' Tommy asked.

'If the tide's in, but it might be cold,' Franceska said, reasonably. It was sunny, we could see that, but also it looked as if there was a bit of a breeze as the trees in the garden swayed gently.

'Anyway, we're only across the road if we need anything from home,' Claire pointed out. 'Pol, we'll pop back for lunch and to see how it's going.'

'Of course, can't wait to get them working,' Polly said, referring to the builders who were due to arrive shortly. 'Right, Henry, Martha, you be good for Claire and Franceska.' They both nodded.

Last night, after the children had gone to bed, Claire, Franceska, Polly and I had sat around the kitchen table, discussing plans for the house and drinking wine. Well I'd actually lain on the table, and dozed while half listening to them. Polly had already hired the builders, and they had done some of the work before we arrived – although, as the cottage looked as if it needed a lot more, I wasn't sure what. But anyway, they were now going to be working under Polly's supervision.

First job was to get the utility room knocked through to the back door so the sandy children could be contained. It had now been christened the 'sand room'. Apart from that, the main job they were starting on was the attic that I hadn't seen. They were going to turn the space, which was apparently huge, into two bedrooms and a bathroom, which would be the children's floor. The idea was that the boys could sleep up there in one room, the girls in another and a bathroom would adjoin the two rooms. They were keen to get that done so the children had their space first. Being a parent myself now, I was learning that parents were like that – always putting the children first. I knew from 'discussions' with the men that the house wasn't being done up extravagantly but Polly knew how to get the best without paying the earth, and they had persuaded the men that if it was worth doing it was worth doing as well as they could. Basically it was costing a lot of money, but at the same time it would definitely be worth more than it was now by the time they finished. It made economic sense, Claire kept saying, but I had no idea what that meant. I just hoped that it was a bit brighter and more comfortable when they finished. All this cat needed from his holiday home.

However, they were all confident that at the end they would have a gorgeous second home and I know Claire spoke dreamily of the children all holidaying here with their families one day. Cynical Jonathan muttered often that it would be sold at some point but I knew when he came here again with the children and saw how much we loved it he'd fall in love too. Anyway, I digress. I watched as the breakfast dishes were cleared away, and then when George went to play with the children, I cleaned myself up and got ready for our day.

We had been out for a runaround and seen the children off for their trip to the beach but I'd had to restrain George once again. He was so eager to go but I'd told him we needed to check it out together, to make sure it was safe for cats. After all, I could see that water was involved, so we needed to be cautious. And Claire hadn't suggested taking us so I didn't want to take any chances.

'George, we'll go a bit later so we can check it out properly,' I said sensibly.

'But I want to go now,' George persisted.

'George, be a good kitten, we can't just do what we want, you know that. Anyway, I promise if you are good today I will take you later.'

'OK,' he conceded but he didn't really like having to give in.

I was just about to lead George back in the house when a van pulled up outside. A stocky man got out and made his way towards us.

'Well hello,' he said, bending down to stroke us both. We both purred and nuzzled into him. He was big and burly, with not much hair. The front door opened and Polly emerged clutching a mug.

'Hey, Colin, nice to see you,' she said. She was wearing flip-flops, her hair was tied back and she was smiling broadly. Polly was beautiful, she used to be a model, and I saw Colin's eyes light up at the sight of her. She had that effect on people.

'Alright, Mrs, I mean Polly. How are you?' he said, striding towards her. We trotted along after him.

'Good, although chaotic. Right, come in and we'll go through the plans again. When are your men getting here? We really are on a tight schedule.' Her forehead wrinkled in worry.

'I've got three lads and the big van on the way, don't you worry.' He was cheerful with an accent I hadn't heard before, but it was nice and friendly; a Devon accent maybe?

We followed them as they headed to the kitchen where Polly showed him what she wanted doing with the utility.

'That won't be a problem. I see what you mean, you want to knock through so you come in the back, straight in there, and don't get a desert of sand in the house.'

'Exactly. We've got six children, as well as the two cats, it can get messy.'

'So, you'll be using the cottage a lot then?' Colin scratched his head.

'Yes, that's the plan. As there are three families there'll be someone in the cottage most of the year I expect. I mean, holidays definitely but also weekends – we want to use it, not just have it empty most of the year. We want it to be a home.'

'That's good, Seabreeze needs some love, that's for sure,' Colin said.

'It'd be good to get the downstairs toilet cordoned off.' It was in the utility space but there was no door on it.

'Right you are.' He seemed agreeable. 'We won't order a new toilet until we order the rest of the bathrooms though, to keep costs down.'

'That's fine, if we can get a door that'll do for now.' Polly beamed. She was in her element. Since going to study interior design when the children reached a certain age, Polly had bloomed. She'd been modelling before she had Henry, and then she'd been a full-time mum to him and Martha. When she first arrived on Edgar Road, Henry was a baby and Polly was suffering from post-natal depression. It had taken a while but she'd recovered, thankfully. Last year, when Matt was made redundant from his job, Polly had thrown herself into interior design work. She had worked long hours in that job, it'd been difficult for both her and Matt, but now she freelanced, which meant she got to pick and choose her jobs a bit more carefully and, although she had some work to do, she was able to do most of it while sorting out the cottage, which was definitely lucky.

I felt exhausted as I followed them round, listening again to what was going to be done. It was another good thing about being a cat, we got to live in houses (well the lucky ones did) without having to worry about all this.

'Right, well when the lads get here we'll get stuck in. It might be best if the kids stay out of the way, and the cats,' he said, pointing at George and me. 'We don't have hard hats to fit cats.' He laughed at his joke, although I didn't get it.

'Don't worry, the children will be out as long as this weather stays, and the cats are very clever,' Polly said, picking George up.

'Fingers crossed the rain stays off,' Colin said.

Yes, paws crossed. If we had to stay out of the way at least the sun should be shining for us.

Shortly after that, a larger van pulled up. It blocked all our cars in, not that we needed them, and three men, younger than Colin, each with more hair, jumped out. Suddenly there was a lot of noise and bustle. It was clear we would be better out of the way. I looked at George, and thought perhaps we could risk checking the beach out now.

'Remember, George, don't leave my side and be very vigilant,' I said as we slid under the gate.

'Yes, Dad, of course,' he replied. His fur was bristling with excitement, I could see how much this meant to him. We stood on the pavement, there were cars driving slowly past, as the road was quite narrow, and there were lots of cars parked on the road opposite. When it was safe we crossed. We both jumped up onto a wall and looked out onto the beach.

Wow, I had never seen anything like it. There was a lot of flat sand, but also these sandy hills which looked like a lot of fun. The sand was yellow in colour, there was grass poking out of the hills, and in the distance I could see the water but it looked as if it was miles away.

However, before we could go further I spotted a real danger.

'Oh, George, look, there's a dog,' I yelled, moving closer to my boy protectively. I saw a solitary dog running around in circles nearby. How annoying, the whole beach could have been ours but a dog was going to ruin it. However, just as I was going to get George and run back to the cottage, a man came up to the owner.

'I'm afraid dogs aren't allowed on the beach during the summer months,' he said, pointing at a sign post behind us.

'But Trevor loves the beach,' the owner replied, looking distraught.

I wanted to squeal for joy. Dogs weren't allowed on the beach and there was no sign about cats.

'I'm not scared of dogs, Dad.' George puffed his little chest out and I moved closer. George claimed not to be scared of anything, which of course scared me. As the owner put the lead on the dog and dragged him, huffily, off the beach, we prepared to join the others.

'George, I am not going to say this again. Dogs are silly creatures, of course they aren't as clever as us cats, but they are bigger and if they're off the lead they might try to hurt us. We can't risk that.'

As if to prove my point, the dog, Trevor, barked aggressively as he was being led away from the beach.

We went to join our family. As we started walking on the sand, I turned to George.

'It's a bit weird,' I said, not really able to articulate what it actually felt like.

'It's, like, very sinky,' George said, as his paws disappeared into the yellow, grainy stuff. It took us a while before we could actually walk properly, but we finally made our way to our families.

'Oh, Alfie and George, I'm not sure that cats are supposed to be on the beach,' Franceska laughed.

'No dogs aren't allowed,' Toby pointed out. 'I read the sign.'

'Good boy,' Claire said. 'But is there a sign for cats?'

'No, no sign for cats,' Toby replied.

'Toby, can I bury your feets?' Summer asked, approaching with a spade. Toby nodded and put his feet out in front of him for her.

'OK, Alfie, George, sit down here with us and don't get into any trouble,' Claire said, pointing to the blanket next to her. Trouble? What on earth could she mean?

We spent a very lovely morning on the beach. It was warm but at times there was a pleasant breeze that ruffled our fur. George let Summer bury his paws but then he didn't like it and squealed a lot. George and I did attract a few funny looks and some people came over to talk to us but Claire and Franceska told them that we liked to go everywhere with them. Some people even took photos of us. And best of all there were no seagulls.

I lay down to enjoy the sunshine as I kept an eye on the children and my kitten. Aleksy was supervising building a very elaborate castle, Tommy was running down to get wetter sand from further down the beach and running back, Summer and Martha were looking for shells to decorate it, and Toby and Henry were in charge of something called a moat. Wow, I thought, this was really something special. Even George was now getting used to the sand and was only sinking a bit, but that was alright because all the children took delight in rescuing him. As I lazily watched everything going on, I felt as warm inside as it was outside.

I did feel a bit hot though, something which didn't seem to bother George, who was basking in the sun. Aleksy was showing off his latest building – it was a sand igloo and he cleverly explained how it was hollow inside. I had to say, with its domed top and entrance hall, it looked quite inviting. While they were finding more wet sand to add to the sides and top, I thought I would see if I could fit in. I wiggled through the entrance with ease. Wow, it was cool, and just comfortable enough. I could hear everyone chattering outside as I lay down and decided to shut my eyes for a quick cat nap.

A little while later, after a refreshing nap, I opened my eyes but I couldn't see anything - it was pitch black. I tried to move but I couldn't, there was pressure pushing down on every side. I wiggled in fear, but I was surrounded by sand. I could barely breathe and I panicked, which made it even worse. The sand igloo must have collapsed, I needed help, now. I opened my mouth to yowl and it filled with sand. As I attempted to spit it out and tried again, I started meowing as loudly as I could, until I was exhausted and my mouth grainy with sand. Finally I could hear voices outside, so I yowled some more, hoping to draw their attention. I tried not to panic any more than I was, as the more I moved the more trapped I seemed to be. I couldn't even swish my tail.

I was breathless from all the screeching and although I

could breathe, I was feeling more terrified by the minute. Even my voice was sounding wrong as I squealed again. If someone didn't come soon I might be living in a sand igloo forever, being washed out to sea, possibly ending up in a far and distant foreign land! I heard the voices coming closer and finally a glimpse of daylight through a crack in the sand.

'See, Aleksy, I told you Alfie must be in there,' Tommy shouted. 'My goodness, he could be hurt!'

'Oh no, poor Alfie, I didn't know, I'm so sorry.' Aleksy's voice was distraught. They kept digging until I was free, and Aleksy took me in his arms, brushing the worst of the sand off. I slowed my breathing down and the panic began to subside. I had to blink a few times so I could see and adjust to the bright light.

The children and George surrounded me, full of concern. Franceska appeared with some drinks, while I tried to shake the rest of the sand off my fur and catch my breath. Claire approached with Summer and Toby – they'd been for a paddle in the water.

'What happened to Alfie?' Claire asked. 'I turn my back for five minutes.' She shook her head.

Five minutes? It was far longer than that, more like hours. Being buried in sand had now been added to my near-death experiences. Others involved a bad man hurting me, almost being run over crossing the road, nearly drowning in a lake, being stuck up a tree – oh and once I was nearly attacked by a seagull. George nuzzled me, whispering that he was so happy to see I was alright. I felt slightly embarrassed; I was constantly warning George of trouble yet it was me who'd put himself in danger.

'He's OK, he was in my sand igloo and then when we were making another castle, it sort of collapsed. We didn't know Alfie was in there.'

'It's usually George who gets into trouble these days,' Claire pointed out. I rested my case.

'We're exhausted,' Claire said as Polly appeared on the lawn. Claire had told us all it was time to go home for a bit to get lunch. I was quite pleased as I was still recovering from being buried alive. Earlier, I had wanted to take George to explore the sand hills, which I heard were called sand dunes, but Claire wouldn't let us out of her sight now. And although I wouldn't let my experience put me off the beach, I knew I would be more careful from now on.

'Chasing the children round in the sun has taken its toll but they love the beach already,' Claire continued.

'And the beach loves us,' Franceska laughed, brushing sand off her legs.

'Right, well let's have a picnic lunch out here. It's a bit dusty in there, although by teatime the kitchen should be usable,' Polly said, coming over to join us.

'What are we doing about lunch then?' Claire asked.

'I thought we could get sandwiches, crisps and cold drinks from the village shop,' Polly said. 'I daren't go into the kitchen. Aleksy, do you want to help me? You can also choose some treats for everyone.'

'Yes, I'll help.' Aleksy stood up proudly, as he went with Polly.

'Any special requests or are you happy with whatever?'

'You know what the kids like, and I'm happy with anything. Do you want some money?'

'No, I've got some. Right, let's go.'

'Yelp!' I said. I wanted something too.

'I'll see what seafood they have for you two, of course,' Polly laughed. 'After all, we are by the sea, so they should have something nice.'

She bent down to give me a pat and I purred. I deserved a treat after my ordeal.

We passed a lovely afternoon on the lawn. It was too hot for us to go back to the beach, I told George. In truth I wasn't ready to revisit it just yet, I was still feeling a little bit anxious. We could see so much from here in the shade of a lovely bush. I did ask George why he hadn't noticed I was missing earlier but he just raised his whiskers and said he was far too busy digging holes, as if that was the most natural answer in the world.

As we watched, there was even more activity on the beach; children, and people on the water, which had moved closer up the beach – Claire said it was the tide coming in. There were some flat boards that people seemed to be standing on. I didn't know what they were, having not seen them before.

'Can I learn to paddleboard?' Aleksy asked. Ah, that's what those people were doing.

'Yes, *kochanie*,' Franceska said. 'We'll find out how to do it and then you and Tommy can learn.'

I hoped they would be careful, water was tricky and although I knew humans seemed to quite like it – the bath, a swimming pool, the sea – us cats sensibly steered clear.

Aleksy set up a game of football for the kids as us adults relaxed on a blanket. Polly went to check on the builders every now and then, Claire dozed off and Franceska read her book. I watched George chasing the football around, pretty unsuccessfully, but I knew he would sleep well tonight. In fact, the sea air was making me sleepy again.

'Dad,' a voice woke me. I looked up to see George standing there. I must have nodded off.

'George.'

'Everyone's gone inside for tea, the builders have gone and I think it's our teatime.' I glanced across at the beach again to see it was emptying. The sky was still bright but I felt hungry so, yes, it must be teatime.

'Let's go then, George, come on, round the back.'

We went through the cat flap and saw there was a doorway into the utility room which hadn't been there before. It was a bit messy but not too bad as we made our way into the kitchen via the 'sand room'. It was good because it took a while for George and I to shake even more sand off our fur – it sure did like to stick and I didn't want Claire to insist on bathing us.

Before we headed into the kitchen I stopped. There was a funny smell again, I could have sworn it was a cat but there was no other feline here apart from me and George so I couldn't understand it. I had a good poke around in the corners but there was no sign of anything, just the smell. I didn't like it though. I lingered for a bit longer, double checking around as I heard George being greeted in the kitchen. Then I heard a lot of laughter. Reluctantly leaving my search, I made my way into the kitchen where I saw George sitting on the kitchen table near Summer. Claire was shrieking but everyone else was laughing. I took a closer look. All the children had ice-cream cones and George had his face in Summer's.

'Look, George likes ice cream,' Henry said, giggling. Summer was holding the cone out to him.

'Don't encourage him, Sum, and you can't eat that now,' Claire chastised, taking the cone off her. But the damage had been done. George was covered in ice cream, and as he licked the ice cream off his face a big grin appeared either side of his ice-cream-white nose.

'This is special local ice cream, made from clotted cream,' Polly explained, reading the tub she had taken it from.

'It's delicious, but I'm not sure we should be feeding it to the cats,' Franceska said.

'It's very cold but I really do like ice cream,' George said to me when no one was listening.

I licked a bit off his head. Um, actually it wasn't bad, I could see the appeal. I saw Claire put the rest of Summer's ice cream onto a plate by the sink. I jumped up and started licking and George joined me. Franceska took her phone out and started taking photos.

'Only we could have cats who get to eat Devon's finest ice cream,' Polly laughed.

'Meow,' I said, as I lapped up the creamy, cold mixture. It was delicious.

'Well I suppose it's their holiday too,' Claire finished. 'Although I am still not sure they should be allowed it.'

'Surely the odd treat?' Franceska said, giving me a big smile.

Our holiday was suddenly looking up.

Chapter
Five

We were all having breakfast in the kitchen when there was a loud, persistent knock at the door.

'Is that the builders already?' Claire asked, looking up from where she was trying to coax Summer to eat some fruit. All the children were sitting nicely at the table, and George was licking porridge off the floor. I was trying, and failing, not to notice him doing so.

'They're not due for an hour, I'll go,' Polly said, making towards the door. I went with her. As she opened the door, we both were taken aback for a moment. Standing on the doorstep was a very glamorous woman, who I first thought was carrying one of those tiny dogs but on closer inspection it was actually a cat. A Persian, I thought, very pretty, but she took one look at me and waved her tail in a hateful way, hissed and started squirming.

'Chanel darling, behave,' the woman said as the cat wiggled in her arms. I stood my ground; this was my ground after all.

'Hello?' Polly said, looking bemused. The woman was tall, very slim and wearing a dress and really high heels. Her blonde hair was long and very neat and she was wearing make-up. I felt a little sorry for Polly – although she is the most beautiful woman I know, she didn't look great in an old T-shirt, cropped leggings, her hair piled messily on top of her head and there was no make-up on her face. The cat was as immaculate as her owner but I didn't like her, she was hostile and, I decided, as she hissed at me again, more than a little bit mean.

'Sorry, sorry.' The lady's voice was confident and a little too loud. 'Allow me to introduce myself. I'm Andrea. I live next door and, well, I wanted to come and meet you, with Chanel of course. I didn't realise you had a cat though,' she said giving me what I can only describe as a 'look'. It was a bit disdainful.

'Oh, hi.' Polly looked at the woman unsurely. 'Nice to meet you. I'm Polly, this is Alfie. We actually have two cats here,' she explained.

'Meow,' I said, trying to tell Chanel I wasn't scared of her. She looked at me as if she'd like to kill me.

'Right, so are you living here now?' Andrea asked. Her grey eyes narrowed and she tried to peer round the door into the house.

'No, not exactly. We've just arrived but we're on holiday. It's a long story.' Finally Polly found her smile.

'Right, well no time like the present.' And somehow Andrea managed to manoeuvre herself around me and Polly and into the house, Chanel still in her arms.

'Um, everyone else is in the kitchen,' Polly said, but Andrea had headed that way already.

Claire was sipping coffee, the children were squabbling and Franceska was trying to clean up but she kept tripping over George who was insistently scrabbling around her feet.

'George, stop,' she chastised.

'Children, shush,' Claire shouted.

'Um, everyone, hello,' Polly interrupted. As they all turned to look at Andrea, everyone went quiet. Even George. 'This is Andrea, she's our neighbour?'

'Well yes, I live in the next house to your left, Beach Villa, and I've come to welcome you.' She didn't sound welcoming. Chanel glared at me and George. George was now still and staring at Chanel, his eyes wide.

'And you've got a cat?' Aleksy said, looking puzzled. 'We love cats.'

'Yes, sorry Chanel is like my baby, my third baby as I have two daughters, but I take her everywhere. I wouldn't have brought her here if I knew you had cats, she doesn't care for other felines.'

'Meow,' Chanel concurred.

'Right, well I'm Claire, this is Franceska and these are our array of children.' Claire smiled, and held out a hand but Andrea was unable to take it because she was still trying to contain a squirming Chanel.

'Lovely to meet you all. I would stay but I think darling Chanel is a little uncomfortable.' As Chanel was hissing and wriggling that seemed to be a bit of an understatement.

'Right,' Claire said, uncertainly.

'But I tell you what, I'll pop back this evening, on my own,' she glared at me as if it was my fault, 'with a bottle of something fizzy and we can have a proper chat.'

'Um?' Franceska said.

'Well we are in a total mess, what with builders and everything.'

'So I see, never mind, I'm happy to slum it,' Andrea trilled. 'I'll be back about eight, I'm guessing all these children will be in bed then.' She laughed, but it sounded a bit menacing. 'Don't worry, I'll see myself out.'

Before anyone could say anything else, she and Chanel were gone.

'My goodness,' Claire said.

'What on earth was that?' Franceska said.

'And we thought that we were the sophisticated Londoners, coming to a little Devon village,' Polly said. 'She looks right out of Knightsbridge. As did her cat.'

'Chanel. What sort of name is that?' Claire mused.

'Did you see the collar? I bet it was real diamonds.'

'Oh God, and she's coming back tonight. I don't know why we didn't say no.' Franceska trembled.

'We didn't get the chance . . . Anyway, it'll be nice to meet some local people,' Polly said unconvincingly.

'Do you think we've got time to get our hair done?' Claire quipped.

'Well, I didn't bring my ballgown with me but I feel that I should have done now,' Polly giggled.

George was scrabbling at my legs to get my attention.

'What?' I hissed.

'That cat, Chanel, she's beautiful,' he said. He looked a little enraptured.

'But not nice, she didn't like us, did she?' I pointed out.

'But everyone likes me. I'm going to be her friend. She's so beautiful, the most beautiful cat in the world.'

I saw then the look in his eyes, which reminded me of myself when I first saw Snowball. My George had developed his first crush.

Andrea was soon forgotten as the builders arrived. One of them was going to finish the doorway into the newly christened 'sand room', while the others went up to the attic. According to Polly they worked hard and didn't drink too much tea – which was apparently a good thing for builders, especially as we had a tight time schedule. As the weather was good, Franceska and Claire once again took the children to the beach. George and I lay on the bonnet of Claire's car – it had the highest roof – and watched them from our vantage point. We said we'd probably go to the beach later but, as it was so close, we didn't feel the urgency any more. So curling up together on the car sunbathing and watching the world go by was definitely a pleasant way to pass the time.

There were a few dogs around, although of course not on the beach, and they were thankfully on leads. It was a busy, lively village; cars kept appearing, looking for places to park, children jumping excitedly out, also lots of people cramming the pavements, all wearing summery clothes and chattering excitedly. I saw that Aleksy had set up some kind of ball game and children were approaching him to play. I hoped they would make some nice friends this summer, I hoped George and I would too—

'Oh it's you,' a hostile voice interrupted me. I looked up to see Chanel standing on the street.

'Hi, hey, how are you?' George gushed. She narrowed her eyes, swishing her tail angrily, and then turned her attention back to me.

'I never go out on my own, not outside my garden anyway, so it's a very big deal that you have made me come here,' she snapped.

'I didn't make you do anything,' I replied, still trying to sound friendly.

'Who do you think you are, coming here?' she hissed.

'Well, I'm Alfie, this is George and this is our holiday

79

house,' I said, not unkindly. I was a firm believer in using charm. Especially with difficult creatures. Chanel was clearly a difficult creature.

'Not for long,' she said, again flicking her tail. 'Mark my words, your days are numbered,' she hissed before turning and leaving.

'What on earth did she mean by that?' I asked. I felt suddenly as if something might be wrong with this otherwise perfect set-up. I blinked, had I misheard her? Her voice had sounded menacing and her words threatening.

I looked at the children, all playing in a big group, Claire and Franceska looking on happily. I saw Polly come to the front door with a cup of tea and make her way over to join them and I saw George preening himself, checking his reflection in the wing mirror of the car. Surely our days weren't numbered, whatever that meant. Our holiday had only just started.

'Oh wow, Dad, I think she likes me,' George said.

'Whatever gave you that idea?' I asked. I didn't want to burst his bubble but that cat really didn't like either of us. I remembered back to when I first met Snowball. She had been quite immune to my charms and I hadn't given up. But then, this cat, well she was no Snowball, or Tiger for that matter, she was just downright horrible.

'It was the way she looked at me, I could just tell,' George sighed. I raised my whiskers but held my tongue. I had a horrible feeling that George's first crush was going to teach him a lot about love – the hard way.

That evening, the house was alive with the sounds of happy children. I pushed Chanel to the back of my mind as they chattered on about their new friends and how tomorrow Aleksy and Tommy had their first paddleboarding lesson. Summer was cross because she couldn't go but, as Claire pointed out, she was too little, and Toby was still a bit scared of the water. Back home Jonathan had started taking him to swimming lessons but it was early days and I totally sympathised with how he felt. Really, I was sure it was more sensible to be scared of water than to actually want to be in it. The builders were long gone but Claire was still trying to clean up the dust, which seemed to be covering everyone and everything.

'Oh God, I need to shower before the queen gets here,' she said. I figured out she was talking about Andrea.

'You know, I think we need to try to get the plumbing sorted soon, the shower is a bit lacklustre,' Polly said, her head back in the plans. 'I'm thinking we can fix it temporarily before we get all the bathrooms done.'

'Polly, you are a marvel with all this house stuff, honestly, I wouldn't know where to start,' Franceska said.

'Yes, well I can't cook remember,' Polly laughed, giving Franceska a hug.

'Also, I have spoken to Colin and we are going to have a shower set up outside, with hot water, to hose the worst of the sand off the kids before they even go into the sand room. What do you think?'

'Genius,' Claire said. 'I love it.' But then she *had* just spent the best part of two hours sweeping both sand and dust up.

'This is going to be the best holiday cottage ever,' Franceska said. 'I am so happy we all did this.'

'So am I,' Claire agreed, a dreamy look on her face. 'I

bet Aunt Claire would be so happy that it was filled with love.'

'Oh gosh, it's nearly seven. Right, Claire, we'll round up the younger ones and get them washed and ready for bed. Frankie, can you continue with the clearing up?' Polly said, jumping up.

'I can, but I'm not sure it's going to make much difference,' Franceska said, taking the broom from Claire and shaking her head at the mess.

By eight, the children were in bed, apart from Aleksy and Tommy who were in the living room watching a DVD. They were the oldest after all so they were allowed to stay up later than the others, especially as it was school holidays. George had gone to bed with Toby as usual and I was hanging out with Aleksy until I heard the knock at the door. I sprang up from Aleksy's lap and went to the door, arriving just before Claire.

Andrea was standing on the doorstep looking dressed for a night out. She wore a dress, again, high heels, her hair was swept up onto her head and she had a lot of make-up on. The smell from her was so strong I felt as if I'd swallowed a mouthful of perfume; it wasn't pleasant.

'Andrea, how lovely to see you again, come in,' Claire said, stepping aside to let her in.

'Likewise,' she replied, but didn't sound as if she meant it.

Claire led Andrea into the kitchen where Polly and Franceska were sitting around the table. Wine glasses had been put out, candles lit and, although it wasn't exactly immaculate, it was tidy and clean-ish at least.

'What a charming kitchen,' Andrea said, wrinkling her nose, as she greeted the others.

'Did you know my Aunt Claire?' Claire asked.

'No, she'd gone before we moved into the village, but she was spoken about. It was a big annoyance to the village that the house was empty for so long. We tried to do something about it but we couldn't seem to get to the bottom of who owned it . . . Until now.'

'Well my aunt was ill, and I think whoever was managing her affairs just did as per her instructions. I used to come here as a child,' Claire explained. Andrea handed her a bottle, and she opened it, pouring four glasses.

'Sorry we don't have flutes, only wine glasses.' Polly looked embarrassed.

'Well, as I said earlier, I'm happy to slum it,' Andrea said, before laughing. Her laugh sounded a little tinkly and fake.

'I'll add them to my list,' Claire said through gritted teeth. She was making a list of things they still needed as she went along.

'How long have you lived here?' Franceska asked, changing the subject.

'Ten years. My husband and I moved here when I had my first child.'

'How many do you have?' Polly asked.

'Two, both girls. Savannah is ten, obviously, and Serafina is eight.'

'Lovely names. And what is the village like now, obviously I haven't been here for so long,' Claire said.

'It's a great village. There's a lovely school for the girls and obviously we live on the beach.'

'Not in those shoes,' Polly said, before clamping her hand over her mouth.

'Oh I don't go to the beach much, all that dreadful sand. But I watch the girls from the safety of my garden. You could do the same.'

'Of course. And we think the village is lovely. We went to a nice pub when we last visited, The Lynstow Arms.'

'The food's good there, of course us locals try to avoid it during the holidays, you know, it's full of tourists,' Andrea said, without a hint of irony, even though she was addressing tourists.

'You must find that annoying,' Claire said, stifling a grin.

'To be honest, we think this is a lovely village and community and we like to keep it that way. We find it unfortunate that Londoners come in and buy up the properties which they hardly ever use. It's sapping the soul from the village.' She said this without a hint of niceness, I thought as I curled up on Claire's lap. I didn't like the turn this was taking; it reminded me of my earlier conversation with Chanel.

'Well the good thing is that this house has three families so we'll use it loads. Weekends, school holidays, you'll probably find there's someone here most of the time.'

'Not quite the same though, is it? You are not going to be a full-time part of the community. Seabreeze Cottage will still be empty a great deal of time.' Her voice had turned cold and I saw Franceska looking alarmed.

'We want to become as much a part of the community as we can,' Claire pushed.

'Absolutely, and we have so many school holidays, as you

know, our kids will grow up here as well,' Polly added.

'I'm sure you mean well. With your building plans and hundreds of children, not to mention the cats, but the point is that I am here to make you an offer.'

'An offer?'

'What kind of offer?'

'I want to buy Seabreeze Cottage. I want to buy it off you right now.'

'But we've started work on it,' Polly said.

'Then stop. Sell it to me, go back to London and if you want to come on holiday then rent somewhere but let this house, this amazing property, go to someone local.'

'But you already have a house, so it'd be a second home for you too?' Polly suddenly sounded annoyed.

'Look, I can't explain everything now but if you sell me this house it will be a home, you can trust me on that one.' She sounded sincere, I almost believed her.

'That's a lovely idea but you know this is a family home for me,' Claire explained. 'And my Aunt Claire was a big part of this community and she wanted me to have the cottage, so that's what I am going to do.' She crossed her arms; nice but firm.

'I will pay you above the asking price.' I noticed a hint of desperation enter Andrea's voice.

'I'm sorry, Andrea, but it's not for sale,' Claire said, stroking me.

'Everything has a price,' Andrea said, staring at Claire with cold grey eyes.

'We don't,' Polly said, going to stand near Claire's chair. 'We want this to be a family home too, but for our families.'

'We'll see. I want this house.' Andrea stood up and glared at each of the women, any hint of friendliness fled. 'And I always get what I want.'

I now understood what Chanel meant. If Andrea had her way, it seemed our days here would in fact be numbered.

Chapter
Six

Thankfully we had made it to the end of our first week on holiday relatively unscathed. Despite the threat from Andrea, so far we were all still here and on the whole having a lovely time. Although Polly, Franceska and Claire had been a little shaken by Andrea's words and her vague threat that she would get Seabreeze Cottage, they had eventually pushed it to the back of their minds and decided she was as much hot air as she was big hair. They said they wouldn't let anyone ruin our perfect holiday. Or get her manicured hands on Seabreeze Cottage, whatever that meant.

Polly had been surveying how much they had got done with the building work and had a review with Colin. We had only five weeks left, so she said they were doing well but couldn't afford any delays.

And thankfully, as it was Friday, the men were coming down for the weekend. Even Tomasz was leaving the restaurants for a couple of days, although to be fair he had managers now and, although he liked to keep a very close eye on them, he was far more willing to take time off nowadays. There was a time when he'd spent so much time at work his family hardly ever saw him, but they seemed to have resolved that, thankfully. I was excited, I'd missed Jonathan, Matt and Tomasz and it would be lovely to have the family all together again for a couple of days.

Unfortunately the weather had turned and although it was warm it was raining. Claire suggested taking the younger children to the local town to have a look around, so they weren't in the way of the builders, and Polly said she was happy to leave them for a bit and go with her, while Franceska was going to stay and try to get everything organised for when everyone came. Despite the fact it was raining, Aleksy and Tommy begged to be allowed to put on wellies and coats and go to the beach, which she said they could, but she would be watching them and they weren't allowed to go too far. They had more freedom here than they did in London, but that was village life, apparently. And Aleksy was very responsible for his age; I thought it would do him good to have more independence to be honest.

Unlike George.

George begged to be allowed out to see Chanel, but I told him no. Not only was it raining but also she was horrible. He argued and whined, a bit like Summer, but I stood firm. I said that when the rain stopped I would take him out for a nice walk but not before. He ran upstairs and sulked under Toby's bed. Kittens!

I decided to help Franceska – or at least keep her company. She seemed happy and I knew that she was looking forward to seeing Tomasz, just as the others were looking forward to seeing their husbands. It hadn't been a bad first week, but it was strange without our men. In fact it made me the man of the house.

While Franceska was watching Aleksy and Tommy play on the beach, I went to the utility room. The builders had finished downstairs for now and were in the attic. I was careful to keep out of their way. They were all very nice, but they had big feet and tools which looked quite dangerous.

The utility room was a bit of a draw to me still, there was definitely an alien smell which kept bugging me. I sniffed around, and felt baffled. I still could have sworn it was the scent of a cat, but not me or George – or even Chanel. And although I hadn't seen another cat around here, the scent hadn't faded while we'd been living here. It was a mystery.

I fleetingly wondered if, when I was sleeping with Claire, another cat was sneaking in through the cat flap and I decided to stay up tonight to make sure. Jonathan would be with Claire anyway and he wasn't as keen on me sleeping on their bed as Claire was – I knew he'd probably banish me to my bed on the landing. I felt a little bit better having a plan of sorts, and I was determined to get to the bottom of the smell, so I decided to go and check on George. Boy that kitten could sulk for England, I thought as I made my way upstairs.

I looked in the boys' room, but there was no sign of him. Not under the bed where Toby slept, or on the bed itself. He hadn't climbed up onto the top bunks either. I felt a bit panicked as I ran around the rest of the upstairs, even braving the builders to check the attic, but he was nowhere to be found. I bounded downstairs, checking every room, but he wasn't there. My heart sank. Not only did I feel panicked but I also believed I knew exactly where George was.

I remembered Andrea saying she was in the house to the left, so I turned in that direction out of the house, feeling the rain soaking into my fur straight away. Wasting no time, I crawled under a hedge, where there seemed to be the best access, and found myself in the neatest garden I'd ever seen. Andrea's house wasn't like ours, it was taller, squarer, the windows were huge. It also looked a bit grander. Why on earth would she want our house when hers was definitely more suited to her? Thankfully, I found George huddled under one of the windowsills. He was sheepish when he saw me.

'Sorry, Dad, but I was going to come back before you'd noticed I'd gone.' Yes, that would work. Honestly, my boy still had a lot to learn.

I wasn't sure how to play this. I knew that he was besotted with the awful Chanel but also I needed him to understand that he shouldn't be out on his own. After all, the last time I left him alone he'd been catnapped, but I also knew that he was a little older now and would want more freedom, a bit like Aleksy. Being a parent was so hard, getting the balance right was difficult.

'George, I do understand you wanted to see Chanel, but we are in a new place and we don't know it very well, so I would be happier if you stayed with me, at least for a while.' I hoped I didn't sound too angry. 'But if you have to go off then you must tell me exactly where you'll be.' I tried to be conciliatory.

'Oh, Dad, I am sorry but she is so beautiful, and I just needed to see her lovely face.' Oh boy, he had it bad.

'And have you seen her?' I asked, softening. I was a romantic cat and so I didn't want to underestimate his feelings. I understood about love, after all.

'Yes, she stood at the window! She was making a lot of noise but I didn't really know what she was trying to say.'

I guessed she was telling him to get lost.

'Did she sound angry?' I asked, treading carefully.

'Well some might say she did, but I think she was just

teasing me. Although she did wave her tail at me angrily before she jumped down and ran off. I sat on the window-sill for a while but she didn't come back.'

'And you got soaked.' Oh my poor boy. 'Look, George, come home with me now, get dried off and warm and I promise that as soon as it clears up we'll go for a lovely walk,' I coaxed.

'OK, I will see her soon though, won't I?' he said.

'Yes, son, you will.' We ran back to the hedge, and I saw George safely through the gap. I was about to follow him when something, or someone, caught my eye. At the back of the house, Andrea was standing under a wooden shelter with what looked like one of our builders. I crawled a little closer, straining my eyes. I was sure it was one of the younger ones, Liam, I think he was called. He was wearing his scruffy builder clothes and a big jacket. She was laughing and then she put a hand on his shoulder and he turned red. What the hell was he doing with her? I was about to move closer when George called out.

'Dad, come on, I'm hungry.'

I took a last look at Liam and Andrea and wondered what on earth they were doing together. I felt as if there was something, something big. Being a perceptive cat, I was pretty sure, what with George's inappropriate crush, Andrea's deter-mination to get her hands on our house, and the funny cat smell in the utility room, there was a lot going on. Mysteries were apaw. I could feel it in my fur.

'I can't believe you dragged us to Devon with the promise of sunshine and it's raining,' Jonathan moaned as he swung Summer around.

'Gosh, is this a record? You've been here five minutes and you're already complaining,' Claire teased.

I rubbed against his legs; I'd missed Jonathan, I'd missed all the men actually.

Polly had picked them up from the train station just after lunch and we had all been incredibly excited when they arrived. The children had been hyper, and George and I could barely contain ourselves. The cottage did suddenly feel smaller with the men in it, but it also felt more like home. Polly showed them the work done so far and introduced them to the builders. I went with them while they inspected the attic. It wasn't looking bad actually. Walls were being built and there was a landing which would lead into each room. As it stretched across the whole house, it was big, but the ceilings were a bit lower, making it perfect for the children I guessed. I was excited suddenly, as I saw the transformation happening. It might take a while – apparently these things did – but you could see the difference already, even within the space of a week. The men seemed to be happy with the work and Jonathan even said, 'Good job,' to Colin. Praise indeed.

It had also been decided that we were going to have fish and chips for supper. There was a local chip shop, which was normal for a seaside village apparently, and George and I were very excited as we were both pretty sure we'd get some fish.

Claire and Jonathan went to collect supper. They had a big umbrella which was kept on the porch, and George and I looked out of the window and saw them go. I felt warm and fuzzy despite the horrible weather; it was going to be such a wonderful weekend. As long as George didn't keep running off to see Chanel, that was.

'You cannot beat fish and chips by the proper sea,' Matt said, as everyone was crowded round the table. They just managed to fit, although it was a squash and Summer had to sit on Jonathan's lap, and Martha on Matt's.

'It's not exactly the sea, darling,' Polly said. 'It's the estuary.'

'Yes but it's water and beach, so near enough surely?' Tomasz said.

'Near enough,' Franceska laughed. 'Isn't this fabulous us all together like this,' she said, beaming.

'We love it here,' Aleksy said. 'We made some friends already and the beach is the coolest thing ever.' His eyes were shining with excitement. 'And, Dad, we went paddleboarding, and it's not as easy as it looks.'

'Really? It does look pretty easy,' Jonathan said.

'Maybe you should try,' Aleksy suggested with a giggle.

'Yes, Jon, why don't I book you a lesson?' Claire suggested with a smile.

'Thanks but I am going to concentrate on relaxing when I'm here. Anyway, I'll leave that to the kids.'

'I agree,' Tomasz said. 'I'm not so fond of the water,' he added.

'Meow,' I agreed.

Later, the men put the children to bed, apart from Aleksy and Tommy, who were told to get washed and ready before being allowed to play on their tablets in the smaller living room. The adults then decamped to the larger living room. Claire and Jonathan were on one sofa, Franceska and Tomasz on the other and Polly and Matt squeezed together on an armchair. I sat on the arm of the sofa, looking around at all the adults I love. There was so much harmony in the air, I felt as if life was calmer than it had been in a long while.

'So how is Edgar Road?' Claire asked. 'I know we've only been away a week but it feels like ages.'

'Nothing much to report. Vic and Heather are making sure we behave ourselves, that's for sure,' Jonathan laughed.

'So how is it down here? I mean, the builders seem to be making progress.'

'Oh they're so much easier to deal with than London builders,' Polly said. 'They turn up when they say and they don't skive. I'm loving Colin.'

'Hey!' Matt laughed. 'The kids seem to love it.' He smiled, indulgently.

'They do, and it might have rained today but we've had three good beach days, and they're all getting on pretty well,' Polly said.

'There is only one fly in the ointment,' Franceska said. I knew Franceska and Tomasz would always be Polish but they certainly had the hang of British sayings.

'What?' her husband asked.

'Oh, there's our neighbour. I'm sure you'll meet her. She's called Andrea and she came to see us,' Claire started.

'That's nice, isn't it?' Jonathan asked.

'No, not only does she look as if she's just stepped out of a beauty salon but she thinks she's the Queen of Sheba,' Polly said.

'She turned up with her cat who's called Chanel,' Franceska added.

'Oh, and she invited herself back when the kids were all asleep, and said she was happy to slum it.'

'OK, so she's a snobby well-heeled woman with a funny-named cat?' Jonathan looked amused.

'She asked to buy the cottage,' Claire replied.

'Oh?' Tomasz looked confused.

'And of course we told her it wasn't for sale,' Polly explained.

'But she said she wouldn't take no for an answer and said she always got what she wanted,' Franceska said, shuddering. Franceska was the most easily intimidated of all the women.

'Did she make you an offer?' Jonathan asked.

'Jon, Seabreeze is not for sale. But she did say she'd pay more than the market value.'

'Why does she want it so much?' Matt asked.

Good question, I thought. I still didn't trust her motives.

'Oh, she banged on about how important it was to her to preserve village life and she didn't like us interlopers taking the best property.'

'She's got a point,' Jonathan said. Judas, I thought.

'Jon, we are going to fall out if you don't stop it. Anyway, I do not believe she wants to buy it out of a sense of community spirit. She owns the big house to the left, she acts as if she owns the village in fact. I think there's more to it.'

'I'm going to ask Colin next week,' Polly said. 'Maybe she knows something we don't.'

'Whatever her motives, Seabreeze is not for sale,' Claire reiterated.

'You love this cottage already, don't you?' Jonathan said, sighing.

'I do, and so do the kids. It's just perfect.'

'Then we won't let anyone buy it off us,' Jonathan said, loyally. I wondered where that had come from.

'You've changed your tune,' Matt said, echoing my thoughts.

'Everyone seems relaxed, the house is going to be gorgeous when it's finished and I for one am suddenly appreciating getting out of London. I had my doubts, mainly financial, but this . . . well, seeing you and the kids so happy seems priceless.' Ah, there was my sentimental Jonathan again. I rubbed against him. 'And what about you, Alfie? Do you and George like it here?'

'Meow!' I nuzzled him to tell him I absolutely did.

'Right, well let's have a toast, to our holiday home.' Jonathan picked up his beer bottle.

'To Seabreeze Cottage,' the others said.

'And to many, many happy holidays here,' Claire finished as they all clinked glasses.

I left them chatting. It was getting late but I wanted to stay awake. I went to the kitchen and ate a little more fish that was in my bowl on the floor. I then went and hid in the utility room. If anyone was visiting us at night, I would be ready for them.

'Yelp!' A voice woke me up and I leapt. I found myself nose to nose with a big cat, who looked a bit like a leopard. He didn't look exactly pleased to see me. What was it with these village cats?

'Hello?' I said. He sprang back and glared at me. 'Do you live here?' I asked.

'I do. I did. But then you arrived. I was hoping you'd leave so I've been watching the house but it seems you're not going anywhere.' He sounded gruff.

'I'm Alfie,' I said, in a friendly manner. 'We don't exactly live here, me and my kitten George, but you see our families own it and we are on holiday.'

'Cats don't go on holiday, even I know that.'

'Well I know most people think that but, guess what, we do! Anyway, it's a long story but we're here for the summer.'

'Right and what am I supposed to do?'

'I don't know, where's your family? You don't belong to Great Aunt Claire, do you?'

'I have no idea who you're talking about. I live here, alone. Or I have done for quite a while now. Very happily I may add.'

'You don't have a family?'

'No.'

'But—'

'Listen, I don't have time for this. I need my sleep. I am out finding food all day and then at night I come back and sleep. It's my life. That's all you need to know.'

'Hey, you can have some of my food. There's bowls out, for me and my kitten George, but we are very good at sharing. Or I am, anyway.'

'Humph. That's kind, but I'm used to looking after myself.' He wasn't exactly warming to me.

'Well if you change your mind . . .' I heard footsteps. 'My humans are coming to clear up, probably before bed, but I won't disturb you if you want to stay here.'

I didn't quite know what else to say or do. The cat wasn't very friendly but then I remembered being homeless and I didn't want to make him think he couldn't stay here. It sounded as if it was his home anyway – well, as far as he was concerned.

'I'll stay out of sight, just until I can find another empty house to live in.' He still didn't sound friendly.

'OK then, sleep well and you know we don't mind you being here. What's your name?' I asked.

'Gilbert,' he replied. He eyed me suspiciously, I raised my whiskers in what was meant to be a welcoming way.

'Alfie, where are you? It's time for us all to turn in,' Jonathan said and I quickly turned to face him, but I didn't need to worry, Gilbert had slunk back into the shadows as if he was never there. If it hadn't been for his scent I would have thought I'd imagined our entire exchange.

Chapter
Seven

'What do you mean, another cat?' George asked the following morning. I'd already checked the utility room but there was no sign of Gilbert.

'He's been living here, I don't know why, he wasn't exactly forthcoming. But he said he doesn't have a family. Anyway, he was hoping we would have left but he's been sneaking in at night and leaving before we get up. I'm hoping to see him again and find out more.'

I was a nosy cat, I'll admit, but I was intrigued by this cat who seemed to think of Seabreeze as his home. I wanted to know why he didn't have a family and also make sure he knew that he could stay here; after all, we weren't going to be here the whole time and it seemed a shame for the house to be totally empty. Most importantly I didn't want Gilbert to be homeless, I still remembered how awful that was. I also thought I might persuade him to make himself known to the humans; I didn't doubt that they would all welcome him the way I wanted to.

'Wow, I can't wait to meet him. But I'd rather go and see Chanel, can we, can we please?' George begged.

Again, I was still unsure how to play this. I wanted to give George the benefit of my wisdom but I also knew that some things had to be learnt first-hand. If I refused he would probably just run off again and I didn't want that, not at all.

'I tell you what, I will take you out for a walk after breakfast

103

and we'll go by her place, but you know if she tells us to go away, we might have to.'

'Oh she doesn't mean it, she likes me really. Anyway, thank you, Dad, I'll eat all my breakfast and then clean up really well.'

That put a spring in his paws. I just hoped I wasn't going to regret it.

After everyone had eaten breakfast, the humans were going to spend the morning on the beach – the sun had returned – and we could join them after our walk/Chanel search. Although we hadn't fallen in love with the sand, we were getting more and more used to it. Our humans packed up food, blankets, buckets and spades and then headed out, leaving George and I alone. The more I thought about his crush on Chanel the more I worried, but at the same time it allowed me to go and check on Andrea. I didn't trust that woman. Not one little bit.

'What are you doing in my garden?' a voice hissed as soon as we crawled through the hedge. We straightened up to see Chanel looking angry as she stood, slowly waving her tail from side to side.

'We were just taking our morning constitutional,' I said, trying to be friendly.

'Is that how you city cats talk?' I had never heard a cat sound so disdainful. 'Well the thing is,' she continued, 'that this is private property, it's my property actually, and I would rather you didn't set paw on it.'

'Hello,' George said as if she hadn't spoken. 'You are looking very beautiful today.'

I tried not to be amused, but it was funny; as if his crush had rendered him deaf.

'What on earth is he talking about?' Chanel looked at me. As if I knew.

We were interrupted by two sets of bare feet approaching and I saw there were two very pretty girls, wearing matching sundresses.

'Ah there you are, Chanel, Mummy wants you,' one said, picking the cat up. George and I had quickly backed into the hedge so they didn't see us.

'Meow,' Chanel said, sweetly, nuzzling the little girl's neck.

'See, I told you,' George said, as they walked off. 'She really is nice.'

Just not to us, I thought. As we made our way back to our garden I was thinking of what a nice day it was. We could definitely join the others on the beach – I'd decided to give it another chance after my experience yesterday. But George had other ideas. He lay in the sun, by the gap in the hedge, and refused to move.

'Won't you come with me, son?' I asked, trying to coax him.

'No thanks, Dad, I'm staying right here so Chanel knows where to find me.'

There was nothing I could do to get George to budge. He had it bad but I did remember what it was like, so I had to try to be understanding. The problem was that Chanel was not only horrible but also too old for him. Way too old.

I really wanted to join the others on the beach but I couldn't leave George. I occupied myself by exploring the garden. It needed work – Polly said the garden would be done last – but there were some nice bushes, which were messy but interesting. Although loath to leave George, I did make my way round the back; what I liked about Seabreeze Cottage was that you could access the back of the house from the front, so I could see if there was any action in the back courtyard. There wasn't, and no sign of Gilbert either.

I was getting a little bit bored of watching George by the time the families returned. They were all laughing and joking, a bit pink from the sun, and of course covered in sand. Claire spread out the blankets on the lawn, and flopped down. Franceska and Tomasz were going to go into town and their boys were going with them as they needed to buy some clothes and bits and pieces. Everyone waved them off as they got into their car and then we passed a pleasant couple of hours in the front garden. Martha and Summer had a picnic with their dolls and teddy bears and Henry and Toby played with a football. Jonathan and Matt joined in at one point while Claire and Polly looked on fondly.

'This is just how I imagined it would be,' Claire said, as I sat next to her.

'George, play ball with us,' Henry said.

'Meow.' George refused to move. Toby tried to persuade him but he wasn't for persuading.

'Oh shall we go and get some of those lovely ice creams?' Polly said.

'Did I hear ice cream?' Matt said.

'Yay!' Toby and Henry shouted.

'There's a van across the road, it does the best ice creams. They're made from local clotted cream, George and Alfie are in love with them too. We'll go.' Claire stood up.

When they returned they handed out the cones. One for each of the kids, an enormous one each for Matt and Jonathan and then Claire held one out to me.

'George, Alfie, want to share an ice cream?' she said. I have never seen George move so quickly in his life. He put his nose straight into the cone, and everyone laughed. Ha, he liked ice cream more than Chanel, there was hope for him yet.

'Who knew cats liked ice cream?' Matt said.

'You'd think it would be too cold,' Jonathan chuckled.

So much for sharing, I thought, but then I would never take that joy away from my boy so I didn't mind too much. I'd wait for the left-overs. If there were any, I thought, as George licked manically at it, his little pink tongue darting back and forth.

'I think it's not a proper holiday without ice-cream cones,' Toby said. 'Even for cats.' Everyone laughed.

I was pretty sure I knew what they were thinking. Everyone seemed to be happier here, or different at least, and even Toby was growing in confidence. It was as if the sun of Seabreeze Cottage was shining down on all of us and it was lovely. If only George would get over Chanel, I thought, as he discarded his ice cream and ran back to the bush. I finished it off and then lay down for a well-earned nap. After all, there were plenty of people around to keep their eye on George and one of my favourite things about this holiday was sleeping in the sun on the lawn.

Aleksy woke me, and I slowly opened my eyes. Blinking in the sun, I meowed and cuddled into him.

'Hi, Alfie,' he said. 'We seemed to have been shopping for

hours. Tommy got so bored he was in trouble – when we got back Mum and Dad said he had to go to his room for a while! Anyway, I am going to set up our cricket set in the garden and our new friends are going to come and play with us after tea. It's going to be ace!' He tickled my fur and I stretched out to encourage him. 'Oh, Alfie, you are such a softy,' he said, laughing.

I followed him around as he set up the game of cricket. When he finished I saw George sneaking out from the hedge. That boy had stamina, I had to give him that.

'Did you see her?' I asked.

'No, Dad, no sign, but then I heard the girls in the garden. They don't like us.'

'What do you mean?' I pricked my ears up. What now?

'Well, I heard them say that their mum didn't want us here, and they definitely didn't want the children here.'

'That's not nice,' I said, carefully.

'Anyway, they said we wouldn't be here for long anyway. What does that mean?'

'I've no idea, George, but I tell you what, I will find out, so don't worry. But if you hear anything else, then tell me.'

'I will. But obviously Chanel won't agree with them, she likes me, I know she does.'

'Um, maybe,' I said. Here we go, I thought. There was something not very nice about all the people living next door and I wasn't pleased about it. We were all so happy here, I couldn't have anything or anyone spoiling it.

Just as we were all finishing our tea there was a knock on the door. Matt went to get it. He came back alone.

'Aleksy and Tommy, there are four children saying they are here to play cricket with you?'

'Oh yes, can we play now, in the garden?' Aleksy said hopefully.

'Of course, if you've finished eating,' Franceska said.

'Can I go?' Toby asked.

'And me?' Henry said.

'Of course, but, Aleksy, you are in charge of the younger ones and keep the front door open. We'll pop out as soon as we've cleaned up,' Claire said.

I noticed Summer and Martha didn't want to go with them.

'Not wanting to play cricket?' Jonathan asked his daughter.

'No, it's a silly game,' she said, folding her arms.

'We had a bit of a disaster when they played on the beach,' Claire whispered in Jonathan's ear. 'Summer couldn't hit the ball and she had a bit of a tantrum.'

'Right, girls, who would like to watch a Disney film as a treat?' Polly trilled, and they jumped up. It seemed much easier to keep everyone happy by the sea.

'Do I watch a film with the girls or play cricket with the boys?' George asked.

'Cricket might be fun, come on, let's go outside.'

I ran out with George on my heels. The game was in full swing. There were two boys, roughly the same ages as Aleksy and Tommy, who were called Simon and Ben, and there were two girls, Millie and Jess. They seemed like nice children. Toby and Henry had to stand around to do what they called 'fielding', which meant they were expected to fetch the ball wherever it landed. I think they got the short straw but didn't seem to notice, and were happy to do so. George said he would help them and he ran after the ball alongside the other boys. It was cute to watch. At one point, Claire and Franceska brought out drinks and then left them – as Jonathan said, it made the kids feel grown up to be allowed to play without adult supervision for once and Claire said they played out like this and on the beach when she was a child without any of her parents or her aunt worrying. So I moved between all my humans, keeping my eye on all of them, which was my favourite thing to do.

I had just reached outside when the gate opened and the two girls from next door appeared.

'Hey,' Aleksy said, waving the cricket bat, 'do you want to join in?'

The local children suddenly went very quiet and looked at their feet.

'No, we don't. And I'm surprised at you.' Savannah, the oldest girl, glared at Simon, Ben, Millie and Jess. 'What do you think you are doing?'

'Uh, we're playing cricket,' Tommy said. Toby, Henry and George were staring at the girls.

'I wasn't talking to you,' Savannah said, nastily. 'You guys,' she pointed at the local children, 'are not allowed to play with them. They don't belong here.'

'No they don't,' Serafina, the younger girl, colluded.

'What on earth?' Aleksy looked appalled. 'We live here, well we do in the holidays, so what is your problem?'

Aleksy used to be quite shy but with my help and the fact he was such a popular boy at his school, he had gained confidence and come out of his shell.

'Um, the thing is that we all go to the same school.' Simon looked awkward.

'And, well, we are all friends,' Ben added, looking unhappy.

'So, we can all play then,' Tommy said a bit aggressively. He was almost as big as Aleksy, despite being a couple of years younger, and he wasn't scared of anyone.

'No, you can't.' Savannah poked him in the chest.

'Oy,' Tommy said. But he backed off. He was a gentleman and wouldn't hit a girl.

'Our friends won't be playing with you again. Come on, right now!' Savannah shouted and the children all mumbled apologies before following her out of the garden.

'We should go home now, anyway,' Jess said, looking embarrassed.

'Shut up, Jess,' Savannah shouted.

'Wow, that wasn't nice,' Henry said. Toby looked devastated.

'Hey, Henry, Toby, don't worry, we can still play. And now they've gone, you can take a turn with the bat.' Aleksy put his arm around the younger boy.

'Finally!' Toby said.

'Well now we know where Chanel gets it from,' I said to George when we were out of earshot.

'What, you mean her beauty? Yes, I see it,' he replied and I raised my whiskers in despair.

Aleksy told Franceska what happened with the children and she was visibly upset. When the children were in bed, or settled in front of the TV, she told the others.

'Like mother, like daughters,' Polly said.

'Oh God, I'm not having them start on the children though,' Claire said.

111

'Don't worry, you know what kids are like,' Jonathan started. 'I know, we'll go and see this Andrea woman and have a word.' He looked pleased with himself.

'What, me and you?' Claire didn't look so pleased.

'No, us men will go. We'll use our charm to tell her that not only can she not buy the cottage but also that the children should all play happily together.'

'Really? All of us?' Tomasz looked unsure.

'Won't we seem intimidating?' Matt asked.

As Polly, Claire and Franceska laughed, I felt a bit sorry for the men. They were about as intimidating as George.

'What?' Matt said again.

'You guys are about as intimidating as a teabag,' Polly finished, wiping tears from her eyes. Everyone was laughing apart from the poor men.

They all headed out before they changed their minds and I couldn't resist, I had to go with them and see this for myself. Thankfully George had already gone upstairs with Toby so I didn't have to worry about him mooning over Chanel as I headed out. The men went through the gate to Andrea's house while I darted under the hedge, waiting by the front door, hidden just out of sight, until I saw them appear. They rang the brass doorbell and waited, as did I. I decided to stay out of sight in case Chanel was there. I didn't feel like antagonising her or having her be rude to me this evening.

Andrea opened the door wearing a low-cut dress, which had a slit up her leg, high heels, full make-up and her long blonde hair shone very brightly. It was almost blinding. I wondered what her secret was; I'd like my fur to gleam like that.

'Hello,' she said, smiling widely. She actually appeared to be friendly.

'So sorry to interrupt you,' Jonathan said. Tomasz didn't seem to know where to look, and Matt was also a bit frozen. Jonathan glared at them. 'I'm Jonathan, this is Matt and Tomasz from Seabreeze Cottage.'

'Oh how lovely to meet you. Of course I've already met your lovely wives, and now you. How are you finding it?' She was so warm and friendly I felt wrong-pawed.

'Well, it's very nice so far,' Matt said. 'And the kids are having such a fun time, just being away from London is so healthy for them.' He was gushing a bit, I thought.

'Oh it is and Lynstow is one of the best places in the world, I am always saying to my husband. Of course that's why we moved here.'

'Is he here?' Tomasz finally found his voice. I think he was more comfortable dealing with men.

'No, I'm afraid he's away on business at the moment. Just little me and the girls, oh and of course Chanel.' Chanel appeared from behind her legs.

'Right, well.' Jonathan was looking awkward again. 'It's just that we wanted to introduce ourselves and also, it's probably nothing, but there was . . . an incident with the children earlier.'

'An incident?' The smile hadn't moved from Andrea's face.

'Yes, some local children were playing in our garden and your girls told them to leave and that they weren't allowed to play with our kids,' Matt explained.

'Someone must have put them up to it. My girls are so sweet, they would never say anything like that. Don't worry, I will have a word and find out who put them up to it, and of course all the children can play together. I am hoping,' she looked directly at Jonathan, then reached out to lightly touch his arm,' that we shall all be the best of friends. I am so happy to have you as neighbours.'

'Right, well that's great, and we'll see you soon?' Jonathan was flustered, Tomasz uncertain and Matt confused.

'I look forward to it.' Andrea smiled again, before she closed the door.

I darted back to Seabreeze Cottage to await the men's return. This was going to be interesting.

'Well?' Claire demanded as Jonathan, Tomasz and Matt trooped in. Franceska was cooking and Polly and Claire were setting the table.

'She's nice,' Jonathan said.

'Very nice,' Matt added.

'Her shoes were nice,' Tomasz said, turning as red as a tomato.

'What do you mean? She's horrible,' Polly snapped.

'No, not to us, she said she was so happy to have us as neighbours and that someone must have put her girls up to being nasty, they would never say anything like that apparently,' Jonathan explained. 'And anyway, she'll sort it out.'

'That's not the case: Aleksy, Tommy, Henry and Toby all corroborated the same story.'

'She didn't say they didn't say it, she said someone must be behind it because they are sweet girls. Anyway, she's going to have a word so it'll all be sorted. And she didn't mention buying the house, just how nice it was to have us living here, so perhaps you got the wrong end of the stick,' Matt added.

Claire, Franceska and Polly exchanged a glance.

'God, why are all men so gullible,' Polly said.

'What do you mean?' Matt asked.

'She's clearly flirting with you and now you think your own wives are liars,' Claire stormed. I actually agreed with her.

'No, of course not, but we're just thinking that you might have got off on the wrong foot, but now it's all going to be fine,' Tomasz said.

'Dazzled by her beauty no doubt,' Franceska added.

'I didn't notice she was—'

'I can't even remember what she looked like—'

'No, not at all—' all the men started objecting at once but Claire silenced them. The damage was done. They had been blinded by Andrea the way George had by Chanel, it was clear for us all to see.

With all the excitement I'd nearly forgotten about Gilbert, but as everyone retired for the evening, and there was no sign of him, I ignored my rumbling tummy and the left-over food that had been so enticingly tipped into my bowl and left it for him. I was too tired to stay up and see if he came back, but I hoped he would, and that he'd eat what I left for him, because I hated to think of any cat being hungry. I had been that cat once and it wasn't nice. I would have left a note for him, but being a cat I couldn't, so leaving him some lovely food would hopefully convey my message: that he was welcome here and I would like to get to know him. The way to a cat's heart is through its stomach after all. You can never have too many friends; the horrible experience with Chanel, Andrea and her daughters proved the truth of that.

Chapter
Eight

The absence of the men was felt keenly on Monday morning. I was secretly excited though, because Gilbert had emptied my bowl, and therefore it was obvious he understood my message. I still hadn't seen him but I thought if I got enough rest today, if George let me, then I would stay up late tonight to have a chat with him. I felt as if it would be great to have a new friend here, and also an ally wouldn't go amiss either.

We had had an uneventful Sunday with no other children sighted, no Andrea, or Chanel, despite George's desperation. The poor kitten was devastated and had insisted on camping out in the hedge watching her house for hours, but to no avail. I had to persuade him back in with the promise of ice cream, and then I had no idea how to get any. Thankfully Summer had a cone which she thought was hilarious to feed him. Jonathan wasn't impressed though, but it was cute and Claire videoed the whole thing. Little George, all eager with his head in an ice-cream cone, pink ice cream all over his fur when he emerged. It took an age to get him properly clean but at least it took his mind off Chanel for a few minutes.

Anyway, when in the afternoon Franceska had driven the men back to the train station we had all been sad to see them go. It was lovely here but it was definitely better when they were all with us. Everyone seemed to agree. We all missed them.

'I thought we might go across the estuary on the ferry today, cheer us up,' Claire suggested.

'Fab idea. I can leave the builders, they are doing a great job with the attic,' Polly agreed. 'And they don't need me at all.'

'It'll be nice to see another new place,' Franceska thirded. 'Right, children, get dressed and we can go out.'

George and I went to the boys' room as they got ready.

'I want to go on a ferry,' George hissed to me. Honestly this kitten was always in need of entertainment.

'We can't and, anyway, the estuary is water, we don't do water,' I said. That was the end of that.

That wasn't the end of that. George was being all cute with Tommy and I knew exactly what his game was. He was rubbing his legs, purring, lying on his back asking to be tickled; he was trying to give Tommy a message.

'Hey, Aleksy, what if we take the cats with us? We can smuggle them in our backpacks, like we used to with Alfie when we were little.' Actually, Aleksy did that only once, but obviously they had never forgotten.

'But, Tommy, we could get into so much trouble if we're caught.' Thankfully Aleksy was sensible. 'But it would be kind of fun to have Alfie and George with us.' I could see Aleksy, who was a clever boy, weighing it up. I really liked adventures but when they involved water, no thank you. 'It would be funny though, like the cats were stowaways. If we get caught we have to say we didn't know the cats were there.' Not that clever then. Who would believe that I would voluntarily go anywhere near water? No one, that's who.

'Yes!' Tomasz high-fived Aleksy. Operation cats on a ferry was a go, whether I liked it or not.

George was so excited as we stayed in the boys' room like we'd been ordered to. The plan was that just as they were ready to go they would say they needed their backpacks, come upstairs and get us. No one would ever find out. I raised my whiskers. I loved a good plan, don't get me wrong, it was what I did, but I didn't have a great feeling about this one.

I tried to quash my misgivings as I peered out of the gap in Aleksy's backpack. This wasn't a bad way to travel, I thought, as the sun shone and we got to see more of the village. We walked past the beach – busy with families – then along to a big wall. There were steps leading down to the water and a boat, which didn't look very big, or safe for that matter, was waiting. I tried to be brave but my fur was quivering. I couldn't see George, who was tucked up in Tommy's backpack, but I hoped he was alright. It felt a bit jerky as they went down the steps.

'God, it's a bit steep,' Claire said.

'Just be careful, children,' Franceska said.

Yes, I thought, please be careful. As the backpack was put on the floor with a gentle thud, I looked around through the small gap. All I could see were legs. There were all of us, plus some other people on the boat. Luckily I couldn't see any water, so I could pretend it wasn't there. I just hoped we didn't sink. When I first met Claire she was sad and watched this film called *Titanic* a lot, so I knew just how precarious boats could be.

I couldn't see George still but I knew he would be excited by this. He didn't share my fears, and actually in some ways that was a good thing. I didn't want him to be scared of everything, but I did want him to sense danger. It was another parenting lesson I was trying hard to get right. The boat ride itself was quite smooth, there were a couple of rocky patches but nothing too bad, I thought as I almost held my breath.

'I love this,' I heard Toby say, and Claire kissed him. 'I've never been on a boat before.'

'Have I?' Summer asked.

'No, darling, this is your first ever boat trip, both of you.' Sometimes I forgot that there was a time when Toby wasn't with us, and I felt emotional. He was such an important part of our family now.

The boat stopped with a jerk and I fell back, but luckily Aleksy had put a jumper in the bag so it was soft for me. Then I felt him pick me up and we were off. As we disembarked I saw us walking up a steep slope where lots of people were playing.

'Let's just find a space on the quay to decamp,' Polly said. Again I was put down on the ground. The quay led down to the water and I could see lots of people were scattered along it, with fishing lines. I perked up. Things were improving. I might not like water but I certainly liked fish.

'What are you doing?' I heard Tommy ask someone.

'Crabbing. We're trying to catch crabs,' a voice replied. Oh, not fish then; I felt disappointed.

'Can we do that?' Aleksy asked.

'Please,' Henry said.

'Gosh, I vaguely remember doing that when I was a kid. Blimey. Right, I'll go to the shop and get lines and buckets. Summer, you can share Toby's.'

'Oh, and Martha and Henry can share. But I don't want any of you getting too close to the edge.' Polly echoed my fears.

'Psst,' a voice said, and I looked to see George's face. Tomasz had put the backpacks next to each other.

'Are you having fun?' I asked.

'The most fun, but can I go crabbing?'

'Best not. Let's stay here and watch for a bit, we don't want to get into trouble,' I hissed.

'OK, Dad.' George sounded happy, which made me happy. I settled down to enjoy the sliver of sunlight coming into the bag and I felt sleepy all of a sudden.

'Alfie,' I heard Aleksy whisper. I opened my eyes. How long had I been sleeping for?

'Meow,' I said, sleepily.

'George is out of the backpack. The adults have taken the little ones to the toilet, and left us and now George is insisting on crabbing with us.' He sounded panicked. I climbed out of the bag, stretched – my legs were a little stiff – and looked for my kitten.

'George,' I said, quietly.

'Yes, Dad.'

'We were only allowed to come if we stayed out of sight,' I explained, trying not to sound impatient.

'Yes, but where's the fun in that?' he said. He had a point. I thought back to when I was younger, before George, and I used to go on many adventures. Yes I got into trouble at times, but at least I had some great experiences. I realised I was getting a bit boring in my old age. I tickled my boy with my tail.

'OK, but listen, stay close to me and watch out for dogs.'

Aleksy looked worried but Tommy thought it was funny as we joined them on the quay to see what this crabbing business was. They had these long orange lines which they were dangling into the water. Beside them were two buckets which contained some funny-looking creatures – crabs – in. Aleksy was putting food on the line, it didn't smell too bad actually, but I tried not to eat it. I was beginning to enjoy myself, when Ben, one of the children from the other day, approached.

'Alright,' he said.

'Hi, Ben,' Aleksy said, sounding friendly.

'Hello.' Tommy was more suspicious.

'Sorry about the other day, those girls, Savannah especially, have started to be a bit bossy. They've always been nice girls, but lately they can be a bit mean. I am sorry though, we were having fun.'

'They seemed really horrible,' Tommy said.

'But they aren't always like that. I think that maybe they were upset that we were playing with you and they weren't. And like I said, recently they have been a bit meaner than normal, and everyone tries to keep the peace with them.' He looked at his sandalled feet.

'You're scared of them?' Tommy asked.

Ben nodded, his face reddening.

'I know what bullies are like,' Aleksy said. He did, I had to go to school with him once to sort out a little boy who was bullying Aleksy. 'But you know, you need to stand up to them.'

'I know, but we've been friends for years, and normally

they are really nice, so we don't really understand.' Ben looked downcast. 'We do want to play with you though. But what if we still meet up on the beach? And now, how about I join you crabbing? My mum is having coffee with one of her friends so I'm a bit bored to be honest.'

'Here,' Aleksy said, handing him his line. 'You have a go.'

I was so proud of my boys. They didn't hold a grudge.

'Oh, your cats are here!' Ben giggled.

'Yes, we stowed them away on the ferry.' Tommy beamed with pride.

Ben stroked both me and George. 'That is so cool!' he said. George, loving the attention, started showing off. He put his head into one of the buckets.

'Yelp!' George sprang up, an angry crab attached to his nose.

'Oh boy,' Aleksy said. 'What do we do?' He looked panicked, as did I. What on earth was this crab doing attaching itself to my kitten?

'Don't wriggle,' Ben said, picking George up and gently removing the crab. He carefully placed it back in the bucket as George rubbed his nose, which looked a bit swollen, with his paw. I backed away from the buckets and nuzzled George.

'Will he be alright?' George was making a very loud noise, I knew it meant that it hurt but there was nothing I could do. Ben cradled him and tried to stroke him. I think we were all glad that he was there. I saw the boys looking worried but then Aleksy laughed.

'Sorry, George, but you did look funny with a crab on your nose,' he giggled. The others joined in and I have to say I did see the funny side. If only someone had taken a photo – that would have gone down a storm on Facebook!

'Yowl!' However, George did not.

We were so caught up in the excitement we didn't notice the others returning.

'What on earth is going on?' Franceska said. Aleksy, Tomasz, Ben, myself and George all looked at them. At least that silenced George.

'Alfie, George, what are you doing here?' Claire snapped. The children giggled.

'Um, we may have accidentally stowed them away,' Tommy said.

'No, they stowed away on their own,' Aleksy corrected, but he was such a good boy he couldn't tell a lie without laughing.

'You boys!' Franceska chastised. 'Right, well there's nothing we can do now, and we are heading back soon anyway. Ice cream?' She smiled and picked me up.

'MEOW!' George said loudly and everyone laughed.

I was glad when we got back to Seabreeze Cottage with no further incidents. Apart from the crab incident – poor George's nose was still a bit swollen – we'd had a very nice day out. Ben had been helpful and I was pleased that they were friends again, although I knew that those girls wouldn't exactly welcome them being so. But as they said, if they played together on the beach – a public place – hopefully there was nothing they could say about that. Although I thought they probably could. I wondered what had happened to them to make them mean – Ben said that they were nice until recently. It was another conundrum for me to add to all the others.

I fleetingly wondered if Chanel had been nice once, but I couldn't see that.

As they all sat down to eat tea, and George and I went to the garden, I felt quite relaxed. Of course, George went straight to the gap in the hedge and crawled through. He struck gold, because Chanel was there, sniffing some of Andrea's very nice flowers.

'Hello!' George said, excitedly. I stayed close to him, just in case. He didn't need any other injuries today.

'Oh it's you,' she said, narrowing her eyes and swishing her tail.

'How are you?' he asked, bouncing around. Honestly, he hadn't quite mastered the art of flirting yet.

'I will be much better when you have gone,' she hissed.

'Hey, there's no need for that,' I said.

'Look, you might be staying next door but this is my house, my garden, and you need to keep out of it.'

'Oh well, you can come to my garden any time,' George said, looking hopeful.

'My owner is going to get rid of all of you, mark my words,' Chanel replied. 'So, it won't be your garden for much longer.'

Again, I felt a shiver in my fur as Chanel stalked off and I herded George back to our side of the hedge.

'Oh, Dad, she's so lovely,' George sighed. 'And I really think she likes me.'

'Did you hear what she said?' I asked.

'Not really. I was too busy looking at her beautiful eyes,' he replied.

There was no hope, none at all.

But it annoyed me that a run-in with Chanel – even if George hadn't noticed it – had ruined what was otherwise a nice day out. Well that and a crab. I had been relieved, by the way, when the boys put the crabs back in the sea. I think they should have been allowed to stay there to be honest – I wasn't sure how kind crabbing actually was. Even if the crabs weren't hurt they were sort of kidnapped, which seemed a little unfair. Anyway, as we went back inside we met Polly on the doorstep with a shopping bag from the little local store.

'Do you think we'll get more ice cream?' George asked hopefully.

'No, I think there's been enough today.' I patted his head with my paw.

Polly opened the door and we followed her into the kitchen.

'Hey,' Claire said, as Polly put the bags down on the counter.

'That woman . . .' Polly fumed.

'Oh, now what happened?' Franceska said.

'Andrea and two of her friends were in the café in the shop and she was pretty nasty.'

'So what she said to the men?'

'Total rubbish. I said to her, "You didn't mention to our husbands that you wanted us out of Seabreeze Cottage," and she replied, sneering through those bright pink lips of hers, "Oh dear, it must have slipped my mind. But mark my words, you'll regret not selling it to me soon enough."'

'You're kidding?' Claire said. 'What did her friends say?'

'They looked embarrassed but didn't speak. Well, one of them tried to introduce herself but Andrea told her to shut up. A bit like the kids, actually, it's like they're scared of her, but I tell you what, that woman is not nice, and we need to watch out.'

'Oh no, I don't like this hostility,' Franceska said, brow furrowing.

'Don't worry, Frankie, we will not be bullied by her.' Polly looked tough.

'There's nothing she can do anyway,' Claire pointed out. 'Yes, she might intimidate us but we're big girls, we can handle it.'

I sincerely hoped they could.

Chapter Nine

I felt slightly despondent as the day drew to a close. The women had managed to push Andrea to the backs of their minds, the children were happy and George, well, he was totally bewitched by Chanel, but I was the realistic one of the family. I could sense when there was trouble ahead and I felt it keenly. That night, I decided to lie in wait for Gilbert. He had been in every night since I'd started leaving him food, although gone by morning, and now it was time for me to speak with him again. I could do with a local ally, and he was my only option.

I waited patiently, playing with a pile of sand that hadn't yet been swept up. I was trying to grow fonder of sand, seeing as we would be here a lot, but I still wasn't sure about it. It was not only grainy but it stuck to everything. I felt as if I couldn't get it off me, no matter how much I cleaned myself.

Just as I was replaying all the events of the holiday so far, I heard the cat flap open and soon Gilbert appeared. He stopped as he saw me. He was an unusual-looking cat; I quite envied his spotty coat.

'Hello,' I said, brushing yet more sand from my paw.

'I should thank you, I suppose,' Gilbert replied, gruffly. 'The food. Most welcome.'

'I was hoping to see you though. You know my family wouldn't mind if they saw you – they love cats and my kitten George would love to meet you.'

'All the same . . . I'm not much of a family cat.'

'But why? I mean, most cats have families. My friend Dustbin, he's a working cat, and he likes being feral but he's the exception and he's sort of part of one of my families anyway,' I gushed.

'Right.' Gilbert was a cat of few words.

'So why don't you have a family?' I pushed.

'Well, I did have a family but they weren't nice. I don't talk about it. Listen, like I said, thank you for the food, I am grateful, normally I have to get my own scraps, so I have enjoyed it, but I don't really want to be around people.'

'Funny you should say that, do you know the next-door neighbours: the cat Chanel and the woman, Andrea?'

'I've seen them about, but as I already said,' he glared at me with his yellow eyes, 'I keep to myself.'

'Well they're not nice.' I'm not easily discouraged. 'And they have threatened us, saying they want this cottage and they want us out. And if that happens, I am guessing they won't just leave it empty for you to live in either.'

'Then I'll find somewhere else.' He really wasn't an easy cat to crack.

'Well you could, but you know this is a nice house and we like it here. We're not giving it up, and I was thinking if you hear anything, anything at all, you might let me know.'

'OK.' He looked at the food bowl, which was quite full. 'I'll keep my ears open, but I can't promise anything. Now if you don't mind, I am hungry.'

'Of course, and I'll leave you alone, I get it. But, just to let you know in the day we go out a lot, the builders are here but they're all upstairs, and anyway you seem quite good at keeping hidden. Just if you wanted to come by then . . .

well, you might almost have the house to yourself and I can always make sure there is food for you.'

'Appreciated.' He started to eat, and I turned to go. 'Oh and Alfie.'

'Yes.' I turned around.

'Thank you.'

I had a good night's sleep after that, curled up on Claire's bed. I wished that Gilbert would meet the family though, they would welcome him after all and I thought that when we weren't here he could sort of act like a guard cat for us. I had a vision of us all becoming the best of friends and he might be able to help me with Andrea as well. I know he wasn't exactly tripping over himself to be my friend, but small steps. One paw at a time.

George woke me by licking my head. I felt warm in my heart and my fur as I stretched out.

'I slept in,' I said.

'I've been up for hours, with Toby and Summer. The others didn't wake quite as early as us but everyone's up now and it's breakfast time.' George bounced up and down excitedly on the bed.

'Good, I'm quite hungry as it happens.' I realised, having given up quite a bit of my food to Gilbert, I was a little bit peckish. As I padded into the kitchen I took in the scene, children munching on toast and porridge, the adults sipping from mugs, and George lapping water out of our water bowl. This was what the holiday was all about, I reminded myself, not the problems that I was fretting about. I tucked into my breakfast, feeling much better.

There was a knock at the door.

'I'll go,' Polly said. 'In case it's Andrea,' she added. I bounded after her.

A woman I'd never seen stood on the doorstep, wearing a big hat and large dark glasses.

'Hello,' Polly said, questioningly.

'Hi, I'm Amber, Ben's mum.' She shuffled awkwardly and glanced furtively around. 'Can I come in?'

Polly led her into the kitchen. The children had all dispersed and I could hear them in the living room with the TV on loudly. George was cleaning himself in the kitchen when we walked in with Amber.

'Hello?' Franceska said.

'This is Amber,' Polly said, as Amber pulled off her hat and glasses. She was very slim with dark hair, pretty but not all over-done like Andrea.

'You were in the cafe yesterday?' Polly narrowed her eyes. Amber nodded.

'Hi,' Claire said. 'Sit down.' She held her hand out and Amber shook it.

'Look, I came to apologise.' She sounded a bit nervous. 'God, if Andrea knew I was here, she'd kill me. Anyway, I don't like the way she's treating you all, and the kids. Ben loved spending time with your boys yesterday and I told him that he is to play with them and not take any notice of the Gold children.'

'Gold children?' Polly asked. She sat down opposite Amber.

'Their surname, Gold.'

'Oh, I didn't know, but it's appropriate, for the way that woman acts,' Polly quipped.

'What is it with her anyway?' Claire asked.

'I'm not sure. Andrea had always been at the centre of village life, or she has been since she moved here. When Savannah was a baby she organised baby and mum groups, she was so supportive, friendly, bringing people together, sorting out a social life for us bored mums, and then when the kids started school she threw herself into the PTA,' Amber explained. 'She's always been at the heart of Lynstow, organising parties and celebrations, she has a bookclub, she's always hosting at her house, and very generous with it. Her husband is successful, you see. But in the last six or so months she has changed, and she's been different . . . She acts as if everything is great when we ask her, but her husband hasn't been seen for ages – apparently he's travelling for business. Anyway, recently she's become obsessed with this house. I have no idea why or why she's changed so much.'

'Just because her husband's rich, it doesn't give her the right to act like she owns the place,' Claire said.

'Quite, but I really think there's more to it than this.' Amber shuddered.

'But what?' Franceska looked terrified.

'I wish I knew. She says everything is perfect but clearly from her behaviour towards you guys it's not.'

'She's been pretty horrid to us,' Franceska said.

'I know but, well, as I said, she's been at the heart of this village for so long, we just, well, we just don't want to fall out. If she needs us, which we think she does, we want to be there for her, but well, we also don't approve of how she's behaved towards you.'

'Why does she want this cottage so much?' Polly asked.

'That I don't know. I was asking Kate, the other woman

you saw us with yesterday, and she's just as flummoxed. Andrea's behaviour has got worse lately, she is becoming a middle-aged mean girl.'

'You're kidding?' Claire was amazed.

'I wish.'

'I still don't understand why she wants this place so much though,' Polly said.

'I wish I knew. She told us she is going to get it, and she spouts all this stuff about how awful it is for out-of-towners to move into the village for the odd weekend and holiday, but I don't buy it myself.'

'Neither do we,' Polly concurred.

'Look, if she knew I was here she'd be furious, but I wanted you to know I am on your side and if there is anything I can do to help, well, short of standing up to Andrea, I will.'

'You know, that's nice of you, and we do appreciate it. Also we won't tell Andrea.' Claire reached out and touched Amber's hand.

Later, after she'd gone, the builders arrived and the women all got ready to take the children out to the beach again. Polly picked me up and gave me a stroke.

'That woman needs bringing down a peg or a million, Alfie,' she said, looking me in the eyes. I blinked my agreement. And I was just the cat to do it.

I needed a plan but was at a loss to what to do. I had George to contend with too; he was pining for Chanel, insisting on sitting under the hedge, and I think Chanel was wise to him because she was avoiding it. He glimpsed her from afar but there was nothing he could do. I tried to reason with him but he was a kitten and therefore reason wasn't one of the most effective tools. While he sulked, lying on the living room window seat, I went upstairs. The builders had made great progress, and the bathroom would be going in soon. Then the floors would be done and the kids could move while they then started on the next floor. It was all working out quite efficiently, as Polly had so cleverly devised. However, when I reached the top floor, I heard a commotion.

'What the hell?' Colin was saying, looking at a hole in the ceiling of one of the rooms.

'It looks as if there's a hole in the roof,' Liam, the builder I'd seen with Andrea, said. 'I'm guessing the whole roof is unstable,' he added. Pete and Mark, the other two builders, looked confused.

'No, it's not, I did the roof myself a couple of months ago, and it was fine. The tiles were all secure and none were broken. There's been no storm, nothing to cause this. This isn't right,' he said, staring at Liam.

'Look, boss, it looks as if the hole's been made from the inside,' Pete pointed out, as he stood on top of the ladder, where there was a hole in the ceiling, fairly small but clear. Pete scooted down the ladder and Colin climbed up.

'Pete's right. OK, Liam, Mark, did one of you do this?' he asked staring at them. 'It's gone right through, which means a couple of tiles need replacing, as well as the ceiling repairing. It's a lot of unnecessary work and Polly is going to go mad.' He was red-faced as the boys shook their heads. But seeing the look on Liam's face, I immediately knew it was him. He had somehow done this! I meowed loudly and scratched him on the leg.

'Ow, blooming cat,' he yelled. They all looked at me. I sat down and started cleaning my paws innocently.

'Liam, was this you?' Colin pushed. Liam turned red and started denying it but he wasn't a great liar. Honestly, it was written all over his face.

'It was an accident,' he mumbled. 'I well, I — I'm sorry,' he blustered.

'How do you accidentally put a hole in the roof?' Colin asked. Liam shrugged. I thought that if my suspicions were right — and they seemed so — and Andrea had put him up to this, she could have picked someone a bit more efficient at sabotage. 'Right, well this is going to set us back so, Liam, you'll be working overtime for no extra money. Pete, keep a close rein on him while I go and sort the tiles out. If you don't buck up your ideas, then you'll be out of a job, Liam.'

'Sorry,' Liam mumbled and I felt pleased with myself. I had sorted that one out. Although I had a bad feeling it was the first of many.

I told George what happened but he was so lovesick he barely registered what I was saying. Or so I thought.

'If I keep a close eye on Chanel, I might be able to find out what her owner is up to,' he pointed out. I was impressed. I hadn't thought of that, but he was right. Kill two birds with one paw so to speak. We would have to stalk Chanel, and that would keep my boy happy as well as hopefully give us more of an idea what was actually going on. And at the same time I could keep an eye on Andrea.

We stopped in the front garden to look at our families all playing on the beach. They seemed to be playing a running game up and down the sand dunes and I was pleased to see the local children were playing with them again. As we headed under the hedge next door I saw that the car normally parked there was gone, and there was no sign of life. So we started to look around. The house, as far as we could see, was empty but it was a big house so I couldn't be sure.

'Come on,' I said to George. We headed to the back, where again, all was quiet. They had a bigger back garden than us, which was lawned like the front. There was a playhouse and I thought it was a shame they weren't nicer children as Summer and Martha would have loved to play in that. Anyway, we found the cat flap in the back door and George and I looked at each other before sneaking in. I know it wasn't exactly right, but hey, we were on a mission.

We found ourselves in a bigger utility space than our sand room – it was all very smart too – and from there we entered the biggest kitchen I'd ever seen. However, there our plans were halted. The door from the kitchen was closed and there was nowhere else to go. I could smell Chanel's scent but there was no sign of her – she was probably out with Andrea. But George was in heaven as he ran around, sniffing the air and prancing on about how the house was as beautiful as she was. I raised my whiskers in despair.

'Look, we better go,' I said. 'They could come back at any time and if they find us here . . .' It was useful to have had a look at the house but, well, I'd seen enough for now.

'Oh I'm sure Chanel will be so happy to see me,' George trilled.

'That may be but come on, Andrea won't, so let's go. We can try to see her later,' I placated. I was a little worried that my new plan to keep an eye on Chanel was going to have a detrimental effect on George but then he was so smitten, I wasn't sure it could get any worse. Anyway, I reflected as we left their very posh house, George wasn't the most successful stalker – so far anyway.

My families fed us and then said they were going to take an early evening walk, before going to the pub to feed the kids. The women were nicely tired after being outside so much, as were the children. Also, having the builders in the house meant they often couldn't face the extra mess of cooking, but of course they could get food in any of the three pubs, the fish and chip shop or the café, so were spoilt for choice.

I could see how healthy this holiday lifestyle was for them all. Well almost. So as George tucked in, the children excitedly put their sand-filled shoes on and the women all looked on indulgently, I vowed I would do whatever it took to make sure all was going to be alright with Seabreeze Cottage. I felt saddened for a moment about my friends in Edgar Road, and I was definitely missing my side-kick Tiger, my partner, my best friend. She would always see me through the bad times and the plans I had to undertake for the sake of my humans. But this time I was alone. Well, I had George – I looked at him licking his whiskers, not sure how much use he was at the moment – and Gilbert who, although he had thawed slightly, had made it clear he wasn't interested in becoming part of our family. This time, I thought, if I had to act, it looked as if I might have to act alone.

Chapter Ten

OK, so it wasn't much of a plan but I decided to follow Liam. I watched him as much as I could and to say he was acting shifty was an understatement. He was working, but if none of the other builders were looking he was behaving in a suspicious fashion; I was worried he was searching for the next thing to sabotage. Of course I was keeping out of his way – after scratching him the other day he wasn't my biggest fan.

Today, George was pining by his hedge, with a promise not to leave the garden, so I was happy when Liam was charged with fixing the tiles on the roof. They had scaffolding fitted to the back of the house, because windows – they called them skylights – had been fitted into the roof already that week. I was managing to keep an eye on both of them; George and Liam. When the tiles were fixed – it turned out he'd only dislodged two – he came back down to the ground.

'Right, mate, now Colin wants us to finish plastering the opening in the utility room.' Mark had also been keeping an eye on Liam, in case he fell or ruined something else, I presumed.

'Alright,' Liam mumbled. They were standing at the back of the house. 'Is this the pipe for the outdoor shower?' he asked, pointing at a copper pipe which ran up the side of the house.

'Yeah, the shower's being fitted later. The plumber's due back this arfto.' They both looked at the pipes. 'Then we have to put down a wooden tray, it's going to be pretty cool,' Mark explained.

'Right, the plastering, I'll just clear up out here and see you in there,' Liam said. I watched from my safe place as he looked around him. Then he took a tool and started hitting the pipe until he had broken it. I could barely believe it. I was right. This was sabotage, blatant sabotage. I wanted to run out and confront him but then he might hurt me, after all I'm a cat not a burly builder. But I needed to figure out how to either put a stop to him or get the others to catch him. But how? I needed to think this one through before Liam destroyed the house.

He whistled as he went inside and I walked to the hedge.

'I saw her!' George said excitedly.

'Where?' I asked.

'Andrea put her in a little bag and took her and the two children out,' he said. 'But I spotted her as she walked past and I am pretty sure she smiled at me.'

Scowled, more likely, I thought, but I let it go.

'Do you fancy going to sunbathe on the car bonnets again?' I asked.

'Yes, I love that.' My kitten bounded over to the car, where we climbed on the bonnet of Claire's – it had the best sun – and we lay down and let our fur luxuriate in the sun's rays. I tried to relax but in fact I was thinking about Liam and why he was trying to destroy our house. And I knew it had something to do with Andrea.

'George,' I said, thinking aloud. 'If when you're, um, waiting for Chanel, you see any of our builders with Andrea, you will tell me, won't you?'

'Why?' George asked.

'I'm not sure but I think they are causing trouble at the house.'

'But why would they do that?'

'Well Andrea's made no secret of the fact that she wants the house for herself.'

'But if she does that then we can't come here any more?'

'No, and you know what that means, don't you?' I was thinking of the kids, of Claire, Polly and Franceska, of the men who seemed so much more relaxed outside of London.

'Yes,' George replied sounding distraught. 'It means I'll never see Chanel again.' OK, well that would have to do.

I did feel bad using my kitten's unrequited love for, quite frankly, a horrible cat to help with my plan, but I was on limited resources. And I knew that George wouldn't just snap out of his crush on Chanel; no matter what I did, it had to run its course. I would be there to mop up his sadness when it did so, anyway. With a rough idea of what to do next, I decided to have a cat nap.

'Alfie, George, you'll have to move.' Claire's voice interrupted my dreams.

'Meow?' I stretched my paws out.

'I'm going to get Jon and Matt. Tomasz can't come this weekend, he's got staff problems at one of the restaurants apparently, but anyway, you'll be pleased to see Jon and Matt.'

I would, although I would miss seeing Tomasz, and I hoped Franceska wasn't too disappointed. She and her husband had had a bit of a rough patch not long ago, because he'd been working too much. It got so bad that she took the boys back to Poland for the whole of the last summer holidays and we were all terribly worried that they wouldn't come back. However, finally Tomasz came to his senses – I helped of course – and went over there to bring his family back and I thought they had sorted that out. Tomasz had been more attentive to his family and the restaurants were more and more successful but Tomasz was getting much better at delegating. I just hoped that this was still the case.

After all, I didn't need any other problems to add to my growing list. I jumped down from the car and watched as George did the same. I saw the children were in the garden, so I ran to them, George on my heels.

'Alfie, George,' Aleksy said. 'We are going to set up a sports day. It's for the younger ones really,' he said as an aside. I knew that Aleksy still loved playing games but at times had to act like he was grown up. It happened to us all, I thought, looking at George. At times when he played with leaves or chased butterflies I had to act as if I was too grown up for such frivolities but in reality you never are!

The children set up their sports day games. There was to be running, an egg and spoon race, and an obstacle course which was set up with anything they could find. It didn't look very safe but apparently the adults had approved it so who was I to argue.

Three of the children from the village, Ben, Jess and Millie, turned up.

'Ah, I found a whistle,' Tommy said, blowing it. 'Let the games begin.'

We had such fun. I sat back a little as George joined in with Summer and Martha's races. Then Toby and Henry had a go, they laughed so much as they kept dropping their eggs, but although George ran hopefully to lick them up, they were hard boiled and it hurt when one dropped on his head. The bigger children took part in running races, and they finished with what they called a relay, where a stick was passed between the runners. But they were having so much fun they weren't being competitive about it at all! I was in my element to see how happily the children were playing together, and I wished that the adults could all get along the same.

But as Savannah and Serafina marched into our garden, I realised I'd spoken too soon.

'What do you think you are doing?' Savannah demanded.

'Who invited you into our garden?' Aleksy responded. He crossed his arms, as did his brother.

'It won't be your garden for long,' Serafina said.

'What do you mean?' Toby looked terrified.

'This house will be ours soon, Mummy said so. So don't get too comfortable,' Savannah said, spitefully. 'And as for you, Millie, Jess and Ben, why are you playing with them? I said you couldn't.'

'We like playing with them,' Ben mumbled, looking at the grass as he said it.

'Yeah, it's not like you can tell them what to do,' Tommy added.

'Fine, play your stupid games, see if we care. But mark my words, you won't be around for much longer and we won't be sorry to see you go.' They turned and left.

'Wow,' Jess said.

'I don't like that they are so horrible.' Toby looked as if

he was going to cry and my heart went to him. The poor kid was so sensitive and hated any kind of arguing, probably because of his past. Aleksy put his arm round him.

'Toby, you're not to worry about them, you've got us now,' he said, and Toby smiled.

'And we are going to play with you, no matter what they say,' Millie added. 'My mum said it was about time we stood up to those two anyway. They've been so mean lately.' Her voice wobbled uncertainly, but I was glad.

'Yeah, when we play with you guys you don't tell us what to do or tell us we're rubbish like they do,' Ben added.

'Those girls need teaching a lesson,' Aleksy said. 'And the best lesson is for us to have so much fun they will want to join in and play with us.'

'Yeah!' All the children high-fived.

George put his paw up to join in, and they all laughed.

'Your cats are so cool,' Jess said, stroking George.

'Meow,' I agreed.

By the time Claire returned with Jonathan and Matt, the children were lying on the grass with ice lollies that Polly and Franceska had given them. Polly was making daisy chains and Franceska was reading her book. They turned and waved as the car pulled into the car port. Jonathan came up and grabbed both Toby and Summer, hugging them at the same time.

'I've missed you guys,' he said. Then he fussed George and I.

Matt kissed Polly, then Martha, but when he tried to hug Henry he squirmed away.

'Too big for a hug from your old dad?' Matt asked and Henry laughed, then launched himself at him.

'So how's the house going?' Matt asked.

'Come with me and I'll show you,' Polly replied. 'Are you OK to watch the kids?' she asked.

'Sure,' Claire said. 'You two go and see the builders, Jon can see everything later.'

'I wish Dad was here,' Aleksy said.

'Me too, *kochanie*, but he has to work. But the good news is that he'll be here soon.'

'I can't wait.' Tommy gave an air punch and I was happy. They weren't in trouble at all, and of course sometimes you had to work. After all, it was their hard work that meant we could all keep Seabreeze Cottage.

Knowing George was being showered with attention, I followed Matt and Polly. But before they could get very far I heard voices coming from the courtyard.

'I don't understand,' a man I knew only as the plumber was saying.

'It doesn't make sense.' Colin was scratching his head, which he seemed to do a lot.

'What's wrong?' Polly asked. 'Colin, you remember Matt?'

'Hi, Matt. Polly, Adrian put in all the pipe work for the outside shower as you know, and today he's come to finish off but the pipe's broken and to be honest we have no idea how it happened.'

'What do you mean?' Matt examined what I had seen Liam do earlier.

'It looks like it was bashed with something, but why?'

Adrian said. 'I'll have to get another piece of pipe. It's not difficult but I'll have to cut it to size, so it means I won't be able to finish until Monday.'

'How could this have happened?' Polly asked.

'I wish I knew, Polly, honestly it makes no sense.' Poor Colin sounded upset.

'OK, well delays happen . . . Anyway, Colin, can we go and see upstairs? Adrian's putting the bathroom in next week so next time you come the children should be in, right?' Polly said, cheerfully. I was glad she wasn't letting the broken pipe get to her.

'Yup, the lads are preparing to paint the bedrooms now, the carpets are going in soon and then that just leaves the bathroom.'

'It's all going well then,' Matt said. 'Come on, let's see the children's floor.'

Our inspection was highly successful. The children were going to love their new rooms. Martha and Summer had the smaller room, but it was going to be painted pink and Polly said she was going to make it like the inside of a palace. The boys' room, which was bigger as it was for four of them, was to be a nice green colour, and they would move the bunk beds up for them to sleep in. The sloping room wasn't that high, but high enough, and the skylights let in the sun, though Polly said they were getting black-out blinds fitted the following week to ensure the children would be able to sleep. My conclusion, as I stepped on Liam's foot and earned a scowl from him, was that Polly had thought of everything and the children's floor would be a success.

'It's going to be great when finished.' Matt echoed my thoughts.

'I just still have so much to do,' Polly said as they went downstairs. 'And these little delays aren't helping. First the ceiling hole, then the pipe. I mean, I know it's not the end of the world but it is irritating when we are on such a tight time schedule.'

'These things happen when you're building though, you know that,' Matt pointed out.

'I know but it worries me. The roof was one of them being a bit careless when they were getting ready to fit the skylight, I get that, but the pipe, how could that have happened?'

'The plumber probably fitted a faulty piece and didn't want to say. Anyway, how about we take the kids for a run on the beach before tea.' Matt grinned. 'You know, I might have been a bit reluctant at first when you came up with this hare-brained plan but it is quite magical here. The beach across the road, the children having a lovely, free time, and the cottage, well it's going to be beautiful. You know, my lovely wife, we were wrong, this is one of your best ideas. As long as it doesn't bankrupt us then I'm so happy we did it.'

'Gosh, Matt, I might need that in writing. And no, it won't bankrupt us because we are all in this together.'

I scampered out to the garden and kept that in mind that, yes, we were all in this together.

As I took my favourite vantage point on the lawn just outside the cottage, I was still thinking that over, how much my families meant to each other, how much they all meant to me. I could see all the way down to the beach, where it looked as if everyone was paddling in the sea, which was quite high, and also I could see George's bottom from under the hedge where he had taken up his post, Chanel-watching once again. I'd suggested he come to the beach but he refused.

It was getting a little cooler as I felt a slight breeze ripple through my fur, and the sun was beginning to fade slightly. I watched and I felt warm inside as I kept thinking about how much we all loved each other and how perfect Seabreeze Cottage was to remind us of that.

'Dad!' An excited George bounded up and I grinned; I was guessing he must have seen Chanel.

'Yes, son?'

'You told me to tell you if I saw anything.'

'I did.' I felt impatient but George hated being rushed when he was relaying anything so I tried not to sound it.

'I saw Chanel, she was with Andrea, who was carrying her. You know, I don't think Chanel likes to walk as she seems to get carried around quite a lot.'

'Right, George, maybe you're right.' It was hard to humour him at times but I'd learnt the hard way not to push. He could string a story out for hours if he put his little mind to it.

'Well, you know that builder you don't like?'

I licked my lips; this was getting interesting. 'Liam?'

'Yes, I saw him.'

'Where?'

'With Andrea. They were round the side of her house. He said something, she said something. She put something in his back pocket. Chanel was nuzzled into her, looking beautiful.'

'What did she put in his back pocket?' I asked, intrigued.

'I don't know, I couldn't see and it was hard to tear myself away from staring at Chanel.'

'Right, was there anything else?' I asked.

'No, not really.'

That evening, I was still mulling over what George had seen. I had seen Liam with Andrea, and as I knew he was the saboteur it was obvious he was doing it for Andrea. If he was in thrall to her the way George was to Chanel, then that would explain how she was getting him to do all this for her and perhaps she was giving him money too, which would explain the pocket thing. It seemed that Andrea was hoping that, with Liam making things go wrong, it would annoy my families. However, to annoy them enough to get them to give up Seabreeze Cottage, they would have to do something a bit worse than making a hole in a roof or a pipe. But then, what if he was going to do just that? What if the ideas were going to get bigger? My thoughts were that Liam, surly as he was, was young and not exactly clever. What I needed to do was to keep an eye on him, but more than that, I had to somehow get him and Andrea caught. Just how, was something I had no clue about, yet anyway.

'Why don't you guys go for a drink?' Franceska said. 'I can stay with the children.'

'Oh, Frankie, we can't leave you here, alone,' Claire said.

'Please do. Look, if all the children are in bed, Aleksy and Tommy look after themselves. I am going to settle down in the small living room with my book. Go out, all of you. It's a good opportunity.' She smiled.

'You've twisted my arm,' Jonathan laughed. 'And so I shall go and organise baths and bed, while you enjoy a glass of wine, in that case.'

It was good really; because the women had the children all week, the men liked to do bath and bedtimes at the weekend.

'Well, you won't hear an argument from me,' Claire said.

'Come on, Jon, let's round them up.' Matt went with him.

'It will be nice to go out for a drink, are you sure that you don't mind?' Polly said when the women were sitting in the big living room with glasses of wine.

'Of course not. You know the downside to this is that we can't go out, we don't have babysitters here yet, so make the most of it. I have a good book, I'm happy for some peace and quiet, no offence,' Franceska laughed.

'None taken. But you're right, I'm going to find a local babysitter so maybe next week, when it's just us again, we can have an evening out. It would be nice to go to the local for something to eat at least,' Claire suggested.

'Good idea. I can always ask Colin,' Polly said.

'What, to babysit?' Franceska asked.

'No, silly, if he knows anyone. He's from the village so he'll probably know everyone.'

'It'll have to be someone who is OK to look after six children,' Claire pointed out.

'Oh come on, the younger ones will be in bed, and Aleksy is so grown up now he'll probably end up looking after the babysitter,' Franceska said. 'It's an easy job.'

'Let's drink to freedom. And maybe we can meet some

more local women who aren't the horrible Andrea, or one of her cronies.' Polly raised her glass.

'Amber was nice the other day.'

'Yes but did you see how terrified she was of being seen here. She came in disguise for goodness sake!'

'OK, yes, but anyway, it'll make a change of scene for us, so let's do it.'

'Right, well I'm going to put some make-up on. If Andrea is in the pub we go to tonight, I don't want to look like a fright next to her,' Claire said, standing up.

'Good point, I'm going to at least brush my hair,' Polly laughed.

'Ah, another reason I am happy to stay in.' Franceska smiled. 'It's been nice not worrying about hair and make-up for a bit.'

'Yes, but, Frankie, we don't want to let ourselves go. After all we are glamorous Londoners,' Polly joked.

'In that case, I better put some lipstick on to read my book.'

I was happy to put my worrying aside for the night. I curled up with Franceska on the old fashioned armchair and snoozed as she read. The younger kids, including George, were in bed and I felt content. It wasn't often that Franceska and I had some alone time any more and it was incredibly nice. With those thoughts I dozed off, thoughts of home and Tiger in my mind.

I woke to hear the door opening and Aleksy and Tommy ran in holding their computer tablet.

'Mum, Dad is on Skype,' they said. I stretched and yawned. As the boys were still up it can't have been too late.

'Thank you, right, you two, get ready for bed, and I'll be up as soon as I've talked to Dad,' she said. The boys left and shut the door. I peered at the screen as Franceska sat down and saw Tomasz's face appear.

'Hello,' he said. He smiled but he looked serious.

'Thank you for calling the boys, I know you must be busy. Is it alright?' she said quietly, her eyes dancing with concern.

'It's OK, we've had to close the restaurant for now, we are going to lose so much money too.'

'You poor thing, it must be stressful.'

What was going on? I looked at Tomasz and my eyes were full of concern now too.

'There is a big mess. Lots of food ruined. Who knew a kitchen flood could cause so much damage.' He looked serious.

'But the insurance is sorting it out, aren't they?'

'They are being difficult. The plumber said three pipes bursting aren't that uncommon but because we need to replace the floor in the kitchen, then everything else I am paying the men to get it fixed quickly. The insurance people sent someone to look but said they would take a while to file a report. We can't wait because we need to get the place open as soon as possible, you know how fickle customers can be. It's not proving very easy. Ugh, it was all going so well, but, Frankie, I'm not sure how long this will take to sort out.'

'And it's so popular, you'll lose so many bookings.' Franceska sounded panicked.

'I know, and the insurance people, well they say they won't be able to get back to us for at least a couple of weeks. I know we have some money in the business but, once we cover the wages and the building works, it's going to be tricky until the insurance pays out. Especially with no money coming into that restaurant, which could take about a month to reopen.'

'Oh, Tomasz, I am sorry. But I know, because we have looked at our policies, that we have good insurance, they have to pay out.'

'Yes, they do but when is the question, and in the meantime we are losing money and also as you know we put all the profits that we don't live on back into the business so there's not a lot . . .' Tomasz sighed.

'I guess the fact we've put our savings into this cottage isn't the best timing.' Franceska stroked me and then I understood. There was a problem with the restaurant and it was costing money and they didn't have much because it was in Seabreeze. This did not sound good.

'No, not good timing but, *kochanie*, don't worry, I will think of something.'

'Make sure you are on the case with the insurance. They always try to make it difficult when they have to give us money but they are quick to take ours. By the way, I haven't told them, none of them, why you are not here, I didn't want the boys to worry.'

'I think it's best we keep it quiet from them. Hopefully by next weekend I'll have more of an idea, and I can have a nice weekend with my family.'

I hoped so too. Paws crossed.

'Ah, look, Frankie and Alfie are both asleep,' Matt laughed. I woke up and yawned. How long had I dropped off for?

Franceska opened her eyes. Her book was resting on me, I noticed as I started to stretch out.

'I must have fallen asleep.' She shook her head. 'Did you have a nice evening?' I saw that Claire and Jonathan were also in the room. Claire was leaning on him and Jonathan had a big smile on his face.

'We did.' Claire's voice was a bit slurry. She did get like that on occasion.

'Guess what, we met Amber and her husband, Dan, in the pub and well, let's just say they were very enlightening about Andrea.' Polly sounded gleeful.

'Really?' Franceska sat up and I pricked my ears.

'Maybe she charmed us after all,' Jonathan said.

'But she was nice though,' Matt offered.

'Yes but it is clear that she wants Seabreeze Cottage, although still no one is sure why. But they said that she is going round the village bad-mouthing us, and saying that we're up to all sorts here. Honestly, she made it sound as if we are criminals or something.'

'Does anyone believe it?' Franceska asked.

'I get the impression that Andrea has been acting up a bit lately,' Jonathan said. 'So, no, I don't think so but they are suspicious of us, being out-of-towners, so we do need to get more involved.'

'How?' Franceska asked.

'Well, Jonathan – after a few pints I might add – told them that we would go to church on Sunday,' Matt said.

'Church?' Franceska looked horrified. 'But we never go to church.'

'Apparently this village is still very much a church-going

village. Anyway it seemed like a good idea. And the best thing is that Andrea goes, so imagine her face when we all turn up!' Jonathan clapped his hands gleefully.

'I don't mind, I like going to church,' Claire said. 'Especially a charming village church. But I'm not sure about the kids.'

'Yes forget Andrea, imagine the look on their faces when they are told they have to go,' Franceska agreed. 'Jonathan, you may end up paying for this one,' she finished.

Chapter
Eleven

Franceska was right. On Sunday morning, Aleksy looked horrified about the idea of going to church rather than the beach; Tommy rebelled against having to wear trousers and proper shoes rather than shorts and bare feet; Summer didn't actually understand so she didn't mind; Martha was the same, she was happy to wear a pretty dress whatever the occasion; Toby had never been to church so he was interested, but Henry complained because he was told he couldn't take his games tablet with him. Even in the cold light of day, the adults questioned the wisdom.

'My head hurts,' Claire said. 'I think I drank too much wine last night.'

'The local cider is probably stronger than in London, which would explain why we thought it was a good idea to go to church,' Matt moaned.

Franceska rolled her eyes, fed everyone a big cooked breakfast, made them drink lots of juice and in the end they were all ready to go, or as ready as they would ever be.

'Meow?' I said as I sat by the front door. I wanted to go with them. Claire crouched down and rubbed my head.

'Alfie, you can't come to church, I don't think they allow pets, but honestly, you'll be much happier here.' I turned to look at George but then I noticed Tommy had him in his zip-up jacket, his little ginger head poking out of the top. I felt jealous and excited at the same time. I knew I was a bit big to fit into the children's jackets these days, so I tried not

165

to mind too much. I looked at Tommy as if to tell him to look after George.

'Don't worry, Alfie, I'll take care of him,' he whispered. I flicked my tail to say I understood. I would have liked to go with them but actually, I was being given some alone time, which I was quite grateful for.

I went to finish off my breakfast, but as I was doing so, I heard the cat flap open and the elusive Gilbert appeared. I knew he had been in the house, but I hadn't seen him since our chat.

'Hi,' I said.

'Alright,' he said. He really was a fine-looking cat, and I wondered, again, why a cat like him would choose to be homeless.

'Well everyone is out, apart from me,' I said.

'I saw them all go, I assumed you were with them, but never mind.' He started sniffing round the food bowls.

'Glad you're pleased to see me,' I joked. Gilbert just looked at me. OK, so not much of a sense of humour this cat. 'Anyway, it's nice to see you,' I continued. 'It's all been a bit hectic here.' I filled him in on the story of Liam and his sabotage and how Andrea wanted the cottage and the exchange that George had seen.

'They don't sound like very nice people,' he concluded when I finished.

'No, they aren't. The children are scared of her children, the women are scared of her, I mean it's ridiculous. But her aim is to get her hands on Seabreeze Cottage as I've said and now I'm getting worried that she really is going to stop at nothing to do so.'

'What do you mean?'

'She's got Liam working for her when he should be working for us, and what else? Gilbert, don't you see? I know you don't much like family life and you don't want to get involved with us here, but if Andrea does get her hands on this place then our days are numbered and so are yours.'

He stopped eating and sat down, licking his paws thoughtfully.

'OK.'

'Look, I get you don't want to tell me why you live here or how you came to live here, and that's fine. I'm a good listener, if I do say so myself, but I'd never pry where I shouldn't. However, this cottage is important to me and my families and it's also important to you as you see it as your home, so surely you wouldn't want her to get it?'

'No, I suppose I wouldn't.'

'So you'll help me?' I felt hope spring up in me. Finally, I might just have an ally.

'I don't see how, but then I also don't see what choice I have. Right, Alfie, what do you need me to do?'

After Gilbert had finished eating and had drunk plenty of water, I gave him a tour of the attic rooms and filled him in on what we knew so far. I had to admit, saying it out loud, it wasn't much.

'Right, so this Liam needs keeping an eye on. You say your boy's helping with that.'

'Yes.' I thought about telling him about George's crush on Chanel but I didn't want to overload him with information. 'And I'm keeping an eye on him too. He's definitely in cahoots but I really would like him caught red-handed with her.'

'That won't be easy. But you know I am good at lying

167

low, as you've already seen. You've been good to me, feeding me and, well, you're not too nosy either, so I'll think about what I can do to help. You never know.'

'Thanks, Gilbert. Look, so this will be the girls' room when it's finished.'

'Nice up here, isn't it?' he said, and it was. There was a patch of floor which the sun shone down on, through the new skylights. 'Don't mind if I do,' Gilbert said as he lay down and stretched out.

'Hey, help yourself. Honestly, if my humans see you they won't mind you being here, they're cool like that.'

'That's as may be but you know I'm not in the market for a family and I wouldn't want them to get any ideas about me going home with you at the end of the holiday.'

I could see why he'd worry; they might think he needed a home and insist on taking him back with us. They were very caring people after all.

'You know what, Gilbert, I think we can sort it so you can be Seabreeze Cottage's guard cat when we're not here.'

'A job? I like the sound of that.' He stretched his spotted limbs out again. 'You know, I could get used to this.'

'Enjoy a spot of sunbathing. I'll leave you to it. They won't come up here anyway, it's not finished.'

'Right you are, Alfie, and I'll have a think about how I can help you, seeing as you've helped me.'

I left happy; it seemed that Gilbert and I had reached an understanding.

My peace was shattered. It was pandemonium as the front door flung open and my families rushed in.

'Tommy, you are very naughty, imagine smuggling George to church. Ah, there you are, Alfie, I hope you weren't too worried,' Franceska said.

'MEOW!' I pretended I was. Aleksy winked at me.

'You have to admit though, Frankie, it was quite funny when George jumped out of the jacket and went to see that Persian cat.'

'Chanel,' Claire added.

'The whole congregation stopped and they were supposed to be singing "All Things Bright and Beautiful". Then Chanel yelped as if she'd been attacked, Andrea screamed and the whole service descended into chaos.' Matt was laughing.

'But, George, why on earth were you fixated on that cat?' Jonathan asked. 'She hissed at you and swiped at you but you didn't move!'

George turned to me as if to say that they had no idea.

'You shouldn't encourage him,' Franceska said but I saw her lips twitching.

'I don't think we should be allowed to go to church again,' Toby said.

'No, I think it's just George who isn't allowed,' Henry told him.

'Oh my, Tommy, that was naughty, you can go to your room now.' Tommy didn't object, he was giggling too much.

'Oh, Frankie, don't be too hard on him, it was priceless just to see the look on Andrea's face,' Polly said.

'Oh and the way she said we had invaded her church and that we ought to be ashamed of ourselves,' Claire added. 'God wouldn't like it!' She had tears running down her cheeks.

'It didn't help that George started running around the pews meowing like a lovesick . . . well, a lovesick cat,' Matt laughed.

'I think the vicar seemed quite pleased, he shook my hand warmly at the end, and said we were welcome any time.' Jonathan smiled.

'She probably terrorises the vicar too,' Polly pointed out.

'Well, I know I said that she was nice when we first met her, but after what I heard last night and what I've seen today, I think that woman would terrorise God,' Matt finished.

Everyone went to get changed and then they decided to drive out to another village which had a cliff railway and yet another beach, and after that they were going to go for something called afternoon tea. Of course George and I weren't invited. The men weren't getting a train back until tomorrow morning, and I guessed they needed to get out of the village for a while to escape from the excitement of church. I was a bit sad that I didn't get to go to church after all; it sounded eventful.

'What shall we do?' I asked George when we were alone.

'I better go and see Chanel.'

'Do you think she's angry about what happened in church?' I asked, trying to sound diplomatic.

'No, but I think I scared her by jumping up at her suddenly, so I should apologise. I mean, I'm sure she would have been very pleased to see me.'

'Even though she hissed at you?'

'It was a very affectionate hiss.'

There was no way I was going to win this one as I went with my boy to take up his hedge vigil once again.

This time, though, there was something for us to see. The two girls were playing in the garden, although they were playing with dolls and being very dainty and quiet. Andrea was with them, lying on a sun lounger and speaking loudly into a phone. I tried to edge as close as I could without being seen.

'Who on earth does he think he is?' Andrea screeched into the handset. Thankfully my hearing was good but I could still hear only one side of the conversation. There was a pause. 'I know I said they'd be gone by now but they are quite mad. Honestly, I mean who takes a cat to church?'

You do, I thought. As the other person spoke – I wished I could hear them but I couldn't – Andrea drank from a large wine glass.

'You're supposed to be on my side,' she snapped. 'I'm doing my best. Those Londoners come and act as if they own the village.'

There was a longer gap this time.

'I know, I know,' she hissed, a bit like her cat. 'I need that house. And I am going to damn well get it. I thought they'd just sell it, I offered a decent sum for the dilapidated hovel, and I know I don't have much time.' Chanel looked a bit surprised as Andrea banged her fist on the sun lounger.

'Of course, and trust me, they'll be gone before you know it,' Andrea replied, throwing the phone down as Chanel nuzzled her in agreement. I felt my fur go cold as I processed the words. Whatever she was doing, she seemed determined to get our house. Our home.

I looked over at George, to see if he'd heard what I had, but he was fast asleep. Some stalker he was turning out to be.

Chapter Twelve

It was hard to believe we were just into our third week in Lynstow, almost half way through our summer break. And in many ways it felt as if we'd been here forever; Seabreeze and the village felt like home. In other ways there seemed to be so much to do that it would never be finished. Matt and Jonathan were gone again, until Friday, when Tomasz would be coming down with them. I was still worried about the conversation between Tomasz and Franceska, I hated it when there were any problems with my families, but I heard no more about it. Franceska was putting a brave face on things, as if nothing was wrong, and if she spoke to Tomasz, which I am sure she did, she did it out of earshot of all of us.

Polly chivvied Colin, saying she wanted to step up the progress. She was slightly panicked that we didn't have long and she didn't trust any major works to take place after we left. With the minor blips that Liam had been responsible for, they were playing a bit of catch-up and Polly said they couldn't tolerate any more delays.

However, the attic was almost finished. A bathroom had been installed, and Liam and Mark were painting the rooms as per Polly's instructions before the carpets were laid. Colin and Pete were working on the outside of the house and I thought that Liam surely couldn't wreak any havoc with the painting, but I kept an eye on him when I could, just in case.

I was sitting upstairs watching Liam like a hawk, or a very

devoted cat at least; I'd made George come with me but he had fallen asleep in a sulk. I was also cleaning myself after having had a small snack but then who said cats can't multi-task? Today Liam was looking so innocent as he painted one of the rooms. He did keep checking his watch though.

'Liam, I'm going to grab a bite to eat, do you want to come?' Mark said.

'Nah, mate, I'm good, I want to get this painting done.' As soon as Mark left he looked at me, then he looked at George who was asleep nearby. I narrowed my eyes at him. What was he doing?

He grabbed a step ladder, put it up near the skylight and opened it. He climbed up and although I am not a fan of heights, I soon realised I had no choice but to follow him. I saw Liam climb out, what was he up to? I climbed up the ladder and perched on the top, looking out. To my absolute horror, Liam was standing on the roof. It didn't look safe but he seemed quite comfortable on it.

'Oh for goodness' sake,' he said when he saw me peering out. I noticed he had a tool with him and I suddenly got the feeling he was going to smash the other skylight window, then make out it couldn't have been him as he was in a different room. That made sense.

Once, when I was in love with Snowball and she was acting as if she was immune to my charms, I decided to perform a grand gesture, climbing a tree in order to woo her. It went wrong when I got so high and realised that I am actually terrified of heights. I froze and then, to cut a long and tragic story short, I had to be rescued by the fire brigade which was very humiliating for a cat like me.

As we glared at each other, I knew that I had no choice, I couldn't let Liam cause any more problems for my family, especially with what I had heard from Franceska and Tomasz – if he did it might be the last straw. I mustered all the courage I could and managed to get out of the skylight; well, if Liam could fit through it I had no problem, but then my stomach lurched and I froze yet again. I looked up and saw the sky, I looked down and everything, cars and people, seemed tiny. I couldn't move as I stood on the ridge of the roof. I couldn't even shuffle back inside but I tried not to let Liam see my fear.

'You're such an annoying cat.' Liam looked angry. I realised how vulnerable I was, he could do anything. My heart started beating quickly. Although, here was the thing with Liam, he was clearly under Andrea's spell but he wasn't dangerous . . . at least, I was pretty sure he wasn't. I really hoped he wasn't. I watched on with horror as he, obviously braver than me when it came to heights, stepped back over me and slid back down the skylight. Thank goodness, I thought as I got ready to follow him.

'I'll get you when I'm ready,' he said and before I had a chance to get through the window, he shut the skylight, leaving me perched very precariously on the roof.

I closed my eyes but that was even more terrifying, so I opened them again. Surely he wouldn't leave me here? I could still see all over the village, it was high, higher than I had ever been – this wasn't good. I clung onto the roof with my paws, and although I could see the skylight, it was closed so I wasn't sure how I would get in, even if I did dare move. I thought about making a noise but there was no point, no one would hear me, the wind would just carry my voice. I hoped George was alright, I felt a bit like I had left him at the mercy of Liam. I might have stopped him from doing any damage but the result was that I was stuck on a roof and my kitten was inside.

No one could see me, so I was literally stuck. The rest of my families were on the beach, which seemed miles away. I knew there would be no point in calling out. No one would see me or hear me.

I inched as close as I could to the skylight, so I could see inside, clinging on for dear life. That was actually less frightening. At least I could see the room. I wondered if I could get anyone's attention – at some point surely they would come looking for me? I could see Liam, who carrying on with the painting, still looking annoyed. Although I was scared and also getting weary with the effort of holding on, I still kept vigil on the skylight, hoping someone would see me. Surely Liam would come and get me – he didn't want to kill me, just because I'd scuppered his plans, surely he wasn't that evil? But it was beyond frustrating. I could feel my legs seizing up from being in the same place for so long. Liam left the room a few times, but I couldn't see any sign of George. Yet again I began wondering if I would ever be rescued.

The sun was hotter up here, I was thirsty, tired, and my whole body ached from the effort of not falling off the roof. Just what was going to become of me?

It felt as if it was getting late, and the sky was darkening in a way which made me think it might fall on my head, when I finally heard voices and Polly and Colin entered the room. I literally splayed myself across the skylight and yowled. The glass was thick though and my voice seemed to disappear into the air.

'Look, Polly I am sorry but, as I said, it's sorted now and he's done a good job painting the room,' Colin was saying, I could hear faintly.

'Fair enough but I'm not exactly thrilled. After all, it was his paint that George stepped in, and he could have ruined the bathroom floor with it, we'd literally only just had it laid.'

What? I thought, how on earth had George got in paint?

'I know and I've given him a ticking-off. And the good news is that the floor is good as new, as is the kitten.' He tried to laugh but he sounded guilty. 'Please, look I know he's made a few mistakes but he's a good lad—' Suddenly he looked up and I bashed my paw as hard as I could on the glass. 'Polly . . .' Polly followed Colin's eyes.

'My God, what is Alfie doing up there?' Polly shouted.

'Hold on.' Colin looked flushed. He grabbed the step ladder, which was perched against the door, unfolded it and climbed up. I carefully inched back as he opened the skylight. He gently took hold of me and, my heart still beating out of my body, he brought me back inside. He gave me to Polly.

'Oh, Alfie, how did you get on the roof? Poor baby, are you alright?' Polly cuddled me, stroking my fur, which calmed me down.

'Liam, get here,' Colin shouted. Liam walked in. He had obviously been cleaning up, he was still holding a cloth covered in blue paint.

'How did Alfie get on the roof?' Polly asked. 'First I find George has trod paint all over the bathroom floor then our other cat is stuck on the roof. And you were working here so how didn't you see it? Just what is going on?' She looked furious as she cuddled me to her. I began to feel safe again.

'He must have climbed out when I wasn't looking. I opened the window so it didn't smell of paint but then I closed it, which is when George must have got in the paint,' he said. I still didn't know quite what George had done.

'Liam, you need to be more careful,' Colin said. Polly and I both glared at him.

Once I'd had some water, and a lot of fussing from Polly, I went to find George who was in the bush looking for Chanel. At least in Lynstow I always seemed to know where the boy was.

'What happened?' I asked.

'That man is a maniac,' George said plaintively. 'He grabbed me from where I was asleep and put me in the paint tray, then he told me to walk across the bathroom floor. I wouldn't so he picked me up and made me.'

'How awful, I wish I'd scratched him or worse. Did he hurt you?'

'No, and at least Polly wasn't cross with me.'

'No, she seemed to blame Liam, which is good. I tell you what, that man is now in big trouble.'

'Is he?' George's eyes were wide.

'Yes, George, this is war.'

After the roof incident, the adults fussed more than normal over me. I have to admit I was terror-stricken every time I thought of it, being on that roof. It was even higher than the tree I'd got stuck up a few years back. But at the same time I didn't want to make too much of a deal about it for George. I just kept warning him about Liam and although of course George said he wasn't scared of him, I reiterated that he should never let himself be alone with him. What if he'd done that to George and not me? What if my kitten was stuck on that roof, what if he'd fallen? I couldn't bear to think about it. Two things were clear. This was more serious than I first thought.

I needed troops, that much was obvious. And Gilbert was my only option. I needed to up my charm offensive with him, so I recruited George.

That night, we waited for him together and when George met Gilbert he was immediately impressed.

'You have a great coat,' he said.

'Thank you.' Gilbert raised his tail. I could tell he was already taken by George, as most cats and people alike tended to be – not counting Chanel and Andrea. 'Right, let's go to the beach. This is going to be fun.'

Gilbert took us across the road, and over the wall which separated the pavement from the beach. He then told us to follow him as he ran up and down the sand dunes.

'Weeeeee,' George said as he flew down.

'Be careful,' I warned.

'It's fine, Alfie, sand is soft, you can't get hurt,' Gilbert pointed out. We had a game of hide and seek where I, loath to leave George, hid with him and Gilbert found us. As the tide was out we sniffed around some boats that were sitting on the wet sand waiting for the water. As the moon shone down on us I realised that this was what we should be doing on our holiday. Not worrying about bad people, but having fun. And Gilbert was right, this *was* fun.

'I love the beach now,' George said as we sat on the wall, in a line, and looked at the large, bright moon.

After the ordeal and the growing unease I was feeling about what was going on, it was a lovely end to the day. I had George, I had a new growing friendship with Gilbert and I was safe. I hadn't fallen off the roof. As I looked at the moon I remembered to count my blessings.

'You're lucky it's summer, the rest of the year they let dogs on here,' Gilbert explained. 'Besides, I love it best at night, when it's pretty empty.' There were some young people lurking around but not many. 'It feels like it belongs to us,' Gilbert said. We sat in silence. Yes, it did feel it belonged to us.

'There are three things I love about this holiday,' George said as we headed home to bed.

'What's that?' I asked.

'The beach, ice cream and Chanel.'

Chapter
Thirteen

Thank goodness for our evening trips to the beach, because on Friday, just before the end of the week after the children had moved up to the attic, and Polly was congratulating the builders on how quickly they were working, another disaster struck.

I had been watching George in the garden. He'd been trying to catch a glimpse of Chanel, yet again. I heard Claire scream from inside the house so I ran back in. I made my way upstairs and saw Claire and Polly with a red-faced Mark.

'You've knocked down the wrong wall,' Claire shrieked.

'Didn't you wonder why there were clothes and everything out which would be covered in dust?' Polly shouted.

Mark's face was ashen. Was Mark now in on the sabotage? I wasn't sure how I was supposed to watch both him and Liam.

'But Liam said it was definitely this wall. I asked him if he was sure.'

Ah, Liam had struck again, but this time he was trying to pin the blame on Mark.

Colin shouted for Liam, who appeared, looking shiftily at his boots. I hadn't thought he would risk doing anything wrong so soon after paint- and roof-gate, but I guess this time he'd been hoping Mark would get the blame. I looked at the big, dusty hole in the wall between where Claire and Polly were sleeping and I knew that this was his fault. To give Liam his due, he had been shouted at so much lately

185

that he must really like Andrea to put himself through this.

'Blimey.' Colin scratched his head, which he was doing a lot lately. 'What have you done?'

'I thought you meant this wall,' Liam mumbled, turning red. He mumbled a lot. 'I told Mark, but Mark could have checked with you.'

Thankfully the children were in the garden with Franceska, so they didn't hear the language that Colin used. Let's just say it was colourful.

'But, I checked with you and you said you were sure,' Mark protested.

'I said the wall between the bedrooms on the left-hand side of the stairs. This is clearly right. Oh God, I am so sorry,' poor Colin said. He looked as if he was going to cry himself.

'Everything is covered in dust and this hole is where you were going to start the plumbing for the en suite bathroom. This is going to cause yet another delay,' Polly stormed. 'And Claire will have to move into one of the other rooms until you get this sorted.' Polly looked angry, Liam looked at his feet, Mark was being so apologetic although it wasn't really his fault, and Colin looked tired. I went over to Liam and jumped as hard as I could onto his foot.

'Ow,' he shouted, scowling at me. I gave him a small swipe with my paw just for good measure. His face turned even redder, if that was possible.

'Don't think the cat likes you,' Colin pointed out.

'Alfie is a very good judge of character.' Claire narrowed her eyes at Liam.

'Right, OK, well, lads, firstly help Claire move everything that's covered in dust, Polly, Liam and Mark will rebuild the wall today as a matter of urgency. If they have to stay late, yet again, then they will so don't worry.' Colin held a hand out as Polly looked like she was going to object. 'I'll stop back to supervise. And the plumber is going to be working on the finishing touches for the kids' bathroom and the outside shower today so he can start work here tomorrow. I promise, it looks bad but we'll have this wall built good as new.'

I left them to it. It seemed to me that whatever Liam was doing, for Andrea, was costing him, rather than us, although it was of course delaying things, which was irritating because we had limited time. I was learning a lot about house renovations this summer it seemed.

Downstairs there was a big picnic going on on the front lawn and the village children were there. Their parents must be used to letting them go out on their own, I supposed; it was so different from life in London. Franceska was supervising everyone, and I saw the girls from next door looking at them from the beach, but with Franceska there, they didn't dare come over and cause trouble.

'Don't you mind that those girls are staring at you all?' Tommy asked the village children, as if he was reading my mind.

'Nah, we're having fun with you guys. They don't like it but we already decided to stand up to them more, so that's what we're doing,' Ben said.

'And then maybe they'll remember how to be nice again,' Millie added.

I admired their bravery, and their optimism, so I decided it was time for me to follow their lead. Liam needed to be stopped and I was going to have to be the cat to do it. Gilbert was returning tonight and so I was determined to ensure I got him to help me. I needed a proper commitment from him. I still didn't know how we would foil them but I knew we would. It was going to happen, if it was the last thing I did on this holiday.

As I went to get George so we could find some butterflies to chase, I knew I would have to come up with something, and fast. Those children, that woman, the cat and Liam, it was making my very restful holiday really rather stressful, but then that was what always seemed to happen when you were a cat like me.

After we'd exhausted ourselves chasing butterflies, I went to join the children while George took a nap. Aleksy and Tomasz had been given permission to go to the beach with the other children, and Toby and Henry weren't pleased about being left behind.

'Please can we go?' Henry had asked Polly.

'The thing is, you guys are younger than them, and so you should only go with an adult,' Polly had explained gently.

The boys were now sitting on the grass and sulking. Well, Henry was sulking and Toby was copying him. Which was cute, but then, as they watched Aleksy and Tomasz and the others running up and down the dunes, I saw that they really did feel they were missing out.

'Will they notice if we just go for a minute?' Henry asked.

'But, what if we get into trouble?' Toby was still afraid of doing anything wrong. Claire and Jonathan often said they wished that he would, because it would show he felt safe with them. I wondered if that was why George was naughty, because he certainly didn't listen to me, but maybe he felt safe with me? It was a strange kind of logic but I found humans tended to that.

'I'll say I made you come with me, don't worry.' Henry was generally a well-behaved boy, and the fact he was willing to take the blame for Toby showed that.

'OK, but only for a little while?'

I toyed with the idea of following them to the beach, but there were a couple of things stopping me. Firstly, George had fallen asleep under the bush, when he was supposed to be looking for Chanel, so I didn't want to be too far from him. And secondly, I felt that if anything happened to the kids, I should be nearby so I could get an adult quickly. I took up my place on the lawn, and had a lovely view to where the children were building elaborate sandcastles. I saw Henry leading a hesitant Toby across the road. I was pleased to see how they looked both ways before doing so. I had learnt to cross the road the hard way – almost getting hit by cars is no fun, I can tell you. I saw Aleksy look a bit reluctant as they joined them and the local children, but in the end both boys got onto their knees and started digging.

All my children were bronzed by the sun, they all looked so healthy, and I could see what Claire meant about this seaside living. I sat up a bit straighter as I saw the group being approached by Savannah and Serafina. Of course, despite my excellent hearing I couldn't make anything out but I saw them looking cross, folding their arms. I saw Aleksy standing in front of Tommy, who could be a little aggressive when pushed. I saw Toby's face crumble – he hated any kind of argument – and the local children looked as if they didn't

189

know what to do. I thought about moving closer but then I thought, perhaps I should get an adult. Before I had time to decide, one of the girls had thrown sand at Toby and he was crying. Aleksy grabbed him in a hug and I saw Tommy throw sand back at the girls. I ran as fast as I could inside the house. I saw Franceska first, and I meowed, yelped and yowled, running round in circles as fast as I could, which was my way of telling them they were needed. Summer and Martha were watching television and I guessed Claire and Polly were still upstairs sorting out the mess.

'What's wrong, Alfie?' Franceska said and I ran outside. I knew she would follow me. As she did, she stood on the lawn and I yowled again.

'Oh goodness, what's going on?' she said as she saw them. Toby was crying in Aleksy's arms and Savannah and Serafina were running off. 'Those boys were not supposed to leave the garden,' she added.

She ran across the road and I saw that she said something to all the children before she took Toby and Henry's hands and started back towards the house. Aleksy and Tommy followed her, looking downcast. I saw the other children wave them off, looking sad.

'What's wrong?' Claire asked, coming out to the garden. 'I saw you out of the bedroom window, Toby, you weren't supposed to go to the beach without a grown-up.' She grabbed Toby and hugged him, as her words gushed out.

'It's my fault,' Henry said. 'I made him come with me.'

Polly had joined them by now. 'Henry, you are in big trouble,' she said. 'Go inside and up to your room to think for now and I'll be up in a bit.'

Henry slunk off.

'What happened, Aleksy?' Franceska asked, sounding concerned.

'Henry and Toby came over and I told them they shouldn't but they begged us to stay. And we were building this really cool sandcastle but the mean girls came over and they were taunting us all, being horrible, and then they threw sand at Toby and it went in his eyes,' Aleksy explained.

'So I threw sand back and then they said that we were horrible and they couldn't wait until we all left,' Tommy added.

'Come on, Toby, let's go and get your eyes washed out,' Claire said, lifting the crying boy up and taking him inside. 'But that's why you shouldn't go to the beach without an adult,' she added.

'The thing is, Mum,' Aleksy said when Toby was inside. 'I think that they knew Toby was the most likely to get upset, as they kept picking on him.'

'That's not nice. Do you think we should go and see Andrea?' Franceska asked.

'Hey, I think I'll go,' said Polly. 'You know Claire gets so upset for Toby and, well, I'm better at confrontation. Can you go and check on Henry for me? Tell him I will deal with him later.'

'Of course, come inside now, boys, Summer and Martha are in the living room, so can you go and sit with them,' Franceska said, taking them inside.

Polly took a deep breath and walked off. I went to the hedge where George had woken up and resumed his vigil.

'Have you seen her?' I asked.

'No, I must have fallen asleep.'

'Right, well Polly is going to see Andrea, there's been a huge drama with the kids.' I explained everything to George. We both decided to risk going nearer the house, as soon as Polly arrived, but we stayed hidden behind a rose bush by the front door. Polly knocked on the door.

'Hello.' Andrea opened the door. She was wearing a pink dress, high heels and full make-up and in her arms was Chanel. The Persian must have sensed us as she tensed and sniffed around.

'She's so pretty,' George breathed before I shushed him.

'Andrea. We have a problem. Your daughters threw sand at one of the children, who is now having his eyes washed out. They also said some horrible things. Now I know you want Seabreeze Cottage and you don't like us but children should not be dragged into this.' Polly didn't hold back or beat around the bush. I was proud of her.

'My girls wouldn't have done that. And anyway, your children are being mean to them. They are playing with their friends and excluding them,' Andrea replied.

'Surely you're not that stupid? They've tried to stop the local children playing with them, they've been saying terrible things and also now throwing sand. I know this is what happened and let me tell you, if it happens again I'm—'

'What? Are you threatening me?' Andrea interrupted. Chanel had spotted George's tail and was yowling and yelping like her owner.

'You're not going to win, and neither are your children,' Polly hissed, sounding as upset as Chanel.

'We'll see about that. If your children are scared of mine,

well then they won't want to stay in the house, will they?'

'God, I knew you were a witch but someone who will involve their children in something like this is despicable.'

'I want that house, and nothing is going to stop me getting it.' Andrea's brows furrowed furiously – even I was scared.

'We'll see about that.' Polly turned and stormed off.

Chanel managed to hiss at us before Andrea carried her back inside and slammed the front door.

That evening Seabreeze Cottage was not a happy place. The children were downhearted by what had happened that day: Toby was still upset, Henry sorry that he'd gone to the beach when he shouldn't, and Aleksy and Tommy were sad that their lovely afternoon playing with their new friends had ended so badly. Only Summer, Martha and George were happy but they didn't really understand what had gone on.

The adults weren't faring any better. Liam was still fixing the wall in Claire's bedroom when the children were put to bed, and so Polly asked him and Colin to leave. Claire would have to sleep in one of the smaller rooms for the night, as would I. When they'd gone, the three of them sat in kitchen drinking wine.

'God, that woman. I swear she is so calm and cold, and she acts as if she'll stop at nothing to get this house,' Polly fumed. She hadn't mentioned her encounter with Andrea until the children were safely in bed.

'God, she's ridiculous, fancy involving the children. What kind of person does that?' Claire stormed.

'An evil one. Why does she want this house so much? Her house is grander, so it can't be to live in.'

'I've got no idea,' Polly said. 'Her house is enormous and Colin says it's one of the few in the village that is a whole house – most are apartments. And there's no sign of this husband either, is there? I wonder if there's a problem there.'

'If she is as mean to him as she is everyone else, then maybe,' Franceska said.

'I wouldn't have thought that she would leave that grand house for this. We love it, I know, but she wouldn't think it good enough for her. No, it's not that but something . . . Anyway, whatever it is, we should find out. No, we need to find out.' Polly crossed her arms determinedly.

'I'm more concerned about the children, I don't want their holiday ruined by those girls. Poor Toby was so upset and then he was so worried about getting into trouble he wet himself, and he hasn't done that for ages.'

'Oh, Claire, poor Toby. I think tomorrow we go out for the day, to another beach, and give the children a nice day a bit away from the village,' Franceska suggested.

'Great idea,' Polly concurred. 'I don't want to leave the builders but Colin's promised to keep a closer eye on Liability Liam.'

'Why doesn't he sack him?' Claire said.

'I think if he does anything else, he might have to. But I think he's well-meaning, just a bit incompetent.'

'Yowl!' No he isn't, I said but no one seemed to hear me.

'Polly, you have been working hard with the house, so you deserve a day off,' Claire said.

'I could do with that, I don't want to sound like a 1950s housewife but I'm really looking forward to seeing Matt this week.'

'I think on Saturday afternoon we send the men to the beach with the kids and we find somewhere to get manicures or something,' Franceska suggested. 'We have earned some pampering.' I noticed that Franceska had been down lately, maybe she needed cheering up.

'Oh yes, let's do something like that! But tomorrow it will be nice to get out of the house as well,' Polly said.

'Alfie, you are in charge tomorrow,' Franceska said, stroking my head.

'Meow.' It was a good job for them that I was, I thought.

And with that in mind, I waited for Gilbert and saw him briefly before I went off to bed.

'They are out all day tomorrow, so come and see us if you like.'

'Alright, I will,' he said, not sounding exactly enthusiastic, but then nowhere near as unenthusiastic as when I'd first met him. It was progress, that was for sure.

Chapter
Fourteen

'But why don't you have a home?' George persisted. He was giving Gilbert the full George third degree. I could see the normally gruff cat struggling. On the one paw he liked to act as if he didn't need anyone but, on the other, he was a bit enamoured with George.

'Life isn't all fish and ice cream, you know,' Gilbert said, softening.

'It's not?' George looked upset. 'I think my life is. Oh and Chanel. Oh and my dad, oh and the families too.'

'Not for me. I had a family, when I was a little lad like you, but it wasn't a happy house.' He stretched his paws out. 'I just realised one day that I would be better off not being there so I left.'

'But why?' It seemed George's 'why' phase was never going to end.

'The family were unhappy. The father would be quite mean, which upset the mother, and there were two children. One of the children would be in trouble a lot with the father. It wasn't nice, and he then tormented me.'

'That sounds horrible,' I said. I could see it was hard for Gilbert to talk about and I didn't want to scare him off as I tried to head George off and stop him asking too many questions. I nudged him a few times but he didn't take the hint.

'I was young and, no, it wasn't bearable. It's so sad the way some humans treat us animals. We don't ask to be their pets yet they think they can treat us badly.' His eyes darkened.

'But anyway, I just got up one day and left home. I hid for a while, and I knew the family were looking for me. They put the posters up.'

'Like the lamppost cats!' George exclaimed excitedly. I explained to Gilbert that we'd had a spate of missing cats in our area and the pictures had gone up on lampposts at an alarming rate. 'Yes. I couldn't understand why they wanted me back when they were so horrible. Well OK, so only the dad and one of the kids was horrible, but they must have known what was going on. I was barely eating and I was terrified. Anyway, I hid for a while then I started making my way further from home. I managed to survive by hunting, after all this is the countryside, and to be honest I found I quite liked my own company. Over time I decided that I liked being so independent and I didn't have any trouble finding food. So when I arrived here and found Seabreeze Cottage deserted, I decided that I would stay here for a while. That has turned out to be a long while because no one was ever here, until you, that is.'

'Well I think that's a great story and now we are here you will stay, won't you?' George asked, nuzzling Gilbert, who purred in response.

'I only have one concern. What happens if your family finds me?'

'Oh they'd love you. Look, our families love cats, the children love cats, they would let you stay. I only worry that they wouldn't want you to be here on your own, and I'm not sure how we would explain to them that you like it here and don't want to be looked after all the time.'

I could see how that might be a problem. They'd probably

want to scoop Gilbert up and take him home with us, or worse, find him a home round here.

'Then I better lie low. I'm glad the house is coming to life but I don't want to move away from here.'

'No, of course not.'

'Well I don't think that would happen,' George interjected. 'It's clear that you live here, and there will be people coming and going from here a lot, so I think the humans will expect you to stay and, maybe, they just might make it easier by ensuring you have food.'

'Do you really think so?' Gilbert asked, uncertainly.

'I do. You belong to Seabreeze Cottage and I think they'll see that. You can be the cottage cat and when no one is here you can look after it for us.'

'That's so sensible, George,' I said proudly. 'I just hope that our families see it that way.' George was so clever at times, and I hoped he got it from me.

'Oh they will,' George replied confidently.

'Look, you've got some free time it seems, so do you want to come with me and I can show you round the area a bit? I know you've seen the beach but we're near some very cool fields and it's a lovely day for a bit of a romp in the countryside,' Gilbert offered.

George looked at me hopefully. I didn't need asking twice.

We made our way through the narrow streets behind the cottage. The ground was quite steep and I could see it would keep you fit living here. Even George huffed a bit. At the top we reached a big road which was busy and took quite a long time to cross. Gilbert then led us into a big green field, where the grass tickled our legs as we made our way through it. As I saw George skittishly jumping from blade of grass to blade of grass I realised this was the first field he'd been in.

'It's not like garden grass,' he said, unsurely.

'No, lad, it's not. But it's great when you get used to it,' Gilbert replied, bounding off.

I had been on a few adventures in the countryside before but I had to say having Gilbert with us made it even more enjoyable. He was a very confident cat, he knew all the best places, where the best bushes for butterfly chasing were, where the animals to be avoided lived, where we could just stop and look at beautiful views and see for miles around. It was breathtaking and the sun chased us, warming our fur.

'This is so much fun,' George squealed with excitement. I told him that he wasn't to try to come here on his own; I couldn't stop being a father, even when we were having a good time.

We were all squeezed under a bush, taking a short break, when Gilbert suddenly sprang up.

'What is it?' I asked.

'There's a dog, I can sense it.' We looked out at the field and saw a large black dog was running around. I started to panic; we had to get away.

'Run,' I said as I started to move.

'Hold on, no need for that,' Gilbert said. 'It's one of the farm dogs, he's friendly with cats, don't worry.'

I'd never heard of dog being friendly with cats but when he did approach us he wasn't aggressive. He nodded his head, swished his tail in greeting and then turned back and ran off. My heart was beating fast, I really didn't think he would be that indifferent. I had been chased by dogs before in London and I'd never encountered one I liked.

'Only one problem,' Gilbert said as my heart started slowing down to normal again.

'What?' George asked.

'Well, the field we need to go through to get home . . . They've moved the sheep in, which explains the presence of the dog.'

'What are sheep?' George asked.

'White fluffy things,' I replied with my superior country knowledge. Gilbert laughed.

'Well the thing is that these sheep are quite aggressive and they don't like anyone being in their fields.'

We looked to where Gilbert was staring and he was right, there was a flock of angry-looking sheep in the middle of the field. I hadn't imagined sheep were mean, they didn't seem to do a lot, as far as I could tell. I had encountered a hostile cow and some very aggressive pigs before, but never sheep.

'What do we do?' I asked, worried for George more than anything.

'We'll run round the side of the field. They'll probably try to chase us but if we stick to the perimeters we can outrun them. Alfie and George you go first, and I'll bring up the rear so that George is sandwiched between us.'

'I'm not scared of the sheeps,' George said, with his usual bravado.

'Well you should be, lad, if they butt you with their heads it can be very painful. Take it from one who knows. Right, when I say go, we go.'

I felt exhilarated and a little scared as I ran as fast as I was able, taking the route Gilbert suggested and made sure George was in front of me. I tried to focus on where I was headed but I couldn't help but sneak a look at the sheep. I could see they had seen us. George was running, speedily, his legs moving quickly. The sheep were all moving towards us and at first it looked as if they were moving slowly but then their speed seemed to increase. As adrenaline flowed through my body I increased my speed and managed to outrun them to get to the edge of the field and safety, just after George.

I joined George at the hedge and ushered him under. We were safe! I looked and saw that Gilbert was a bit cornered though. As if he had sacrificed himself for us. I didn't know what to do. I turned to George.

'Make as much noise as you can,' I said. The sheep wouldn't fit under the hedge so my plan was that if we made enough of a racket they would be distracted, and therefore Gilbert could come to safety.

'Yowl,' I said as loudly as I could. George joined me. We yowled and yelped and meowed until our voices were hoarse. But as the sheep turned their attention to us, Gilbert made his escape.

We collapsed on a small patch of grass the other side of the field.

'Oh, Dad, that was exciting,' said George. I wished he had a little more of a honed sense of danger, to be honest.

'It was scary,' I chastised. 'We could have become sheep food.'

'Unlikely, they seem to like grass,' Gilbert said. 'They would have just knocked us around a bit but, you know, thank you for saving me, because it would have hurt if they'd got to me.'

'Why don't they like you?' I asked.

'It's not personal, they just protect themselves. They're like a family and they see us as intruders, I guess. Farm animals can be a hazard of living here, but I wouldn't have it any other way.'

I totally understood that. We walked home slowly, trying to recover our breath. I was still feeling the terror of being in a dangerous situation. George seemed unfazed, he just saw everything as exciting, and Gilbert seemed normal, not at all wobbly like I was. I was just thankful that the walk home was all downhill.

We spent the rest of the afternoon in the backyard, while George went to see if he could spot Chanel.

'Why on earth does he do that?' Gilbert asked.

'First crush,' I replied.

'No accounting for taste. Her or her owner.'

'Talking of "that woman", I really need to discover what she's up to more than ever now. The kids are now getting involved and that's not good. I know my adult humans can look after themselves but the children, the younger ones and especially Toby, can't.'

'Do you want me to do some surveillance and see if I can find anything out?' Gilbert asked.

'Would you?' I could barely believe it. I had been trying to engage Gilbert for some time and now it looked as if he was finally, properly, onboard. I knew with him by my side we would foil any plan that Andrea and Liam came up with. Well hopefully.

'You almost saved my life, it's the least I can do,' Gilbert replied. 'And also, I quite like having you and the lad around. I might be self-sufficient but there's nothing wrong with friends.'

Although he still sounded his usual gruff self, I felt touched. And after all, he couldn't be any worse at surveillance than George, who was already fast asleep.

It was much later when I heard the commotion of everyone returning home. We were all inside, having a break from the sun, as I rushed to greet everyone. They came into the back, all taking turns to use the outdoor shower to get the sand off before putting all their towels and beach accessories into the sand room.

'See, this works pretty well,' Polly said, pleased.

'It was a great idea, the shower especially,' Claire added, giving Polly a squeeze.

'And we can contain the mess with the sand room,' Franceska said, smiling. 'Well almost,' she laughed as Summer tipped up a bucket which was still full of sand onto the floor.

'We're supposed to leave the sand at the beach,' Toby laughed. It was a phrase that he had heard the adults say many times. I felt happy again; they had obviously all had a lovely time. As the children chattered and bickered over getting cleaned up, Claire took an armful of washing which she put in the machine, Franceska piled up the buckets and spades and Polly ushered the almost sand-free children inside. I realised that this was the perfect time to introduce Gilbert to everyone . . . but when I turned around he had disappeared.

Chapter
Fifteen

'So, here's what I thought we'd do,' Jonathan said to Matt and Tomasz. They had arrived the previous evening and everyone had been pleased to see them, especially me. It had been a fraught week and although it ended well, I thought having the guys around might just bolster everyone's mood. It was funny how much I actually missed them. I knew the others did too from the way they talked. We, like that funny flock of sheep, were a family and it didn't feel quite right when part of our family were missing.

I looked worriedly at Tomasz but he showed no sign of being anything but his usual self. I did notice Franceska shooting him worried glances at times but they didn't talk about it, or if they did it was out of earshot of everyone, including me. He didn't mention the problems at the restaurant to anyone and I secretly hoped that maybe he had sorted them out already.

'What?' Matt asked, looking suspicious. It was Saturday afternoon and Polly, Claire and Franceska had gone to a spa; the men had agreed they needed a well-deserved break and some pampering. Well, I could have done with some too, but then clearly cat pampering wasn't on the cards! George and I were going to keep our eyes and ears open today, it was time to move 'project Andrea' on, in that I needed to find out just what she was up to, so I knew what we were dealing with and what we would need to do about it. Gilbert being onboard was reassuring, as was having our men back, even if only for a couple of days.

'OK, so we are going to go round to see this Andrea and sort out, once and for all, the situation with her, the children and our house.' Jonathan looked pleased with himself.

'You are sure that's a good idea?' Tomasz looked uncertain, and I agreed with him. I thought it was possibly a terrible idea.

'Our wives might string us up if we go and see her behind their backs,' Matt pointed out. Again, I agreed.

'No, but you see, it's not behind their backs. They are going to be having a lovely time and we will sort this situation out and be heroes when they return.'

I licked my paws; this wasn't going to end well.

'Jon, I have to take Aleksy and Tommy paddleboarding this afternoon, or at least stand on the beach and watch them, I promised,' Tomasz said, looking relieved. He had a get out of jail – or Andrea – card. Matt shot him an annoyed look.

'OK, well we will both go and take the younger children.'

'I don't know—' Matt started.

'Perhaps not a good idea to take Toby – he was very upset and maybe he will be more upset by seeing them?' Tomasz made an excellent point.

'Um, maybe you're right, can you take Toby with you?' Jonathan asked. Which possibly wasn't what Tomasz meant.

'Well, I guess . . .' He shuffled his feet uncomfortably.

'The thing is, Jon, if Toby goes, Henry will want to go too,' Matt persisted.

'Oh, Tomasz won't mind. Right, I'll get the girls ready and we'll be off.'

Tomasz and Matt looked at each other and both shook their heads. But I knew, as did they, there was no arguing with Jonathan when he made his mind up.

I was torn. I wanted to go and see the boys on their paddleboards. They were these flat things which looked a bit like ironing boards without legs and floated in the water while you stood on them and paddled. But I knew I would really need to go with the others to Andrea's, and of course George would want to go too, in the hope of seeing Chanel. Paddleboarding would have to wait for another day, as I saw Tomasz, clutching Toby and Henry's hands, set off with Aleksy and Tommy who were in their wetsuits ready to go.

As Jonathan, Matt and the girls headed next door, I shuffled through the hedge. I assumed that George would already be there. It seemed silly to go the long way round when we didn't need to. I joined them at the front door, where there was no sign of George. I was a bit surprised as Jonathan petted me.

'Glad you decided to join us, after all I am sure you think this is a good idea,' he said.

'Yowl.' I really didn't.

There was a flash of annoyance on Andrea's face as she opened the door, followed by a moment where she rearranged her features into a smile.

'Well this is a nice surprise,' she said. Chanel hissed nastily. Goodness, she didn't waste any time. I was almost glad that George wasn't here.

'Look, Andrea,' Jonathan started. Matt stared at me, and I knew what he was thinking. 'We thought it might be a good idea to clear the air. I know there have been a few problems.'

'Really? I wasn't aware of any problems,' she countered. I had to admire her composure, as she was blatantly lying.

'Well you know the thing about you saying you want the cottage, and then the incident yesterday with your girls upsetting Toby, I thought we should have a reasonable chat and sort it out.'

'Me too,' Summer said. 'I want to sort it out,' she said, without any idea what she was talking about.

'And me,' Martha added. Matt shook his head.

Andrea shrugged. 'Look, the girls are out at the moment, but why don't you come in, I've got some fresh lemonade in the kitchen and we can have a civilised chat. I do find standing on the doorstep a little bit common.'

'Thank you, we'd love to come in,' Jonathan said. Andrea stood back and Martha and Summer went in eagerly, Jonathan behind them with Matt reluctantly bringing up the rear.

'Oh.' Andrea stopped. 'I'd rather your cat didn't come in, it does so upset Chanel.' She shut the door on me, almost catching my paw in the process.

I knew the kitchen was round the back, so I decided to go and see if I could hear any of their conversation. I struck gold, as one of the kitchen windows was open and, although I didn't dare jump up on the windowsill, because I'd probably be shooed away, I found a point by the open window where I could hear everything, even if I couldn't see it.

Andrea was speaking. 'I am so sorry about Toby, you see it was a bit of a misunderstanding. My girls are so sweet but some of the other village children have been unfair, refusing to let them join in their games with your children and, well, they were ever so upset as you can imagine. I know it was wrong of Savannah to accidentally throw some sand at Toby but she was very emotional and you know what children are like.'

'How do you accidentally throw sand at someone?' Matt asked, just as I thought the same.

'Well you know, it wasn't malicious. I have told the girls that even if everyone is being horrible to them they must rise above it and not react.'

'Our children are not horrible though, I can assure you of that,' Jonathan said.

'Well, of course they probably don't mean to be, but being left out is very hurtful,' Andrea persisted. I wished I could see Jonathan and Matt's faces, I hoped that they weren't buying this rubbish but I feared they might be.

'How about we speak to our children and tell them to be nice to your girls and you do the same?' Jonathan suggested.

Really? It would be that easy? Sometimes I wondered about my humans.

'But not me, you don't need to speak to me,' Summer said.

'She's adorable,' Andrea laughed. 'And so pretty, both of you are very pretty girls.'

'Well thank you,' Matt said. Oh goodness they were falling for it. 'But what about the house?' he quickly added. Phew. 'You said you wanted it no matter what it cost.'

'Oh I did, and I meant financially. You see, I have tried to have a reasonable chat with your wives. I hate to sound sexist but I do find men much easier to deal with in these matters,' Andrea chirped. She sounded as if she was flirting with both

Jonathan and Matt, which I was annoyed about. 'I would love that house, the village means so much to me and my family and we really don't like the idea of houses here being used only for holidays, it diminishes our community, and of course I like to do my bit for the community. I would love to own Seabreeze, and if I did it would really be to help the village.' She almost sounded believable, I thought, but I didn't trust her at all.

'Yes but we are three families who will be sharing the cottage, so it will be used a lot of the time. And we love this place, and will be spending money locally, so that's surely good for the village?' Jonathan added.

'Of course and if your wife, or wives, had explained it as simply as that I would have been delighted. I mean, I just want you to know that you are all very welcome here and I am the first to open my arms to new people, but if you ever change your mind the offer is there.'

'You are very reasonable,' Jonathan said. 'Is your husband around? Maybe you could both come over for drinks one evening?'

'That would be lovely, only my husband is travelling a lot for business at the moment, so he's barely here, but hopefully later in the summer, before you all go back to London.'

'Hiss,' a voice interrupted my eavesdropping. I looked up to see Chanel at the window. 'You've heard enough, you can go now,' she said.

With that she was gone.

I decided to find George. He would be furious about missing Chanel but then it was probably a good thing. It seemed that the more awful she was to him, the more he liked her. I checked the cottage but there was no sign of him, so I went to sit on the car bonnet. From there I spotted the others on the beach and saw that George was with them. Aleksy and Tommy were in the water with their paddleboards and Tomasz was on the sand with Henry and Toby, watching, with George standing next to them. I ran across to the beach, dodging all the families sitting on the sand, before reaching the shore and greeting them all. Tommy, who was standing on the board, paddled over to us, jumped off and came to see us.

'Alfie, did you see me? I am getting really good.'

'Not as good as Aleksy,' Henry said, innocently, which made Tommy scowl.

'I am as good as him.' He puffed out his chest. Tommy was more competitive than Aleksy, who was the more sensitive of the brothers. It was a surprise to everyone that Aleksy was so good at paddleboarding, but nice, because with most sports he was in Tommy's shadow a bit.

'Come on, it's not a competition,' Tomasz said.

'Well, watch me, I'll show you how good I am.' Tommy brought the board up to the shore while he huffed at us all. I was rubbing against Toby's leg when Tommy started pushing the board back into the water.

'Oh look, George is on the board!' Toby exclaimed.

'Meow,' I said, angrily. He must have jumped on the board and as Tommy had been pushing it back in the water, looking at us and telling us to watch him, he obviously hadn't noticed him. Oh my nerves had been shot to pieces in the last few days. This was too much. I yowled as much as I could, and then Tommy finally turned round and noticed George.

'Tommy, bring George back,' Tomasz yelled as loudly as he could. Tommy didn't turn round though. Instead he got on the board, on his knees, and started paddling, wobbling everywhere. George was standing on the front of the board and if I didn't know better I would have said he was enjoying himself. He stood, watching the water, not huddling close to Tommy, which was what I would be doing. It was apparent that Tommy wasn't great with the paddleboard, which was rocking quite violently, and then there was a huge splash.

'MEOW!' I shouted. What about George? Thankfully, he was still on the board as Tommy's head emerged from the water.

'He has very good balance, Tomasz,' Henry said.

'He does, even for a cat,' Tomasz agreed.

Aleksy paddled over to them and I watched, horrified, as George looked over at him, then leapt from one board to the other. As Aleksy turned his board around and headed back to the shore, I could hear both boys laughing, although the wind was making it sound faint. I was glad to see George was on Aleksy's board now – it made me feel a bit more reassured.

George made the shore safely, where Tomasz used a towel to dry him off a bit, before we all headed home.

'George, you shouldn't have done that,' I chastised as soon as we were alone. 'Cats are not meant to go near water.'

'I love water, Dad,' George said excitedly.

What? Whoever heard of a cat who liked water?

'And I love paddleboarding,' he went on. 'It was so much fun. You should try it.'

'Not unless I can paddleboard on dry land,' I replied, giving up. George was a stubborn kitten and now it seemed that, as well as liking Chanel, which was bad for him, he liked water, which was even worse for him. I had no idea what to do about that.

If only humans could be as sensible as I was. Tomasz and Matt were right, as was I. The women were furious that they had gone to speak to Andrea, and they were, quite rightly, refusing to buy her reasonable act.

'She's going to talk to the girls and make sure they are nice but she said they're being left out as well, which upsets them,' Jonathan said.

'That's not true.' Franceska was angry. 'Aleksy, he tell me what they say to them, they are nasty and they tried to get all the children not to play.'

'Maybe their mother is just fooled by them,' Matt suggested.

'Oh God, you are such an idiot,' Polly stormed.

'What on earth were you thinking? Going to see her?' Claire was practically screeching. Luckily the children were all in bed and that included George.

'I just thought we could clear up the unpleasantness.' Jonathan at least had the grace to look sheepish.

'And she did explain she wanted the cottage because she couldn't bear it to be empty so much. But when we explained it wouldn't be, she said she was delighted for us to be her neighbours.'

'And she said what a wonderful job you were doing with the renovations,' Jonathan added.

'And you believed her?' Polly stormed.

'Why wouldn't we?' Both Matt and Jonathan were looking a bit ashamed by now.

'Honestly, a pretty face and you believe anything.'

'I hadn't noticed she was pretty,' Matt said quickly.

'Yeah right,' Polly answered.

'Well, she does have nice hair,' Jonathan added and Claire swiped him.

'You guys are deluded if you think she was actually as reasonable as you say. She's playing you and it's embarrassing to see that you fell for it so easily.'

'Look, let's just give her the benefit of the doubt. Please?' Jonathan was red-faced and rubbing his arm where Claire had hit him a bit harder than she possibly intended.

'If you say so, but if there is another incident then you guys cannot doubt us,' Polly said. 'We don't lie and our children don't lie. Andrea is a middle-aged mean girl and she's bringing up her daughters to be mean girls.'

'OK, look let's leave it, we're only here for a short time and I don't want to argue,' Matt said reasonably. 'But honestly, if anything else happens, I promise we'll have your backs.'

'Yes, as long as the lady with nice hair doesn't turn your heads yet again,' Claire retorted.

Later, I could feel the tension in the air as Tomasz, who had cooked dinner, cleared his throat.

'Look, guys, the timing isn't good and I've tried to put it off but we have a problem.' I almost couldn't bear to listen.

'What's up, mate?' Jonathan said. Franceska was staring at her plate and refusing to meet anyone's questioning glances.

'We had a flood at the restaurant, it's not good. We have had to close and it'll be a couple more weeks at the least, plus the insurance company is dragging its feet.' He looked so sad my heart went out to him.

'Oh, Tomasz, that's terrible, we didn't realise. Frankie, why didn't you say?' Polly said.

'Because I didn't want to make more problems,' Franceska replied.

'What do you mean?' Claire asked.

'The money we put in here, our savings, we might need it after all. I am so sorry but I have wages to pay, and the business accounts are all tied up for the time being, so I need to find some cash, and soon.' Tomasz rubbed his head, anxiously.

'But the insurance has to pay out,' Matt said, reasonably.

'Yes, eventually it will, but I and my business partner are having issues with them. Look, we love this place, and I wouldn't want to lose it, the boys love their paddleboarding, but we do have a temporary cash flow problem and I don't know how to fix it.'

'Can we just bridge it, temporarily?' Claire asked, looking at Jonathan.

'Darling, we'd have to borrow money, which takes time, unless we go to a loan shark, I don't think it's feasible. Tomasz, how long do we have before you need the money and how much?'

Franceska named a figure, which meant nothing to me but everyone took a sharp intake of breath, and she started crying. Tomasz put his arm around her.

'If there was any way, we would try to find it,' Tomasz

said. 'But we literally have about two weeks until we are in trouble.'

'Oh God, we can't lose the cottage, not now,' Claire said, tears in her eyes.

'We are so sorry,' Franceska said. But no one went to reassure her and the party broke up soon after.

I was very upset, so I lingered in the hope that Gilbert would appear, and he did.

'I wanted to introduce you to our families,' I said. 'Although tonight wasn't a good night.' I wanted to Gilbert to meet them at their best and they certainly weren't right now.

'I know but I got cold paws. I'm still nervous around humans and I'm sure yours are nice, but you know I'm not ready to trust again.' I felt sad for him and what he had been through, although we had all had our tough roads to tread, I guessed.

'Anyway, it's your choice and I respect that. But I am worried about them.' I filled him in on the drama that had unfolded.

'I saw that neighbour and she was talking with that young builder, the one you don't like.'

'Liam?'

'Yes that's his name. I heard her speaking to him on the phone while she stood in the garden not that long ago. She looked around her furtively, checking no one was around, but I heard her tell him that his "little acts of sabotage" were unsatisfactory and he better "up his game".'

'What does that even mean?' I asked.

'No idea. We know what he's done but your families haven't agreed to sell the cottage.'

'But what does she mean by upping his game?'

'The mystery deepens.'

'The thing is, we need to follow him at all times to see what he's up to, and what with George and his crush and the kids and the humans, I'm just not sure I can do that.'

'Alfie, I can help. I mean, I'm quite good at hiding so I'll track him, at least for a while, especially when he's alone. And if I can't for any reason I'll let you know and you can take over.'

'Gilbert, that would be amazing, a huge weight off my mind.'

'Well I got used to hiding, being invisible, it helps with survival.' He looked sad.

'I hate to think of you being so alone. I told you about my homeless time, and well, I hated it. I wish you could see that being part of a family isn't all bad. My family isn't.'

'I'm sure you're right.' He grinned sadly and I nuzzled him. 'And maybe soon I'll be able to let myself believe it.'

It made me so cross that a handsome, lovely cat like Gilbert had had such a hard time. He was my friend now so that meant I would do all I could to ensure that things improved. Yes, he was going to help me with Andrea and Liam, but in return I was going to help him see that people weren't all bad. I only wished that the truth was that none of them were, but we all knew that that wasn't the case. With the news that Tomasz and Franceska had imparted on top of that, well, I had a very bad feeling in my fur. Very bad indeed.

Chapter
Sixteen

The men had left but the house had been strained since Tomasz and Franceska's announcement. Before they went, Tomasz promised to see if there was anything he could do and Matt and Jonathan had offered help but I caught Claire crying when she and Jonathan were alone. Jonathan tried to reassure her but Claire said that if Franceska and Tomasz needed to pull their money out, then they might have to sell the cottage to the horrible Andrea. And she said she couldn't bear to give up their dream. Jonathan promised he would do whatever he could but a heavy cloud hung over them.

The tension between the adults was clear. It was as if no one blamed Tomasz and Franceska but they were unhappy so the easy relationship had changed. Franceska and Claire seemed to be avoiding each other – and living in the same house that wasn't easy. I needed to keep an eye on this one. The optimistic part of me thought that perhaps it would all be sorted but the other part suspected I would have to be the one to do so. Again, there was a lot to do for this cat, and although I had Gilbert and my kitten to help (although I was not sure how much help lovesick George would actually be), it still seemed my problems were mounting.

It had rained for the past two days and the children were largely housebound, as was I. George, however, still insisted on sitting under the hedge, despite constantly coming in drenched and miserable after not catching even a glimpse of Chanel. Today I'd finally persuaded him to stay with me and the children in the big living room. The adults had got a selection of films for us to watch and we all snuggled up on the sofas watching and eating popcorn, which was a real treat, as we'd only just finished breakfast. The kids were enjoying lazing around, eating treats, and watching films. The one currently showing was called *Despicable Me*, chosen because it was suitable for all of them, and of course us cats. I was quite enjoying it although George, who was sitting with Summer and Martha, seemed a little bit lovesick still.

The point was that we never did this at home so it was still like being on holiday even when we were inside. Seabreeze had that effect on us. It made everything feel like a holiday. I was quite keen on licking the popcorn, as was George it seemed, and the kids took great delight in feeding us. I snuggled down more and realised holidays could be a lot of different things.

But there was a cloud over our lovely holiday home, and not just a rain cloud. The women were all uneasy. It felt that the friendships that had been so strong almost from the moment I got my families together were now under threat. Franceska was in her bedroom, it was clear she wanted to be alone. Claire and Polly were supposed to be ordering furniture but they said they didn't know if they should now that the future of their shared cottage was in question. I knew Franceska felt guilty, although it wasn't her fault, and I also knew that Claire was so upset at the idea of losing the cottage she didn't know how to act. Polly was trying to keep the peace but although they weren't arguing, or angry with each other, they were all sad and quiet. The atmosphere inside Seabreeze almost matched the weather outside. Which was why I was keeping well away and in with the children.

'You know how Mum seemed a bit sad earlier?' Aleksy said quietly to his brother.

'Yes,' Tommy said. 'So did Claire.'

'Well what about if we put a play on for the mums to cheer them up?'

I meowed. What a good idea.

'Guys,' Tommy said, loudly, 'we're going to put on a play for our mums.'

'Yay!' Toby said.

'Can I be a spaceman?' Henry asked.

'I want to be a princess,' Martha chipped in.

'Me too,' Summer agreed.

'And can Alfie and George be in it too?' Toby asked.

'Of course,' Aleksy replied.

I was going to make my acting debut it seemed.

'Can I go out, Dad?' George asked after lunch. I looked at the children who were going to the living room to do more rehearsals for the play. Although we were in it, it seemed we had very little to actually do, so I was sure we wouldn't be missed. But still it was awful out there as the rain persisted.

'I'd rather not, it's still quite wet out there.' I was a fair weather cat.

'But can I go to the hedge to look for Chanel then?' he pushed.

'OK, but you know what, I'll come with you, I'm not happy with you being alone in this weather.' My thoughts were that if George got too wet I could drag him back inside – not literally of course. I would have been happier in the warm but I didn't want to be a bad parent.

When the others had gone I followed with George; we ran quickly to the hedge and nestled in. Looking at Andrea's house I assumed she was inside; Chanel was definitely a fair weather cat, a bit like me in that respect.

'I just wish I could see her,' George said.

'I know, but the weather is terrible, so I'm not sure she'll come out.' My poor kitten looked so dejected, I had to think of a way to cheer him up. 'Tell you what, if you come home now maybe we can play hide and seek.' As he bounded off, I followed. Thankfully that seemed to do the trick.

When we got home, George urged me to hide, so I went upstairs where I found another commotion. I went to the doorway of the adults' bathroom to see Liam with his head hanging down. There was a broken window, and glass all over the floor.

'What the hell have you done?' the plumber asked. 'How can you manage to put a wrench through a window?'

Colin approached, looking annoyed.

'Liam, again?' he asked.

'I slipped,' Liam whined, sounding like a little boy, 'and the wrench smashed the window. You said you were replacing the windows anyway.'

If it hadn't been for the glass all over the floor I would have gone up to him and swished my tail or something.

'We are but not until the end of the summer. It's booked in before we paint the house as the last job. Honestly, boy, you're a liability,' Colin said, still shaking his head.

'What shall we do? I've got to get the fixtures all working today,' the plumber said.

'I've got some sheet glass in the van. Liam, go and get it and you'll have to stay late and fix it. But first clean up the glass – if any of the kids or the cats get cut you'll be for it.'

I followed Colin downstairs where he found Polly looking at fabric samples in the smaller living room.

'Can I have a word?' he asked.

'Sure.' Polly smiled.

'It's Liam, I'm afraid. He slipped and put a wrench through the bathroom window.'

'What?'

'Yelp!' I tried to tell them that he probably did it on purpose but it fell on deaf ears.

'He's a calamity I know, but we're going to fix it up so it'll be fine until the double glazing goes in. Luckily you've got two windows in that bathroom but for now, only one will open. I'm so sorry.' Colin looked upset, and I felt sorry for him. He didn't know that one of his workers was trying to sabotage his job, which actually could have a really detrimental effect on him, couldn't it?

'Colin, that's just the latest in the long list of things that Liam has done to mess up, cause delays and general trouble on this job. Can't you get rid of him? The others are working here so well but he's more trouble than he's worth. I can't afford not to be on schedule, we've got to go in a few weeks for school, and you know I want the bulk of the work done by then.' Polly sounded kind, she wasn't a shouter, or nasty like Andrea, but she had a fed-up edge to her voice.

'I know and if it was anyone else I would. Look, Polly, I know this isn't your problem but Liam is my brother's lad, and my brother's been unwell, he had to give up work, so well, they rely on Liam's pay packet. I've been swallowing up the extra costs, apart from his time of course, but I really can't sack him. I'll take full responsibility for him but I don't want my brother and sister-in-law to have any more stress.'

'OK, I understand, but you know I can't have him bringing the house to ruins.' Polly smiled sadly and touched Colin on the arm. 'I am sorry for your brother, but maybe you can get Liam to do jobs where he can't damage anything.'

'Good idea. Or I'll give him some play tools like Henry and Toby have!'

'Not a bad thought, he can borrow theirs,' she laughed.

'Thank you so much for understanding, it really is good of you.' Colin's mouth curled down, sadly. And suddenly I felt sorry for Liam although I wasn't happy with him but again, as George, my very astute kitten, said, things aren't always what they seem.

After tea that evening, we put on our play. Aleksy was the director, and he also narrated the (very thin) storyline. The play was about the royal family who visited the beach. It was a little bit strange and didn't make total sense, but then neither did life.

'I'm a princess,' seemed to be Summer's only line, which she repeated.

'I'm a royal prince,' Toby added. Tommy was the king, and he re-enacted the paddleboard incident with George, only without a paddleboard. Henry was the spaceman servant to the royal family. It was quite funny and the women all clapped very loudly, but I could tell they were putting a brave face on things. My only part was to be the royal cat and I joined in, quite happily; we needed some light relief. Aleksy even tied a towel around me to be a royal robe and I was pleased to see the women smile as the play reached its final scene. Even if things were still strained, everyone appeared to be happier than they had been before as they broke into another round of applause, and the three women were momentarily united as they cheered us all.

As I moved on from my acting debut, I went to find Gilbert. In my time I had learnt to trust my instincts and when I felt something in my fur, well, let's say I believed those feelings.

'Alright, Alfie,' Gilbert said. His gruff greeting was warmer each time I saw him.

'Did you see Liam break the window today?' I asked, no time for small talk.

'I did, I found a good spot to watch him from, the idiot broke it on purpose, but that's not all. When I was following him earlier his phone rang and he went to where he thought no one was listening but, of course, I was. Anyway, I heard him say Andrea's name and I imagine she was shouting at him as he was flinching quite a lot. In actual fact, he seemed scared of her, but asked if they could have dinner . . . Well anyway, she must have said yes because he smiled and then he went and smashed the window.'

'He might be next door right now!' I said.

'He might.'

'What are we waiting for?' I made to go to the back door.

'Where's George?'

'Fast asleep, he stays with Toby all night, and anyway we won't necessarily need to be long.'

'OK, Alfie, I'm right behind you.'

We circled the house before we hit gold. There was a room with full-length doors. The doors had curtains but they weren't completely closed and we could see inside. As we peered in, we saw that Andrea was on a very comfortable-looking sofa, holding a glass. Chanel was perched on the arm of the sofa and opposite her sat Liam, wearing clothes that were smarter than we had ever seen him wearing. He looked quite nice, his hair was neat and he looked clean.

The problem was that the doors shut out any sound so we couldn't hear what was being said, although I could see Andrea's lips moving a lot and Liam just sitting there looking besotted.

I noticed that Chanel seemed to sense there was something amiss as she made her way to the glass doors and we quickly darted back so she couldn't see us. She sniffed a bit, before baring her teeth then leaving.

'Isn't Liam a bit young for Andrea? I know I'm a cat but she seems a lot older than him,' Gilbert said as we started to head home.

'I think so.' I wasn't an expert, but I was pretty sure that Andrea was using Liam to get to us and it looked as if he had a crush on her just as George did on Chanel. 'But then Chanel is too old for George but he's so besotted he won't listen to me.'

'It must be the same for Liam,' Gilbert said.

'Yes but if he is trying to help her get us out of the cottage, then how are we going to stop him?' I felt as if Andrea was in charge of too many aspects of our lives.

'I don't know but if I stay close to him I can try to make sure that he doesn't do anything too bad. You know, when he broke the window I wasn't expecting that but if I had I could have tripped him up or something.'

'Or if you can't do anything then try to come and find me if you can, or yowl so loudly that the humans all come running.'

'But then they'll find me.' Gilbert was still uncertain.

'They have to meet you at some point,' I told him.

'Humph,' was his reply and I knew I was winning. With him at least.

Once again, I felt that things were mounting up and, for the first time this holiday, I missed Edgar Road badly. I missed Tiger and my other friends. I missed not having anyone to ask advice from; although I now had Gilbert, it wasn't quite the same as having my usual cat gang. I was feeling as if things were threatening to slip out of control and our idyllic holiday home was under threat. The worst thing was that my humans were still oblivious to all this. They thought that Franceska and Tomasz were the only threat to keeping the cottage. Yes they knew that Andrea wanted the house, they knew her children were mean and they thought that Liam was one of the most incompetent builders they'd come across, but apart from that they had no idea that there was a plan underway, a plan I was pretty sure was going to turn our holiday upside down. I couldn't believe it had only been a few short weeks since we had come here, it felt as if we belonged here in so many ways. I wanted what Claire wanted, I wanted our families to have this wonderful holiday home for many years to come, even after I was no longer around. I wanted it for them so badly that I knew I would have to play a big part in making sure it happened.

Chapter Seventeen

Franceska was unloading the car and George was hindering her by circling her legs. I was trying to stop him, which somehow meant I was circling her legs too.

'George, Alfie, you guys are going to send me flying,' Franceska chastised. At least the sun had finally come out again and, although things weren't back to normal with Franceska and Claire, they had cleared the air a bit, deciding not to worry until they knew the whole situation.

'Meow.' George was proud of himself although I wasn't sure why.

Franceska took the last bag out of the boot of the car and put it down. 'I'll go and get the boys to bring the shopping in, wait there.'

We weren't sure why she wanted us to wait but we did as we were told. Aleksy and Tommy ran out and grabbed the bags then ran back in, ignoring us completely.

'Meow,' I shouted.

'Sorry Alfie but Mum said if we took the shopping in we could go to the beach,' Aleksy said excitedly as he ran back to the house.

Us cats couldn't compete with the beach.

Franceska returned. 'Right, boys, I am locking the car and then I'm making lunch. Hungry?'

'Yowl.' Yes I was. We were about to turn back to the house when I spotted Andrea and Chanel approaching.

'It's Chanel.' George hopped from paw to paw excitedly.

As Andrea stopped, the Persian gave us her usual dirty scowl, which I think George saw as a loving blink.

'Ah, it's the Polish one,' she said, unkindly. Franceska turned to her, looking confused and then angry.

'I have a name, it's Franceska,' she replied, her voice shaking a little.

'Of course, whatever. Anyway, I'm glad I ran into you, I want to speak to you all. Together.'

'What do you mean?' Franceska asked.

'You and the other two women, we need to sit down and talk. We need to resolve this.' Andrea was wearing a bright pink dress, lots of jewellery and high heels. As usual her hair was very tidy, and didn't move in the breeze, and Chanel was sitting bearing her teeth at us in one of her arms. I was immediately on my guard. George was trying to catch Chanel's eyes by being cute but she was blatantly ignoring him.

'We do?' Franceska looked at the house as if hoping someone else would come and rescue her.

'Yes, we need to resolve the issue about the house,' Andrea pushed.

'I didn't realise there was an issue. You asked to buy the house, we said no. End of story.' Franceska's face reddened; she could be sensitive at times so it was nice to see she was holding her own.

'It's not the end of the story. When the husbands, well two of them, came to see me it was clear that there is definitely not an end of story. I hate it when women go running to their husbands as if they can't cope themselves.'

'That is not what happened. That was about the children. Anyway, I don't need to speak to you about this, I told you we don't want to sell the house and we definitely don't need any trouble. If there is a problem we will talk to you, not our husbands. In fact Claire and Polly were cross with them for coming to see you. So we shall leave it at that.'

'Are you saying you won't sell the house to me?' Andrea narrowed her eyes.

'We have said that all along. The renovations are well underway, we have only a few weeks left before the end of summer, and honestly, we would all like to enjoy our holiday.'

'We'll see about that.'

As Andrea turned and trotted off in her heels we could feel the threat hanging in the air.

Franceska went back inside and I waited patiently with George as he looked wistfully after Chanel. Aleksy and Tommy ran out of the front door and stopped to pet us.

'We're going to the beach.'

'Why don't you come?' Tommy asked.

'Meow.' We could go.

'Cool and we'll take care of you,' Aleksy said. He and Tommy looked at each other, then Tommy picked up George and Aleksy picked me up and off we went.

They found a spot in the sand dunes, and Aleksy put me down. I was getting quite used to the sand now, finding it easier the more we came here; I would possibly be a sand expert by the end of the holiday. As the boys sat down, flicking off their sandals, George started sinking into the sand. It was cute, but he did it on purpose, I could see, as he pushed his paws down.

'George, don't do that,' Tommy said, picking him up and brushing the sand off. We took a few moments to enjoy the sun and the grass in the dunes tickled us in the gentle wind. Just as the boys were deciding what to do, Savannah and Serafina approached. This was not good. We had already had to encounter their mother, now them.

'What are you doing?' they asked.

'Well, we are just hanging out, obviously,' Aleksy replied.

'How exciting. Anyway, I wanted to say, don't expect to see any of your other friends, because they are coming to my house. My mum has organised it and you are definitely not invited.'

'We wouldn't want to come anyway,' Tommy said. He poked his tongue out at her, which I felt was a bit childish but then I guess he was a child.

I hissed to tell Tommy to shush but he didn't seem to hear me.

'Tommy, don't waste your time talking to them,' Aleksy said. He turned to George and picked him up, stroking him.

'You boys are so boring,' Savannah said, and used her foot to flick sand up at us. I felt it cover me and Tommy.

'Oi!' Tommy shouted.

'Yowl!' I said; it wasn't a pleasant feeling. The girls walked away laughing.

'I really don't like them,' Aleksy said.

'Me either, but never mind, I've got some money for ice cream. Shall we get some?'

'Meow!' George said excitedly.

'OK, George, we can get some for you too,' Aleksy laughed.

We spent a pleasant time on the beach. George and I shared an ice cream and sunbathed, enjoying spending time with

Aleksy and Tommy, but all too soon Franceska appeared at the beach wall and shouted that it was time for us to go home to tea.

The house was empty when we got back.

'Where is everyone?' Aleksy asked.

'Claire and Polly have taken the others for a walk to burn off some energy.' So, they were still avoiding each other a bit.

George went to the sand room to clean up and to find some shade and I drank a lot of water, being thirsty from the sunny afternoon. Aleksy told his mum how the girls had been and she told him to ignore them but I knew that was easier said than done. Colin appeared and, as Franceska made tea for the builders, they chatted over the day's work.

'No accidents so far,' he said. 'But you know we have a lot of work to do still, so let's hope it stays that way.'

'Will the house be finished before we leave?' Franceska looked anxious and I wondered what she and Tomasz had decided to do.

'It should mainly be. As you know, the downstairs is being done after you go, only because the new kitchen will be a big job as we will be knocking the rooms through, and then we just have the windows and the painting and it'll all be ready the next time you're here.' Colin smiled.

'Um,' Franceska said, looking thoughtful.

'Well, I hope you'll be overjoyed with the finished house. It's amazing what the attic rooms and now the second floor has done for the house already. The whole village is buzzing with what a good job you've done.'

'Well I wish they would talk to us more, I mean it seems

that when we go to the local shop or to the beach people are scared to speak with us.'

'Well, it might be because of Andrea,' Colin said.

'What, because she speaks so badly of us to the rest of the village?'

'Look. I'm sure it's all hot air, but you know, why don't you take the children to the pub for tea tonight, about six? I'm in there, my wife is coming down and I'll introduce you to a few people. It would be good for you to make friends in the village.'

'Would you? That would be great. It would be nice if we can make some friends.'

'Honestly, not all of us are like Andrea, and you've been here long enough, it's about time you saw that for yourselves. But it's a small village and, well, I guess the locals are more cautious with new people. Anyway, come to the pub tonight, bring the kiddies with you, and you'll see.'

'Thank you, Colin. That would be very nice and the children love to go for tea at the pub.' Franceska looked happy and I thought she had made a sensible move. Getting out of the house, meeting new people, it might be just what they needed. Just as the children had made friends, it was perhaps time that the grown-ups did too.

'You know what would go down a treat?' Colin had turned to go, stopped and then faced Franceska again.

'What?'

'If, when the house is nearly ready, you invite some villagers over to have a look. They're all curious and it would be a nice way to break the ice and let them have a nose around.'

'Great idea. We could do tea and cakes and have, like, an

open house! Colin, that is such a good idea – they can see then how much we love Seabreeze Cottage and Lynstow, so they will feel happier about us being here.'

'You got it, love.' Colin left to go back to work. I rubbed up against Colin's legs. I could tell that he was definitely one of the good guys.

The children were excited to go out to eat but George and I weren't invited and the boys had been warned in no uncertain terms not to sneak us out. I didn't mind, I fancied a quiet evening in with my boy, even if he had other ideas.

'Can I go and wait for Chanel?' he said. Really, all George did was either lie under the bush hoping for a glimpse of her, or hide behind a plant by her back door, and more often than not he fell asleep before he even saw her. So, neither tactic proved very successful, or at least hadn't so far. I really didn't want to go out again and I thought perhaps, now he was growing up, I shouldn't have to.

'If you promise to be home before it's dark, or I'll have to come looking for you,' I warned.

'Of course, Dad.' He raised his whiskers, gave me a thank-you nuzzle and was off. I settled down in a nice spot on the big living room sofa. It was warm and cosy and before I knew it I'd dozed off.

I was woken by a tail tickle and I opened my eyes to see George.

'Oh good boy, you came home on time,' I said, looking out of the window where the sky was darkening.

'Yes and it was no good, I didn't see Chanel but I did see

Andrea, she was pacing up and down angrily, shouting down the phone.'

'Who was she talking to? Was it Liam?'

'I don't know but she said that things were getting desperate and she was scared.'

'She doesn't act scared though, does she?' I was thinking aloud.

'People act in different ways, for different reasons, you taught me that,' my wise kitten replied.

I had taught him a lot. When my first love, Snowball, moved in next door to me on Edgar Road, her whole family acted a bit rude, including her, and they didn't ever want to talk to us. When they did they made it clear that they didn't want anything to do with us, and it did look as if they had something to hide. It turned out they'd had a very bad experience which had left them scared of making friends and I wondered if Andrea was in a similar situation – it might be that her fear was making her mean. I could sometimes be a bit judgmental; perhaps I needed to listen to George more. If Andrea was doing this because she was scared then maybe she wasn't all bad and we could get to the nicer version of her. I just didn't know how. Going through Chanel the way I did with Snowball certainly wasn't an option. That cat wasn't scared, she was just downright rude.

As George and I were thinking about what to do next, the door opened and the children burst in, shattering our peace and quiet. Or mine anyway. George hopped down and began mewing at them excitedly.

'But I'm not even tired,' Summer was shouting, in a way which suggested she really was.

'Me neither,' Martha concurred. Although Martha was older than Summer, she often let Summer take the lead. For the most part she was laid-back, whereas Summer was the bossiest person I knew.

'Bed, both of you,' Claire said, coming in the room, 'and Toby and Henry too. Upstairs now, before I get cross.' She was giggling as she spoke, which suggested she wasn't that cross at all.

The younger children were hustled upstairs and Aleksy and Tommy were allowed to go to the small sitting room and watch some TV for a while.

Franceska came in to join us with a bottle of wine and three glasses. She collapsed on the sofa next to me, absently stroking my fur. She seemed happy and I was looking forward to hearing what a success the evening had been.

We didn't have long to wait as Polly and Claire came in.

'That was quick,' Franceska said, with a smile.

'Well, I couldn't be bothered to bath them so we just got them into their PJs and into bed quickly.' Polly smiled. 'They were all too tired to argue the minute they saw their beds.'

'I shouldn't drink when in charge of my children though,' Claire laughed, as she took a full glass from Franceska.

'Look, I am sorry about the spanner we threw in the works, with the restaurant. I know Tomasz is still trying to sort it and I want to keep this house very much, so I just want to say sorry and I hope it doesn't ruin everything.' She looked suddenly tearful. 'We are doing everything we can to make sure we can keep the cottage, you need to know this.'

'Oh, Frankie, I am sorry,' Claire said. 'None of this is your fault, or Tomasz'. I just love Seabreeze so much, and I was worried about losing it but after tonight, well I feel like we can sort it out . . . Somehow we will keep the house.' Claire hugged Franceska. 'I'm so sorry that I was cold with you, you know how emotional I get, but our friendship is more important than anything.'

'To me too.' Franceska's eyes glistened with tears.

'And what a fun evening though. I mean, Frankie, you are a genius getting us to meet the locals,' Polly took the conversation in a more upbeat direction. I felt relief flood my fur, it seemed that the women had got over the hump for now.

'It was Colin's idea.' Franceska smiled. 'He said the villagers were very nice.'

'They were and the idea of having an open house when the cottage is nearly finished is also good. They all seemed to be keen to have a look around.'

'Again, Colin. But he's right, with the Andrea situation, it might be good to have the locals on our side.'

'He's a lovely man,' Claire said. 'I feel that we've made progress, they all seemed to like the idea that we'd be in the house a lot, and when you said that we were looking for someone local to be a kind of caretaker I thought they were all going to line up there and then, Pol,' Claire said.

'Well, we do need someone, they can do the beds ready for when we're coming, and when it's empty I like the idea of someone giving it a clean every week too.' Franceska added.

'It's very sensible. But I think that Colin's sister-in-law might want the job,' Polly said.

'Liam's mum?' Claire looked faintly horrified.

'She might not be as hopeless as him and Colin told me

246

they are struggling for any extra cash, so I said I would talk to you.' Polly seemed to have talked through a lot with Colin.

'Hey, let's meet her, if Colin vouches for her . . .' Claire said. She was in a good mood; I couldn't help thinking it was the wine.

'And they promise not to let Liam be here alone,' Polly laughed.

'But wasn't it nice to meet the women too?' Claire said. 'I mean, I know we met Amber before but the others . . . They are all clearly terrified of Andrea but actually they're nice and seemed more than happy to be friendly with us.'

'Not sure if they would in front of *her*, though,' Franceska said. 'Look, I know that we're OK but I am sorry. I was just so terrified that we might have to take the money back to keep the business afloat, I can't bear it.'

'Oh, Frankie, honestly, let's forget it for now, I still feel terrible that I've been a bit moody with you,' Claire said. 'We were so excited and we all stretched ourselves to afford it, so please, don't worry.'

'Look, this place has already become a home to us, in the month we've been here it's become like home to us all. So we will figure it out, the restaurant, Andrea, everything, I promise that.'

'Let's drink to that.' Claire raised her glass. 'To Seabreeze and Lynstow and many, many happy holidays here.'

Chapter Eighteen

'I get it, this is what it's all about,' George said excitedly. He had his head in an empty box and was pushing it around the kitchen table, much to the delight of Summer and Toby.

'What?' I asked quietly, making sure our families couldn't hear.

'The holiday, Seabreeze Cottage, all of our families having a very lovely time,' he said.

'You are so wise for one so young.' I had taught him well, after all.

It was the day when our families had invited half the village, or so it seemed, round to Seabreeze Cottage for food and drinks. We still had a few weeks left here before we had to go back to Edgar Road. The builders had doubled in number and been working extra hard since the night the women had gone to the pub and the men had taken an extra day off work and were coming down on Thursday night. It was all exciting, and they had worked out that instead of just worrying about Andrea they should embrace village life. I only wished I had thought of it.

George bumped into the table leg, eliciting lots of giggles from Toby.

'George, get out of the box, and Alfie, we don't want you getting under foot today,' Franceska chastised as she prepared a mountain of food.

'Yes, Alfie,' Claire reiterated. Honestly, why was it always me, not George? 'The men are taking the children out for the morning so we can get organised. Can you do the same with George?'

'Can we go sit in the hedge?' George asked quietly as I used my nose to try to nudge the box off him.

'Fine,' I agreed. After all, I had no better plan on how to spend time getting out from under everyone's feet. I decided not to be offended, after all I understood how important today was for everyone.

The men had come down and had some very good news. Jonathan had put Tomasz in touch with a friend of his, who was something to do with the law, and he had threatened the insurance company on their behalf. Apparently there'd been a bit of arguing and going backwards and forwards but the insurance company had finally agreed to pay for all the damage and lost wages. Tomasz and his business manager had then gone to the bank who had given them a temporary loan to cover the costs, so their stake in Seabreeze was safe. The celebratory mood returned and if it hadn't been for Andrea and Liam I would also have been jumping for joy.

Jonathan, Matt and Tomasz had been so amazed by the transformation that they were overjoyed. The second floor was finished and now was home to three big bedrooms, a refurbished and expanded bathroom, and a master suite with en suite shower room. The only thing was that some of the furniture hadn't arrived yet but they didn't seem to mind that. Bit by bit, it was becoming a home, but more than that a home that represented each of my families. The children's rooms were amazing, and now the other bedrooms were too. Claire and Jonathan's room was painted in a blue colour that they both loved, and all the curtains and accessories matched. Polly and Matt's room had a more modern feel, whereas Franceska and Tomasz had gone a totally different way and opted for a seaside feel – with stripy wallpaper, driftwood and shells, it did look a lot like a beach hut in fact. It was my favourite room because it felt as if it belonged. But I understood how each room was part of my families and that I loved. It meant that they were going to make this cottage a second home and it was feeling that way already.

Oh and Gilbert had been wonderful, he'd been on Liam-watch but Liam hadn't had the opportunity to ruin anything else. Gilbert had even heard him on the phone, we assumed to Andrea, saying he was never alone in the house long enough to do anything. It seemed our plan was working, well sort of. And Gilbert was warming more and more each day to the idea of meeting our families so now I knew it was just a matter of time.

George and I made our way outside. It was a warm, not hot, day, with a cool sea breeze (I now understood the name of the cottage) gently brushing our fur. We made our way to the hedge and shuffled through. I found my favourite spot, ground soft, leaves shading me, and George sat as near as he could get to Chanel's garden without being spotted. There was nothing to see, which we seemed to get a lot, but I saw George was looking so hopeful so I settled down for the duration. At least it wasn't raining and there were worse ways for a cat to pass some time.

I had almost dropped off for a cat nap when George jumped up, stretching excitedly.

'She's here, Dad, she's here.' Before I had managed to open

both of my eyes he had run off across the lawn to where Chanel stood, glaring. I thought it best I follow him.

'Hey!' George said, excitedly. For once Andrea wasn't around, and Chanel was on her own. A rare occurrence.

'What are you doing sitting in my hedge?' she asked. She flicked her tail, fixing her green eyes on us. Yes, she was a sophisticated-looking cat but she had the meanest eyes I had ever seen. Even Salmon had nothing on her.

'Technically, it's our hedge too,' I said. I wasn't going to let her intimidate me. Well, only a bit as she inched towards us.

'Not for long.' She arched her back.

'You are so lovely,' George gushed. I nudged him, but there was nothing I could do.

'Go away,' she hissed.

'We will go but before we do, I want to know why your owner wants our house so badly.'

'Why should I tell you?'

'Look, Chanel.' I squared up to her. I didn't intend on doing anything, I knew violence didn't solve anything and I was the least violent cat ever, couldn't really even hunt, but I didn't want her to know that. 'I just want to know. We know about Liam, we know that Andrea's under pressure and that she has to sort things out soon. So what exactly is going on?' I bared my teeth for good measure.

'So, so pretty,' George said, tilting his head.

'How do you know all that?' Chanel asked. I had wrong-pawed her.

'We know, that's all that matters. We're on to you, and so you can either tell us what is going on or not but know this, we will find out.'

'And your fur is the most beautiful I have ever seen,' George added. We both looked at him.

'Listen, none of this is any of your business, it's my family and our problem. Yes, we do need your house and there is a very good reason for it, but I am not at liberty to share with you. You might do well to keep your nose out of our business. And while you're at it, take the annoying kitten away with you.' She turned on her paws and ran back towards the house.

'Come on, George, I think it's probably time we went,' I said.

'I think she really likes me, Dad,' he replied. 'I mean, more than she did at first even!'

What could I do?

The lawn had been transformed. The dining table had been moved outside, which had taken Tomasz, Matt and Jonathan a lot of arguing to get it through the door. But now it was on the lawn, laden with an abundance of food. Colin had brought over some other tables, and every chair we had, plus some of Colin's, littered the lawn, along with picnic blankets. The children were playing outside and Seabreeze Cottage was open for our party, or whatever it was we were having.

Colin and his wife Fiona, a lovely warm woman who loved cats, were already here. They were having a cup of tea and chatting.

'It's funny how you brought your cats with you on holiday,' Fiona said.

'Ah, well they're like family to us, we couldn't not, and anyway they are so good, they haven't run off or caused any problems.' Claire bent down and petted me. I purred, although that wasn't strictly true. I looked over to where George was eating ice cream out of Summer's bowl. I would have to ignore that for now.

'Well it's lovely. Right, there's our Shelley coming.' Some more people were approaching. 'She'd be ideal to look after this place when you're away.'

'Oh yes, we were looking forward to meeting her,' Claire said and she and Jonathan smiled as they were all introduced.

It was a lot for a cat to take in. There seemed to be so many people in the garden that there was barely any grass visible. As well as Colin's family, there were other people who I had never seen, some old, some young. Amber, the woman who had come to apologise for Andrea's behaviour, was again apologising for not spending time with us. It seemed she had been looking after her sick mum but now she was back they were all planning on having lunch together. Amber said she didn't care what Andrea said any more. Then there were the village children, and their parents, who again, now they had stepped out of Andrea's shadow, were really nice.

'Do you think we should go and see if Andrea wants to come?' Matt asked.

'I wouldn't,' Vicky replied. 'She knows where we are, she's probably watching from one of her rooms.' They all looked up at Andrea's house but there was no sign of anyone there.

'And we did put an invite through her door,' Polly said. 'Not that she deserved it after the way she talked to Frankie, but we are trying to be neighbourly.'

'Well, you know I was a bit dubious at first, I mean that

you would spend all this money on the house and barely use it, sorry,' Kate, another of the village ladies, said.

'Well that was the idea Andrea tried to plant in our heads anyway,' Amber explained.

'Oh don't worry, you'll be sick of the sight of us we'll be here so much,' Polly laughed.

'Speak for yourself, you won't be able to get enough of me,' Matt joked and they all smiled.

'By the way, I wanted to find a gardener when the house is finished.' Polly quickly changed the subject. 'We have some plans for getting plants all round the side, and then we can look at the furniture.'

'Oh look no further,' Kate said. She turned to a young woman. 'Chrissy, come here.' Chrissy joined us.

'This is my sister, Chrissy, she has a garden design business and she lives in the village,' Kate explained. Polly then took Chrissy round the garden, explaining what they were looking for.

The village seemed to have sprung to life in our garden and I felt incredibly content as I watched the party unfold. Everyone was eating, drinking and chatting. Jonathan had met a guy who was involved in the local football team so they were talking football for ages, and Aleksy and Tommy's paddleboard instructor popped in too. We met Liam's parents: Shelley, who was very sweet and who seemed keen to be our caretaker when we were away – as well as Liam's dad, who had a walking stick. He kept admiring the work that had been done while his son was looking awkward as Colin got him to help by giving guided tours of the house. Everyone was complimentary.

The children were playing without a cross word. As well as Ben, Jess and Millie, there were other children I hadn't met yet. Younger ones were playing with Summer and Martha and there were a couple still in prams. Summer was besotted by one of the babies, and Martha was trailing Millie around, asking her to plait her hair for her.

The men were all laughing and joking and, at one point, Jonathan almost tried to buy a boat from Colin, but luckily Claire stopped him.

'Maybe I'll buy one next summer,' he said. I sincerely hoped not. That was just asking for trouble.

I saw my humans blossoming once more. The stress that Polly, Claire and Franceska seemed to have been feeling looked as if it was melting away in the sun and as everyone bonded I felt we really were part of Lynstow. And it was as if it was meant to be.

It was an exhausting but lovely afternoon and I was only sad that I couldn't find Gilbert. I was hoping, yet again, to introduce him to the family while everyone was together, and I decided that I would see him tonight and tell him that that was what we were going to do. It was time to be forceful. I knew that if he stayed here when we went back to London Shelley could make sure he was well fed, and then he would definitely be part of the family. I just had to convince him of that. I was pretty sure my family would see it the way George and I did as well. The only problem now was convincing Gilbert.

It also meant I had to keep a close eye on Liam at the party. I was unsure if Gilbert was there, but hiding, although

I couldn't sense him so it seemed unlikely. However, Liam behaved, and his family were there, as well as the other builders, so he was occupied at all times. Only once did I see him sneak off, and following him, discovered he had merely gone to the downstairs loo. Nevertheless, I sat outside and waited for him. It didn't hurt for him to think that I was on to him and from the way he looked at me, slightly frightened, I think he did.

There was a lot to do in our time left at Seabreeze Cottage before the children had to go back to school, I had to ensure that Gilbert was alright, that Andrea stopped trying to take our house, and that Liam didn't manage to knock it down. It seemed an awful lot but I was going to make sure I did it.

'Dad, I think I need to go inside,' George said, joining me by the front door where I sat watching the fun.

'What's wrong?' I asked, concerned. George looked a little shattered.

'I'm a bit hot but mainly it's very tiring being this cute.'

'Of course it is.' I smiled and led him inside for a rest.

Chapter Nineteen

The clean-up operation took most of the next day, because some of the party guests remained into the night, with the children practically falling asleep in their clothes, the adults enjoying far too many drinks and George and I trying to stay awake to take care of everyone. When I tried to get George to go to bed he refused until Toby did, so he was overtired – well, we were all overtired actually.

The downside to this plan was that the adults all woke up feeling a bit worse for wear, the children were tired and grumpy having not had enough sleep and the house was a total mess. This was not a situation for a cat to worry about though so instead I cleaned my paws, made sure George was thoroughly groomed and then we went to relax.

Last night, after everyone had finally gone to bed, I'd seen Gilbert and we'd enjoyed some left-overs together. Probably because of the sardines I managed to extract a promise from him that this evening, just before the sun set, he would finally let me introduce him to my families. The men were going back to London on Monday, and wouldn't be back until the following weekend, so it was important that Gilbert met them tonight. Especially as they were all so happy at the moment. The adults had made plenty of friends and the children had made even more. In fact, the women were planning on going to lunch with Amber, Vicky and Kate this week; they all seemed to get on pretty well. There was no sign of Andrea, which was always a good thing, although George was pining for Chanel, which wasn't.

'Right, well I'm convinced,' Jonathan said as the last of the mess was finally cleared away.

'Convinced about what?' Claire asked.

'This place, the village, us spending our weekends, holidays, or most of them, here. I see it now,' Jonathan replied.

'I agree,' Tomasz joined in. 'I wasn't totally sure this was a good idea at first. I mean, the cottage, and the money, and then with the restaurant problems, but the children have had such a lovely time, one we wouldn't be able to have in London. Aleksy is doing so well with his paddleboarding.' Tomasz looked happy again, which was so wonderful to see. 'I want to spend as much time here as we can.'

'I know, Tommy is miffed as it's the first sport that Aleksy is better than him at,' Franceska laughed. 'And we know we have increased the value of this place already. If you think about it, the money we're spending on it, spread over all the holidays we would take, is well worth it.'

'More than worth it,' Polly sighed. 'I feel so restful here, I mean, I know we've been working flat out and it's been a bit stressful at times but, on the whole, just getting up in the morning and looking out at the sea makes me feel so calm.'

'So, we are all in love with Seabreeze Cottage?' Matt laughed.

'Meow,' I said. Yes we all were.

We were sitting on the lawn on a big picnic blanket. Well, I was sitting, Jonathan was lying, Claire next to him, Matt was across from us, supervising a game of cricket with the chil-

dren, although Aleksy and Tommy had been allowed to go
to the beach with their new friends. Polly was leaning against
an oversized cushion, and Franceska was propped up against
Tomasz. George was trying to help with the cricket game
but he kept getting hit with the ball which, instead of encour-
aging him to keep out of the way, was having the opposite
effect. He seemed to think it was a game. Luckily the ball
was soft. At least it wouldn't knock him out, and it was too
much to hope it would knock any sense into him regarding
Chanel, of course.

Speak of the devil. The gate opened and in came Andrea,
resplendent in a fitted turquoise dress with high heels, and
her halo of blonde hair, carrying an angry-looking Chanel.
George immediately stopped what he was doing to gape. Of
course this meant he got hit again by the ball. He was a bit
embarrassed that Chanel witnessed it though. He made his
way to where I was lying on the rug, and we waited for
Andrea and Chanel to join us.

'Hello,' Jonathan said, sounding friendly. Claire tried to
hide a scowl.

'Hi, I'm terribly sorry to disturb you,' Andrea said, sounding
nice, well nicer than normal anyway. The three women
exchanged glances, looking as surprised as I felt.

'That's OK. I would say take a seat but we don't have any,'
Matt laughed. Polly did not seem happy because the men
were all looking at Andrea with something of a soppy look
on their faces, a bit like the way George looked at Chanel,
I thought. Oh goodness, I hoped they weren't in love with
her, they were all married after all.

'Ha, of course. I would sit on the rug, but in this dress . . .'

I swear I saw Jonathan blush. I flicked my tail in annoyance. 'Anyway, I won't keep you, but I wanted to apologise for not being able to make your little . . . thingy yesterday, but I was so busy and the girls weren't feeling great, so we didn't think it was a good idea. However, to make it up to you I wanted to invite you all over next weekend. Saturday. I'll make a big picnic lunch and some of my friends will join us. It'll be lovely.' She almost seemed as if she wanted to spend time with us. I wasn't sure if I could believe what I was hearing. Or could I?

'Wow, thank you, that does sound nice,' Tomasz said. Then he looked at the picnic blanket as if he knew he might not have chosen the best words.

'Well you know, there's no secret that I wanted to buy your cottage, but it's clear that you have done a wonderful job in making it your holiday home, and so it's time for me to be neighbourly.'

'I guess we can come, but listen, Andrea, if your girls are horrible to our children . . .' Polly warned.

'I promise they won't be. I did explain to your very reasonable – not to mention handsome – husbands that it was a misunderstanding, my girls were feeling a bit jealous. Anyway, let's not rake over that again.' She smiled. No, this was not sincere. I was pretty sure of it, could feel it in the tips of my claws.

'No, let's not,' Claire said between gritted teeth.

'So you'll all come, Saturday, about one?' Andrea looked hopeful. I wondered if the others thought she was genuine in her desire to make amends. I was pretty sure the guys were, but the women weren't. Or perhaps more accurately the men wanted it to be genuine.

'Of course we will, we'll look forward to it,' Jonathan said. All the women grinned, broadly, but it was the kind of grin that said, 'Oh no we won't look forward to it at all.'

George followed them to the gate, making his cute eyes at Chanel who was determinedly ignoring him. He went right to the gate, but then, as they shut it behind them, he lay down, looking defeated.

'Hey,' I said, nuzzling him.

'Why did that woman have to take her away?' he said sadly, resting his head on his paws. 'I could tell Chanel wanted to spend some time with me but that woman always stops her.'

'Of course she does,' I replied, slightly lost for words. And I gave him the same kind of grin that the ladies had given Andrea.

I found Gilbert nervously grooming himself by the back door. Everyone was in the kitchen. The children were sitting round the table, the adults scattered around performing various tasks: Claire coaxing Summer to eat vegetables, Jonathan next to Toby, Polly stirring something on the hob, Tomasz in the corner of the room reading a newspaper and Matt making hot drinks.

'I'm not sure about this,' Gilbert said.

'Well I am, there's no time like the present. Now come on, don't be a sissy.' It was a word I heard a lot from the kids. George had been primed and he was waiting by the opening between the kitchen and the sand room. I took a deep breath and walked through, making sure Gilbert was with me. The three of us stood in a line and I opened my lungs.

'MEOW!' I cried as loudly as I could. Everyone stopped what they were doing and looked at us.

'Oh my, who is this?' Franceska rushed towards us and picked Gilbert up. He looked a bit startled and squirmed in her arms, but then after a while he let her stroke his head. I was relieved. Everyone crowded round.

'Mum, he looks like a leopard,' Tommy said, coming over. All the children and adults made a fuss of him and he looked so surprised that I felt a bit sad that he wasn't used to this treatment. This was how *all* cats should be treated.

'So, Alfie, he's a friend?' Jonathan asked me. 'Alfie does have a lot of cat friends,' he added.

'I always thought cats were solitary but not our Alfie, he always has someone in tow,' Matt added.

'Meow,' I confirmed; yes he was my friend.

'Do you think he belongs to one of the neighbours?' Claire asked. 'He hasn't got a collar.'

'Definitely not Andrea's,' Polly added.

I knew it wouldn't be easy to explain who Gilbert was or why he was here but I also knew we had to try.

'Meow,' I said, and I ran to the sand room. There I ran around in circles trying to explain.

'He lives in the sand room?' Franceska asked. Bingo!

'You know, I did wonder, there were cat hairs in there when we first got here,' Claire said. 'I felt as if it smelt a bit like a cat as well, but of course we never saw him.' She stroked Gilbert's neck, and he actually purred.

'So you think he lives in the cottage?' Matt asked.

'Meow.' Honestly it wasn't easy, was it?

'But it's been empty for years so that would mean he was living here alone,' Polly said.

They all started discussing Gilbert, where he may and may not have been living, and I saw him start to make his way back through to the sand room. I ran after him.

'I knew this would happen,' he said, sounding sad. 'They want to know who I belong to, humans aren't used to us just belonging to ourselves. I knew it was a mistake to come.'

'No,' I insisted. 'Look, they will discuss it but at the end of the day this is your home, and they will realise that. We'll help them realise it. Please trust me. You have been really helpful with the Liam situation and everything, trust me, they will realise you belong here and that you are Seabreeze Cottage's very own cat,' I begged. I wasn't certain about much but I was about this.

After a while, I persuaded him to return.

'Well as you said, he's got no collar, and he hasn't been around much, or maybe he only comes in normally when we're all asleep,' Jonathan started. 'So my guess is that he's used to being here, on his own and, look, we're in the country, plenty of cats survive without pouched food you know.'

I jumped onto Jonathan's lap and nuzzled him to tell him he was right.

'I know, but I hate to think he doesn't have a family to fuss over him,' Claire said.

'But, Claire, look at our Dustbin, he loves living in our yard, if we try to take him inside he really doesn't like it,' Franceska pointed out.

'So it's likely that the cat lives here?' Claire sounded uncertain.

'Meow, meow, meow,' I said, which meant yes, that's exactly where he lives.

'But what if we take him back to London?' Matt suggested.

'Yowl!' I screeched. That meant no.

'He's a beach and country cat, not a city cat,' Jonathan pointed out. 'Look, he's not skinny, or malnourished, he looks healthy, my vote is that we get him checked out with a vet, make sure he is OK, and has all his immunisations, and then we let him live here. We'll be here a lot between us and Shelley is going to be taking care of the place, she only lives down the road so she can look after him, but I really think it would be mean to not let him live here, especially as he seems so at home.'

'The vet?' Gilbert hissed. OK, I hadn't thought of that one.

'A necessary evil,' I hissed back. It really was, although I felt a bit sorry for him. 'Just think, you'll have a quick check and then you will have the run of Seabreeze Cottage when we're in London, and when we're here, think of all the fun we'll have.'

'You make a good point, Alfie, but still the vet. Even I remember how intrusive they can be.'

But as Gilbert went back to the kitchen and let Tomasz lift him onto his lap I knew I'd won; he had fallen in love with my families, just as I knew he would. After all, who wouldn't?

'What is his name?' Tomasz said, stroking him. Ah, that was something we hadn't thought of.

'You know, my aunt had a big ginger cat when I was little. He was called Gilbert. Let's call him that,' Claire said and I was stunned into silence.

★   ★   ★

'I told you it would be alright,' I said later when we were alone. 'But what about the name thing?' I was still a little shaken by that.

'It must be one of those coincidences,' Gilbert said. I shook my fur. It was obvious that he wasn't the ginger Gilbert who was not only ginger but would have been incredibly old by now, but what were the odds?

'It is still strange, as if you belong here, like the cat before you,' I said. 'Like Seabreeze Cottage always has to have a cat called Gilbert or something.'

We were in the backyard, looking at the moon and enjoying some peace and quiet. George had been so excited by having Gilbert officially around that he had insisted we take him to the beach before bed and George had run around enough to tire himself out. After putting him to bed, I found Gilbert, eating in the kitchen, officially this time. It made my heart swell. After dinner we went for a walk around the garden together.

'It's all worked out perfectly,' I said.

'I know and thank you. When you first moved here I thought I'd have to find a new home, and I'm so glad I didn't, because I love Seabreeze Cottage.'

'I know, it really does get to you, doesn't it?'

'It's more than a house, Alfie, it's special. That's what I thought when I first came here and I still think it now!'

We were disturbed from our musings by a noise the other side of the hedge. I darted into the hedge, Gilbert on my paws. It wasn't as easy to get through as our usual gap but we fought our way so we could see into Andrea's garden. She was sitting on the terrace, drinking, and Liam was with her.

'Can we get closer?' I asked.

'Follow me,' Gilbert said, and moved stealthily nearer, so we could hear them.

'I thought you'd forgotten all that stuff,' Liam was saying. 'I can't do anything to the house, I'm being watched like a hawk, Andrea.'

'Of course I haven't. And if you want to be with me you will do as I ask.'

I had to concede she looked beautiful in the moonlight. For once, there was no sight of Chanel.

'I love you.' Liam looked sad. 'But I don't know what more I can do.'

'Liam, I have told you the predicament I'm in. It's getting worse. My husband, sorry, soon to be ex-husband is piling on the pressure. I need to sell this house but I can't if I don't have anywhere to go. Don't you see how desperate I am?' Her voice trembled with panic.

'But, again, Andrea, I don't see what I can do. There must be somewhere else?'

'No. there isn't. I want you to take these.' Andrea handed something to him. Both her voice and her face hardened.

'Matches? Why are you giving me matches? I don't smoke.'

'No, but the house will when you set a little fire,' Andrea said quietly.

I felt sick as I looked at Gilbert, who looked equally horrified.

'No, there's no way I can do that,' Liam said, shaking his head, which was a relief. 'I won't be an arsonist.'

'Listen, on Saturday afternoon they'll all be here, the house will be empty, so you can go in and set a fire. There won't be too much damage as you don't need to leave it too long. Then you can call the fire brigade, anonymously of course. And you can start the fire in the kitchen which hasn't even been done yet.' She paused, as if to let her words sink in. 'But, it'll have done enough damage to make them want to get away from here.'

'But, Andrea, why would you burn down a house that you want to live in?' Liam asked, quite reasonably I thought.

'Because I'm desperate, Liam! Haven't you heard a word I said? My husband is threatening me, my girls need a home, and minimum disruption to their lives. Having their dad move out has been hard enough on them, I won't let them suffer any more. No one will be hurt, but they won't want to stay here after a fire. It's the perfect solution.'

So that was why she had invited everyone over on Saturday. Oh goodness, I was right not to trust her.

'It's crazy. I am not going to do that. I could go to jail.'

I saw Andrea shudder at that. 'Liam, I'm beyond desperate, I would never ask you if I had any other options.' Her voice sounded teary.

'As I said, Andrea, I am not going to jail over this.'

'You won't, and it won't be a bad fire. I'll be your alibi, I promise no one will know it was you.'

'But you said the neighbours will all be with you.'

'And I'll say that you were working upstairs doing something for me, I'll think of something.' She sounded insistent. 'Liam, darling, don't worry about the details, what I need you to worry about is how you can get into the house when they are all here, I'll take care of the rest.' She leant over and kissed him for what seemed like a very long time.

'I don't know, I mean I'm not happy about it. Not only is it illegal and dangerous but the families have been good to me . . .'

'But I'll be much better to you, do this for me and I will take proper care of you.' When Andrea smiled at him, I felt my fur stand on end. 'We will be together, officially, I promise, you just have to do this one small thing.'

I wasn't sure but it did seem as if Andrea could be persuasive, and she also had Liam twisted round her little finger. He was clearly besotted; though it was dark I could see it in his eyes and in the way he was sitting, and for the first time I felt sorry for him. She was a powerful woman and he didn't stand a chance. But then again, I was a powerful cat and therefore they didn't stand a chance. Well I hoped they didn't. If Liam agreed to what Andrea asked, then our holiday home, and Gilbert's home, was in jeopardy.

'I will not allow them to set fire to Seabreeze Cottage,' I said angrily when Gilbert and I were back home, my legs shaking with anger.

'Me either, it is my home, Alfie, not my holiday home but my home.' Gilbert looked as furious as I felt.

'I know. But how are we going to stop all this?'

I had no clear idea, I couldn't stop the families from going to Andrea's, that wouldn't work, so we would have to come up with another way. I was thinking through my past plans, but I couldn't get hurt like I did once, or stuck up a tree, or lose George again, like the last plan I had hatched. No, whatever we did, I was not putting George at risk again.

'Look, we know when they are planning on doing it –

although I still don't know if Liam will go through with it – but on Saturday, when the humans are all next door, we will somehow have to stop Liam from setting fire to the house.' Gilbert sounded so confident that I began to feel better.

'That's true, he's quite incompetent so he might not even be able to burn the house down!' I liked to look on the bright side.

'But whatever, I will guard the house, you will switch between the party and here, because George will clearly want to be near Chanel, and we will sort it. If I have to scratch, or hurt Liam, I will, Alfie, don't worry, we won't let this happen.'

'So we have a plan?' It wasn't a very solid one but it was something. And Gilbert did have sharp claws, and he was used to living on his wits, which meant he was a much tougher cat than I was. I could see that as a team maybe, just maybe, we could do it.

'We do.' And it was a very simple plan, which, given those I'd had to carry out in my past, was a huge relief. I mean, two cats, one man and a potential fire.

What could go wrong?

Chapter
Twenty

The week seemed painfully long. I felt as if I was waiting and waiting, but at last it was Saturday and the day of Andrea's party and Liam's arson attempt. I felt sick to my fur with the stress of it all but I was doing my best to keep calm and ensure that George didn't sense the danger that we, or at least Seabreeze Cottage, faced.

In fact the arson attempt would affect all of us, because the children were having the summer of their lives, the cottage was being transformed into a home which had a part of each of us in it, and everyone was so happy. Jonathan had even said to Claire that she was right and they would never want to sell Seabreeze Cottage. If it hadn't been for Andrea it would have been a happy ending. But with only just over a week left of this holiday, I worried that the outcome would be different to that which each of us expected.

Gilbert, a true member of our family now, had been keeping tabs on Liam. Honestly, he would have made an excellent stalker, not like my poor George who had spent the best part of the week mooning after Chanel. Anyway, Liam had not given anything away. He was still working at the house but he was never left alone, and so he was causing no problems. He didn't have the chance. He did go and see Andrea a couple of times but they had talked in the house and so Gilbert couldn't hear what was being said.

Our loose plan still stood. Gilbert would guard the house

and I would veer between the party and home. If he needed me, Gilbert knew where he'd find me and vice versa. We would be a team. I still didn't want to get George involved though, he was too little to worry about such things, and of course I was his parent so I wanted to protect him from the bad in the world. I knew I wouldn't always be able to, I felt sad but realistic, but I wanted him to enjoy his kittenhood for as long as he could.

The good thing was that Tomasz, Matt and Jonathan all had a week off so they were going to be staying with us all week! It would make the house a bit full, but I liked that. There were going to be lots of trips to the beach, fish and chips and ice cream in our last week, I was sure.

Claire, Franceska and Polly were all wearing dresses, they did look lovely, and the children were also quite neatly dressed . . . for now, I knew it wouldn't last. The men were wearing their summer casual clothes – shorts, T-shirts or, in Jonathan's case, a short-sleeved shirt – and George and I had made an extra effort with our grooming. Especially George, he had groomed his fur so it was practically gleaming. I knew Chanel was wrong for him, too old for one, and he was too young for love, but he was going to be a heartbreaker when he was older, that was for sure.

We made a good-looking group, I thought as we set off. Instead of going through our hedge we decided to arrive with the humans, though Tommy carried George, as if he didn't trust him not to run off – how little he knew. George wasn't going anywhere but to see his crush. As we walked through the front gate and into Andrea's garden, they were all there to greet us: Andrea, her daughters, and the village children, along with Amber, Kate and Vicky and their husbands, who were now friends of ours.

'Ah, here's our guests of honour,' Andrea said loudly. Claire looked behind her to make sure that there weren't any other guests she could be talking about.

'Thank you,' Jonathan said, giving Andrea a kiss on her cheek and holding out the bag they had brought with them, which contained wine I think. 'Where shall I put this?' he asked.

Of course, Andrea was holding Chanel. George managed to leap from Tommy's arms into Jonathan's, nearly making him drop the wine, but also bringing him close to Chanel.

'Meow,' he said, trying to sound flirtatious I think. She turned her nose up and looked away. He seemed happy with that.

'George,' Jonathan chastised, putting him on the grass.

'Oh follow me and we can put that in the kitchen.' Andrea smiled at Jonathan and led him into the house.

'Why do I think he'll never come out alive?' Claire whispered to Polly, who laughed.

The children all immediately ran off and I told George to go and keep an eye on Toby. He was nervous and had confided in George (who had then told me) that he hadn't wanted to come today, he was scared of the girls. George, who wanted to trail after Chanel, reluctantly agreed.

'If Chanel sees how great you are with the children she'll think more of you,' I said, feeling once again that I was a terrible cat. But it wasn't just that I was trying to deceive George, it was also that I didn't want him spending too much time with Chanel, who would just continue to be horrible to him, and

I genuinely did need him to keep an eye on Toby, especially as I would be busy waiting for Liam to strike.

'Do you think?'

'Absolutely.' I didn't of course, but it did the trick as George bounded off to look after Toby.

It was one of the hottest days we'd had so far. The children all wore hats but even they weren't running around as much as normal and the adults were sitting around on chairs that Andrea had arranged on the lawn, sweating and chatting. I was desperate for shade but I couldn't risk missing anything. Never mind the house, my fur felt as if it was going to catch on fire. Nevertheless, I ran back to see Gilbert, who reported that nothing had happened so far, then I ran back to the party where George was being fussed over by most of the children, though I saw him stealing glances at Chanel, who was sitting with Andrea, ignoring him still. Poor kitten. The women were all getting on but I could see that Andrea was more comfortable with the men, as she flirted with each of them.

'Oh you do look as if you have a lovely tan,' she told Jonathan, who looked a bit too pleased with himself. 'Matt, would you be a darling and top up the drinks, after all you do it so well.' And to Tomasz: 'You must give me the recipe for that dip you brought over, it is simply the most divine thing I have ever tasted.' Tomasz blushed and Franceska glared; she had made the dip. The other women's husbands all got the same 'Andrea' treatment.

But at the same time, Claire was chatting to Fiona, Polly was talking to Kate, Vicky and Amber, so it was all fine. Or so I hoped.

I had to get some shade so I went to take a quick lie-down under a bush. Unfortunately the heat and the worry had made me tired and, without realising it, I dozed off.

'Alfie,' a voice hissed. I blinked my eyes open and looked at Gilbert.

I jumped up. 'Oh no, I'm terrible, I can't believe I fell asleep. What's happened?' I looked at the lawn; the party was still in full swing and I couldn't see anything wrong.

'Look, come with me, quickly.'

I followed Gilbert back home. 'What's going on?' I asked.

'Well, here's the thing, Toby and George ran in the house. Toby was crying. There are no adults and I think that perhaps they don't know that he's gone.'

'Liam?' I asked.

'No sign.'

I ran up to the boys' room where Toby was huddled on his bed, sobbing, and George was snuggled up next to him.

'Meow?' I said, in order to ask George what happened. He hopped off the bed and followed me so we were out of earshot.

'Those girls were horrible to him again, they teased him about being adopted,' George said. 'But no one saw him when he ran back home, he went through our gap in the hedge,' he explained. 'It was a bit tight but he wriggled through. I followed him because I couldn't leave him alone.'

'Did anyone else see this?'

'No, they waited until he was alone, well apart from me.'

'You did well, George, and I'll go and get Claire and Jonathan now.'

I left Gilbert in charge as I went back to the party. I felt so sick now, not because of Andrea but because of her daughters. How did children get so mean? I remembered when I had to go and sort out a bully at Aleksy's school a few years ago; the boy had been unhappy but that is not an excuse for being horrible to other children. I was so furious and I knew that Claire and Jonathan would be too.

When I got to the garden, I quickly found Claire, sitting next to Polly with a plate of food in her hand.

'Meow!' I shouted, jumping on her lap. I had learnt from past experience that subtlety didn't get results.

'Alfie, I've got food,' she shouted, dropping it.

'Yowl.' I put my paw on her chest, which I knew normally got her attention.

'What's wrong?'

'Meow.' Claire stood up, and looked around.

'Where's Toby?' she asked. 'Jonathan, where's Toby?' she shouted really loudly. All the guests fell silent.

'I can't find him,' Henry said, running over.

'Do you know where he is?' Polly asked.

'No, the last time I saw him he was with Serafina and Savannah, but . . .' Henry looked as if he might cry. 'I think George is with him because he's not here either.'

'Hey, it's OK, Henry, can everyone search the garden,' Jonathan said, taking control.

'Savannah, Serafina, do you have any idea where he is?' Andrea asked. The two girls, with their long hair and matching dresses, looked as if butter wouldn't melt. Serafina shrugged.

'He said he wanted to go home,' Savannah said.

'Why? Why did he want to go home?' Claire asked, sounding angry.

'Please don't shout at my girls,' Andrea said, smoothly.

'My son is missing, I am a little stressed. If he has—'

'Claire, let's go back to the cottage, he's probably there if that's what he said,' Jonathan said, calmly as he put his arm around her.

'Oh, you mean he might be in the cottage, alone?' Andrea said as if it had just occurred to her and the colour drained from her face.

But Claire was already out of her chair.

I knew what I had to do.

I ran as fast as I could, taking the quickest route to the house through the hedge. Gilbert came to meet me. He just looked at me and I noted the horror in his eyes.

'What?' I asked.

'I was just coming to find you, Liam's there.' I followed him through the back door and into the kitchen. I felt my heart almost stop.

Liam was stood by the kitchen table, holding a rag and a lit match. There was a funny smell. I glanced at Gilbert.

'Is Toby still here?' I asked.

'Yes and George, upstairs.'

'Oh my goodness.' I felt sick.

'What should we do?' he asked. 'Go to George?'

'No, we need to stop Liam,' I replied. 'We'll have to jump at him, it's the only thing.' Before Liam could notice us we both launched ourselves at him. I managed to jump up onto his chest, digging my claws in, Gilbert leapt onto his shoulder where he scratched his face, as hard as he could.

'Ugggggh!' Liam shouted and he dropped the lit rag onto

the table as he tried to bat us both off. Gilbert clung and scratched him again.

I had to put the fire out before it took hold, so I jumped onto the kitchen table, feeling the heat from the flaming rag, which thankfully hadn't yet spread. I went to a jug of flowers, pushed it near the rag and, with a big shove, managed to push it over. Water dripped everywhere and the fire fizzled out. The relief was immense. Gilbert finally let go of Liam and jumped down onto the floor. Liam looked shocked as he touched his face which was bleeding. Gilbert and I shared a congratulatory look, although my heart was still pounding.

We had foiled the plan. We had saved the cottage and, more importantly, George and Toby. Before I could go and upstairs to check on them, the door burst open.

'What are you doing here?' Claire demanded. Liam was definitely not her favourite person.

'Um,' Liam mumbled.

'How did you get in?' Jonathan asked.

'Back door,' Liam said.

'We never lock it, which is why I think Toby's probably upstairs. Speaking of which . . .' Claire ran off.

Jonathan looked as if he was going to follow her but then he glared at Liam. He was still deciding what to do when a phone started ringing. It was on the kitchen table, but had escaped getting soaked by the flower water. I looked at the horror on Liam's face and then I nudged it with my paw towards Jonathan.

'Why is Andrea calling you?' he asked as he picked up the ringing phone. 'And why are there flowers and water all over the table?'

Liam, who I didn't think could get any paler, looked as if he had no colour left in him. Jonathan looked at the phone, I wanted him to answer it but he didn't.

'I'm going to check on my son,' he said. 'You stay here. If you move an inch I will kill you.'

Liam sat down on a chair. We both decided to stay and guard our hostage.

The flower jug was lying on its side and it hid the rag that Liam had tried to start a fire with. Liam still looked horrified, but he collected up the flowers, shoved them back in the jug, then he mopped up the water with some kitchen towels and quickly hid the rag in his pocket. There was a faint smell of smoke in the air, and Liam had to clean a black mark off the table, but it looked as if he would get away with it. And I wasn't sure what we could do about that, but the important thing was that the fire didn't get going and hopefully now they could put a stop to Liam and Andrea once and for all.

It felt like ages before Claire and Jonathan came back downstairs. Liam had his head in his hands. Gilbert and I remained silent.

'Meow?' It was my way of seeing if everything was alright.

'Toby is better, calmer, but I suggested he play in his room with George so we can sort this out. I don't want him upset any more than he already is,' Claire said.

Jonathan turned to Liam. 'So, are you going to tell us what you were doing here?'

'And what happened to your face?' Claire asked. She looked at me, then at Gilbert.

'Well, you see, I thought I might have left some tools

here . . .' Liam started. 'I had to do some work for my mum and, well, anyway I needed a, a screwdriver, which I couldn't find so I came here, but no one was in, so I'm sorry but I just let myself in. The cats must have thought I was up to no good so they attacked me . . .' Liam trailed off. It didn't sound feasible even to me.

'Good cats,' Claire said.

'So why was Andrea calling you?' Jonathan asked, folding his arms.

'I don't know, I mean I work for her sometimes.'

Yes you do, I thought.

'Really?' Jonathan looked doubtful.

'Well that's fine. I'll just call your mum to check; after all she's going to be looking after the cottage for us soon.' Claire stared at Liam, until he looked as if he'd be sick.

'No,' he shouted a bit too loudly. 'Please don't.'

There was a commotion at the back door and Polly, Matt and Tomasz bundled in.

'Thank goodness Toby is here,' Polly said. 'Thanks for calling and, before you ask, Franceska has all the other children in sight, so don't worry.'

'Is he alright?' Matt asked.

'No, he's distraught. He says he hates it here, and wants to go back to London. Those girls teased him for being adopted and they called him names, anyway, I'll go into that with Andrea, but we reassured him for now. I wish we hadn't gone to her house.' Claire, who seemed so in control, burst into tears. Polly wrapped her arms around her.

'What's he doing here?' Tomasz said, as if he had just noticed Liam.

'That's what we'd like to know,' Jonathan said. 'He says he came to find some tools, but then when we said we'd call his mother to check out his story he told us not to.'

'Right, buddy.' Tomasz, who was the biggest of the men, sat down next to Liam. 'You better tell us what you were doing here before I call the police and have you arrested.' Liam flinched.

'Wait.' Andrea suddenly appeared from the back door.

'What the hell are you doing here?' Claire shouted. 'This is all your fault. Toby is in such a state, your daughters called him terrible names and said he didn't belong anywhere because he was adopted, what kind of children say that?'

For the first time since we'd met her, Andrea had the grace to look guilty.

'I know, I'm sorry—'

'What, no excuses, no ridiculous stories about how your girls wouldn't do that.'

'Unfortunately they did say that, I'm not going to pretend.' Andrea sat down at the table, looking defeated. 'And the fact that Liam's here is my fault too.'

'You better explain,' Polly said, sitting down. Andrea went to sit on the other side of Liam. Tomasz moved to the other side of the table. I sat on Polly's lap. Andrea and Liam glanced at each other as they faced Jonathan, Claire, Matt, Polly and Tomasz. Jonathan had his arms crossed, Claire was still tearful, Polly fuming and Matt and Tomasz looked ready for a fight. Gilbert had placed himself on the floor by the door, as if to stop them getting out.

'I didn't want it to go this far, you have to believe that,' Andrea started.

'What exactly?' Jonathan asked.

'I told you I wanted to buy Seabreeze Cottage, I didn't tell the truth about why.' She looked awkward. Liam squeezed her hand. 'My husband, I said he's away on business but actually, well, the truth is that he's left me.'

'Left you?' Jonathan asked.

'Yes, for another woman. It's been very hard, on me, and especially on the girls. They don't understand where he is, or why they never see him any more. I mean, he's not even been here for ages, since he moved to London with his mistress, it's as if the girls don't exist for him.' I saw actual tears in Andrea's eyes.

'That's terrible,' Matt said, running his hand through his hair.

'Yes, but what does it have to do with Seabreeze?' Polly asked. I wanted to know that too.

'My husband wants to sell the house and, to cut a long story short, I desperately need to say in Lynstow, for the girls' sake. I can't bear to take them away from the village, not after everything they've been through.'

'Oh for goodness' sake, get on with it,' Polly said, irritably.

'I thought that if I got this cottage I could afford it, because of the work that needed doing, and at least keep the girls in the same village, same school, near their friends.'

'Hold on, you were going to live here?'

'Yes, I was going to buy this cottage, do it up – at least as much as I could afford to – but then you guys came here and started doing work.' Andrea looked annoyed for a moment as if it was our fault her plan had gone awry. Which it was actually, well mine and Gilbert's and Toby's, I supposed.

'Right, let me get this straight. You could only afford it

before we started work on it yet you still persisted in trying to get your hands on it?' Claire asked, her face ashen.

'Yes, I thought that you wouldn't like it here, and you'd want to get out so I could persuade you to sell it to me quickly you know cash buyer, no estate agent fees. But you wouldn't. So, I was desperate.'

'Which is where Liam comes in, I'm guessing,' Tomasz said. He was still looking furious.

'I'm sorry,' Liam mumbled. I flicked my tail at him.

'It wasn't meant to get out of hand, I just needed the house. I still do.' Andrea wiped tears away, I checked and they were real. 'I thought if I made your lives a bit miserable you'd change your mind, decide Lynstow wasn't the ideal holiday destination after all and sell to me. I was offering a good price.'

'It's not about money. So, Liam, all the mistakes?' Polly asked.

'Yes, they were for Andrea,' Liam admitted. 'But you were so cross and, well, I wasn't the best at sabotage. Colin made sure I was watched like a hawk so I had to give it up. It was like that damn cat kept foiling me, which I don't understand.'

'Meow.' Of course you don't.

Andrea shook her head. 'It was just meant to delay the work, cost money, annoy you all and, well, get you to pack up, but nothing seemed to work, and to be honest, I got desperate. It's not just about money for me, there's the girls . . .'

'Please tell me you didn't get your children involved in your plan?'

'No, of course, I might be a total cow but I wouldn't do that. No, what happened was that the girls overheard me talking to my lawyer saying how you guys moving into the cottage was ruining everything and I wished you weren't around. I said if you left then everything would be fine for us again.' She put her head in her hands. 'I'm sorry, I really didn't want them to be mean but when they were, well I can't say I tried to stop them. But with Toby, I feel truly terrible about that.'

'OK, I get it.' Jonathan held his hand up. 'You were in trouble, you needed the cottage, so you got this goof of a man to try to sabotage our build. It didn't work. So what is he doing here now?'

The silence felt endless. Andrea glanced at Liam who looked as if he was going to cry. Then she took his hand. I looked at Gilbert who was staring at the box of matches. Still no one else noticed them.

'You know, I am this close to calling the police,' Polly said. She was often the feistiest in these situations. Matt was more laid-back although even he looked shocked. Tomasz's eyes were flecked with anger and Claire was crying, so it was down to Polly and Jonathan really.

'Please don't. I know my daughters have behaved badly but they don't deserve to lose their mum as well as their dad, and Liam, well none of this was Liam's fault. He has a crush on me and I'm afraid I used that.'

Liam frowned. 'But you said we'd be together, when you got the cottage.'

'Oh dear, you've been played,' Polly said.

'Liam, I was desperate, I still am. I felt that Seabreeze Cottage was the only way to keep what's left of my family together. I know it was wrong but you were so keen on me. And to be honest, I'm possibly almost old enough to be your mother.'

'I'm quite sure you are more than old enough,' Polly bit.

'But I loved you.' Liam looked so crestfallen I actually felt sorry for him.

'This is a very interesting nonexistent love story, but what were you doing here now?' Jonathan pushed.

'He was just going to . . .' Andrea looked at him and mouthed that she was sorry. 'You know, nobble the build when no one was around. The idea was that you'd come in Monday, everything would start going wrong, and you'd all get so fed up that you would agree to sell to me.'

Liam looked relieved as Andrea finished. They weren't going to confess about the fire and I wasn't sure if I wanted to draw attention to it or not. On the one paw they deserved to be caught, on the other, neither were exactly master criminals. And Andrea had obviously been desperate. I didn't condone her actions but I almost understood. She thought she was doing it for her family and I would do anything for my families. Me getting stuck on the roof was proof of that.

I jumped off the table and I went to where Liam had dropped the matches. I put my paw over them. I had a big decision to make for a cat. If I drew my humans' attention to them they would see exactly what Andrea and Liam had planned and probably have no option but to call the police. And of course they would think about how Toby had been here, alone with George, and what could have happened and it would give us all nightmares. But on the other paw, Andrea had put a stop to it as soon as she heard that Toby was here and Liam wasn't acting like an arsonist, so I wasn't sure he would have gone through with it anyway. Besides, Gilbert and I had stopped him, hadn't we? Just as we planned.

I looked at Gilbert, trying to ask what he thought. We went to the back of the room to have a chat.

'All's OK at the moment, isn't it?' he said.

'I think it would hurt everyone if they thought that they actually would set fire to the place,' I replied.

'And look at him, he doesn't look as if he'd have been capable of going through with it. And with me attached to him he couldn't anyway.' We both seemed in agreement and, while the adults were still arguing about what to do, I walked back and pushed the matches under the cooker with my paw so they would, for now, remain unseen.

'You did a brilliant job, Gilbert,' I said.

'You too, Alfie,' he replied.

'I don't see why you should get away with this,' Polly was saying.

'I haven't, believe me. I haven't got the cottage and I don't have a husband,' Andrea said and she started to cry again.

'Liam, you can't work here any more. I won't have you in this house, not after what you've done,' Polly said.

'That's reasonable,' Liam said. 'I guess you'll tell Colin.'

'Unless you want to?'

He shook his head.

'And I want your girls to apologise to Toby,' Jonathan added.

'Of course.' Finally, I thought, Andrea seemed defeated. 'But if you change your mind about selling this place . . .' she added as she stood up and left the house with a heart-broken Liam trailing after her.

'She's unbelievable,' Polly said.

'She's desperate I think,' Tomasz added.

'It's kind of ruined it, though, don't you think?' I was

surprised to hear Claire say those words. 'The cottage, the summer, the idea they wanted us out, and Toby, well it all feels like such a mess.'

With that she burst into tears again. I saw they weren't just about this, but about Toby, her son, who was so hurt by the cruel words of two children, about her holidays as a child when she hadn't had to deal with the complexities of adulthood. And Seabreeze, which had already undergone such a huge transformation but still had a way to go, which we'd thought was our home but suddenly, it didn't feel like it. It had all been tainted.

Franceska burst in with the rest of the children. 'I kept them in our garden as long as I could, but they wanted to see their parents,' she said. 'Is all OK?'

'Yes, but we'll tell you later,' Claire said.

'Can I just say.' Aleksy stood forward. 'That we did love it here, but with Toby, and those horrible girls and their horrible mum, everyone seems miserable and, well, we all just want to go home.'

The adults looked shocked.

'But, *kochanie*, you were having such a good time with your new friends,' Franceska said.

'We were, but now we've seen you all arguing with that woman and then with Toby being so upset, and Savannah and Serafina being so horrible, we just don't think it's worth it. Not for this.' He looked round the kitchen table at the adults. It was clear that everyone was unhappy.

'Aleksy speaks for all of us,' Tommy added.

'Let's just go home,' Summer said, coming to sit on her mum's lap. 'Mummy's sad and I don't like that. Toby's sad and I don't like that.'

'Some things just aren't worth it,' Aleksy said. And everyone looked shocked.

'Out of the mouths of babes,' Matt said, as he pulled Martha onto his lap.

'Claire?' Jonathan said.

'When Toby ran off, and when for a moment I didn't know if he was safe, I felt so sick, and if it's being here that's done that, then maybe the kids are right, maybe we should go home.'

I made my way over to Gilbert and we went into the sand room to have another chat.

'Do you think they all mean it?' he asked.

'It's been dramatic for them, this thing with Toby, finding out that the house was being sabotaged, it really will have shaken them up,' I said.

'But if they sell the house to Andrea . . .'

'I know, you'll be homeless.'

'No, I wasn't just thinking that, I mean I would, but that's not the worst thing – I have been before and I will again. No, it's that Seabreeze is a special house, a home, and you guys belong here. Your families have loved being here for the most part. I know today has been shocking and I think we were right not to draw attention to the matches as they would probably be packing right now, but we need them to remember how much they've loved being here.'

'You're right, we need to save Seabreeze, and our families and we need to save the summer.' We had foiled Andrea and her plotting, and poor Liam, but that, it seemed, wasn't enough. We had to make everyone fall back in love with Seabreeze Cottage.

But of course, I had no idea how.

Chapter
Twenty-One

It was our last few days and since the incident there had been many grown-up conversations and children's whispers behind closed doors. The adults still had no idea what to do. Polly was adamant they should make Seabreeze Cottage work; she said she couldn't bear to let the beautiful cottage go when they'd come so far. I tended to agree with her. Claire felt torn between her children who had fallen out of love with the place, and her childhood holidays. She couldn't bear to see the house which characterised childhood holidays be lived in by someone else. The men, as usual, supported the women but Franceska sided with Polly; she was determined that Seabreeze should be a holiday home for us all and she didn't want to let Andrea and her family ruin it. She was trying hard to rally the adults to her way of thinking, but with the builders still traipsing in every day (though Liam had been replaced), and the fact everyone was tired, and still a bit down, it wasn't working.

Colin was profusely apologetic and working his men even harder than usual. Final decorating was going on, and even George was managing to keep out of trouble as the house underwent its transformation, though he was oblivious to the dilemma that we were all facing.

'OK,' Franceska said, one evening when the children were in bed, tired out from a lovely trip to the beach. 'We need to decide, we have less than a week left. Do we keep Seabreeze or not?'

'It's the kids I'm worried about, they keep saying they want to go home,' Claire sighed. 'But then I think of the lovely time everyone had when we threw that party. We really felt part of the village then. So I'm not sure.'

'Look, Aleksy is worried for Toby, we all are I know, but he thinks that the girls will continue being mean to all of them and Toby can't handle it. But I think Toby is doing OK now. The kids love the beach, they like their other friends, so why can't we move on from the incident?' Tomasz asked in his usual reasonable way.

'You know, I think that I might have an idea,' Jonathan said. 'We told Andrea we wanted her girls to apologise, well they haven't yet. How about if we get an apology for all the children and then, when they have assurances that the girls won't terrorise them any more, they might feel differently?'

'And this from the man who first wanted to sell the cottage,' Polly teased.

'It's a good idea, mate. But who is going to call Andrea?' Matt asked.

Everyone, including me, stared at Polly.

Gilbert and I had spent a bit more time together; he was now a fully paid-up part of the family. That was the terrible thing: Seabreeze Cottage felt like our family home, the first place I had managed to have all the humans I loved under one roof, and not only could I not bear to think I wouldn't come back, we were both worried about him losing his home. However, he was a tougher cat than I, so he was bearing it well.

George was upset because everyone was upset and when

he heard the children talking about wanting to go home, he was distraught.

'But if we go home, then what about Chanel?' he had asked.

'George, I'm sorry but you're a big boy now so I have to be honest with you. If we go home, then you won't see Chanel again.'

I had realised my mistake immediately, as George looked so incredibly upset. Since then he had taken to spending more time in the bush looking for Chanel, but the whole family had been lying low so there had been no sign of her.

'Of course I'll miss paddleboarding and the beach,' Aleksy said. He had taken to holding meetings in his bedroom with all the children. I wasn't sure that Summer and Martha really understood but they liked to be involved, even if they did spend most of the time playing with their dolls rather than listening.

'I will too, but I won't miss those horrible girls,' Tommy said.

'Or me,' Toby added.

'No, but there are more of us than there are of them,' Henry pointed out. 'So, if they are ever horrible to us again we can stand up to them.' Henry was perhaps turning out a bit like Polly.

'Yes, but then their mother upsets our mothers. I know it's been going on all summer and when Toby ran away . . .'

'I didn't mean to run away, I just wanted to come home,' Toby said, sadly.

'Did you hear what he just said?' Henry asked. 'He said

he wanted to come home, this is our home, our other home, maybe we need to remember that.'

'Meow.' I nuzzled Henry, he was clever.

'Yes, but we need everyone to be happy here,' Aleksy said. 'And I'm just not sure that's possible.'

I felt as if both the adults and children were going round in circles and I could only hope the big apology would do the trick for all of them. It was a lot to pin my hope on but it was all I had.

The grown-ups felt that it would be easier to have all the children in the garden for the apology. Andrea, who had been largely avoiding us, had agreed to anything they asked, she was just relieved not to be in more trouble. And I hoped she felt guilty about Liam too. George had decided that Chanel, on hearing about the girls' apology, would probably use the opportunity to apologise to him for not falling in love with him – no, no idea how that kitten's mind worked either – so he had groomed himself and was waiting eagerly for the appointed time.

Gilbert, who went out most days, said he would stay around, 'just in case'. He really was coming round to my way of thinking as regards humans. As I told him, we didn't necessarily need them to take care of us but they needed us to take care of them.

So, it was clearly going to be a bit intimidating for the girls and the adults weren't going to make it any easier as everyone waited on the lawn for them to come over. They did, right on time. The girls were dressed more casually than normal in shorts and T-shirts, and although Andrea looked immaculate she wasn't quite as dressed up as normal either.

'Love how she's trying to look poor for us,' Polly hissed to her husband.

'They don't look remotely poor,' Matt shot back.

'Exactly,' Polly said.

'Hello.' Andrea approached us. We did look a bit like a big gang, all gathered on the lawn. Claire was holding onto Toby, because of course he was nervous about seeing the girls, and Jonathan was carrying Summer. Everyone else was standing as if we were in a group photo, the kind they take at weddings.

'Hi,' Jonathan said, sounding stiff.

'Look, before the girls say anything, I would like to say a few words—'

'Meow!' George had gone up to Andrea, because Chanel was nowhere to be seen.

'Oh hello, cat.' Andrea patted his head awkwardly. 'I didn't bring Chanel because I didn't want to upset your cats.' She looked at all of us. 'What kind of cats are they anyway?'

George had lain down, sulking, and put his head in his paws.

'Um, really? You wanted to say a few words about our cats?' Polly snapped.

'Sorry, no sorry. I wanted to say that I appreciate your understanding the other day and I am so sorry for how I behaved. I'm not proud of myself, I know I've been terrible and unwelcoming as well as unneighbourly. So, I hope that we can start again.'

I wasn't sure if I trusted her but she did sound as if she meant what she said.

'And can I just say, we do appreciate your honesty,' Matt said.

'But no more,' Franceska added. 'No more games.' She snuggled into Tomasz, who put a protective arm around her.

'No, of course not and, with that, the girls have something to say.'

For the first time the girls looked like children. Serafina hung her head and Savannah looked as if she had been crying.

'We are sorry we were so horrible,' Savannah said. 'We didn't mean it but we thought that if you stayed in the cottage we would have to leave our school and also how would our daddy know where we were? We might never see him again.'

She burst into sobs. As Andrea rushed to comfort her, I felt very sad for her, she must be missing her dad, they both must. I couldn't condone their behaviour but I did understand a bit now.

We all stood around slightly awkwardly, but then a surprising thing happened. Toby ran towards Savannah and took her hand.

'I would miss my daddy if I didn't see him. That's my daddy.' He pointed at Jonathan, who looked choked. 'So I 'cept your apology, but please don't be horrible again, it's not our fault.'

Serafina gave him a big hug. 'Thanks, and I promise we won't be horrible. We want to be your friends, after all you do have the best games, don't they, Savvy?' she said.

'Yes.' Savannah was still crying but the gulps were subsiding slightly.

Claire came over to Toby. 'Well done, Tobe, that was very nice of you,' she said.

'It was, you are all very good people.' Andrea was looking ashamed again. 'And honestly, girls, it's not their fault that

Daddy isn't here, I was just cross when I said that, but we need to be nice to everyone.'

'But, Mummy, you always say nice people never win,' Serafina chirped up. We stared at Andrea, who had the grace to appear embarrassed.

'I shouldn't have said that, and I was wrong, because all these families who live at Seabreeze are nice and look, girls, they *are* winners.' Andrea hugged both the girls. 'From now on we'll all be nice, even me.'

'That I can't wait to see,' Polly said, then she clamped her hand over her mouth. 'Sorry, I meant to say that we should all draw a line under this, forgive and forget. Girls, pretend you've met our children for the first time and start over, and we should do the same with you, Andrea.'

'I am so grateful for that.'

The girls chatted to the children, and Summer and Martha begged them to make daisy chains, which they did. The boys, who were less interested in flowers, set up a football game and I felt my heart swell again as they all played beautifully on the lawn of Seabreeze Cottage.

Franceska and Polly went inside to make some drinks and they came out with tea and biscuits, juice for the children and they even brought our water bowl out in case we needed a drink. I did, as I lapped some water; it was very thirsty work all this making friends. It was nearly teatime and I was hungry as well. I hoped we wouldn't have to wait too long for our food.

Andrea went to get Chanel but said she would be right back. Which reminded me that I needed to make sure that George had a drink, it was so hot. I went, expecting to find him under the hedge on Chanel-watch, but he was nowhere to be seen. Feeling panicked again, I circled the garden, checking all the places he might be, but he seemed to have disappeared completely. I couldn't believe I had let him go missing again. What kind of parent was I? I ran to find Gilbert.

'What's wrong?' Gilbert said.

'It's George, he's not here,' I said.

'I'll check the house, shall I?' Gilbert suggested.

'You can but I'm pretty sure he's not in there.'

'Well, where would he have gone?' As I started to fret, an earth-shattering shriek interrupted me. We ran back to the front lawn to find Andrea had returned, ashen-faced.

'What's wrong?' Claire asked.

'It's Chanel, she's nowhere to be seen and she never leaves home without me.'

I glanced at Gilbert. It suddenly made sense. I had suggested to George that he would never see Chanel again and now look what had happened. He had obviously gone off with her, although somehow I couldn't see them running away together. More like Chanel running away from him. Oh no, just what had George done?

It was chaos as it always is when humans try to solve a problem. Andrea was hysterical, the girls looked frightened and everyone was talking at once.

Jonathan called order. 'Look, let's organise a search. Firstly, you are sure she's not at your house or in the garden?' he sensibly asked Andrea.

'I'm certain, I checked everywhere. Chanel doesn't leave the garden without me. Oh, what if she's been stolen?' Her eyes widened.

It would be a brave person who stole that cat, I thought, but of course I stayed quiet.

'Meow,' I said. Had no one noticed that George wasn't here?

'Oh goodness, Alfie, where's George?' Claire asked.

'Meow.' I had no idea, although I was pretty sure if we found Chanel we'd find him.

'Aleksy, Tommy, can you check the house, so at least if they're not inside we can rule it out,' Tomasz said. The boys ran off.

'Right, Claire, Franceska and Andrea, you guys should look together.' Jonathan started organising everyone. 'Matt and I will search, and Tomasz, perhaps you, Aleksy and Tommy can form the third search party.'

'Shall I stay with the kids?' Polly asked.

'Is that OK?' Claire said.

'Fine and if either of them come here I'll phone you.'

'Andrea, where do you suggest we look?'

'I honestly don't know, she doesn't go out without me.' She was visibly shaking with distress; she obviously loved that cat very much, which made me soften towards her a bit.

'How about we go to one end of the village and start there. Jon and Matt go to the other, and Tomasz take the boys to search the beach?' Franceska suggested, sensibly.

'OK, good plan.'

'Meow?' I said.

'Alfie, if you come with us you might get lost too,' Claire said. 'I'd rather you stayed here.' She had no chance.

Aleksy and Tommy returned and confirmed that the cats weren't in the house, so everyone split into their groups, ready to search. Gilbert was with me and I knew as soon as they left we'd go off ourselves, we would be a group. We couldn't just leave it to the humans, of course.

We set off a little while after the humans, which I thought was the best bet, so they didn't notice us. The village was quieter, it being early evening, and we soon reached the entrance to the beach, where I stopped, breathless and still fretting.

'Hello,' a tabby cat approached me.

'Hi,' I replied, still catching my breath.

'I'm Lily,' she said. 'I just moved here.'

'Well that's all very nice but we're in the middle of an emergency,' Gilbert cut in, sounding gruff.

'Oh dear. What kind of emergency?' she asked. 'Is it to do with fish?'

'No, I've lost my kitten,' I said. 'He's small and ginger and I think he might have been with, or at least chasing, a Persian cat.' My words rushed out in a jumble.

'Oh yes I saw them. I tried to stop them for a chat but they just ran past me. Bit rude I thought.' She tipped her head to one side. 'I mean, I was only trying to be friendly, it's not easy being the new cat, I can tell you.'

'Where, where did they go?' I asked, trying not to sound irritated.

'They headed onto the beach. The Persian was running ahead, and the kitten, cute isn't he? Well anyway he was trying to chase her but he was quite far behind. Little legs I suppose.'

I looked at Gilbert. 'You go to the beach, I'll go and round up the humans,' I said.

'Can I come?' Lily asked. Gilbert raised his whiskers but didn't reply as he took off and she followed him anyway.

Everyone was outside our house, I guess they'd run up and down the road and drawn a blank.

'Meow!' I shouted. Then I ran around in circles a few times.

'I think Alfie wants us to follow him,' Aleksy said.

'Don't be absurd, he's just a cat,' Andrea said.

'No, Alfie isn't just a cat, not at all,' Tommy replied. 'Come on, guys, let's follow Alfie. He knows what he's doing.'

I got to the beach first where we found George, Gilbert and Lily, and there were two things I immediately noticed. The stretch we were on was devoid of people and the water was quite high. Not being a fan of water, I ventured onto the sand tentatively.

'George?' I asked.

'It's Chanel, she's over there,' George said, vaguely waving a paw.

'Where?' I couldn't see her anywhere.

'She's in the water,' Lily said. 'I mean, a cat in water, who'd have thought it? Although of course technically she's in a boat on the water but still—'

'Shush,' Gilbert said. 'George, explain.'

'She's in that boat, Dad, look.' I followed George's eyes and he was right. Chanel was looking out of the side of a boat, looking terrified as it floated on the water, and it was moving further and further away from the shore.

'Oh no, she's at sea,' I said. 'What do we do? How do we make the humans see her?' I asked.

'Hold on, they're coming,' Gilbert said, calmly. 'They'll see her. And I think I can hear her.' We all listened and yes, there was a sound of a cat crying being carried through the air.

'What happened?' I asked.

'Well, you said I might never see her again so I went to tell her and she kept hiding from me, so I realised that she wanted to play hide and seek, and anyway, I am guessing that she was hiding in that boat when I followed her but it was already floating away. She's very good at hiding.'

I tried not to let my exasperation show.

'I don't think she was playing hide and seek,' Lily said.

'Who are you?' George asked as if he'd just noticed her.

'Lily, nice to meet you.'

'Guys, listen, we need to focus,' Gilbert said. 'What are we going to do about Chanel?'

'I'll go and get her,' George said.

'Don't you dare, you'll end up drowned, or worse,' I said. 'No, George, I forbid it. The humans will get her.'

At last they all ran towards us, Andrea trying to take her shoes off as she ran like a mad woman. They all lined up beside us and looked towards the water.

'Why are we staring at the water?' Andrea said, putting her hand up to shield herself from the burning evening sun.

'Oh, look, there's your cat, in that boat there,' Aleksy shouted. They all looked and finally saw what we wanted them to see.

'Oh no, oh no!' Andrea started to breathe funny. 'What are we going to do, my baby is floating away.'

'When's the tide coming back?' Tomasz asked.

'Not for hours. She can't stay out there until then.' Andrea was hysterical, Franceska took hold of her as if she might faint.

'Do you have a boat?' Matt asked.

'No, of course I don't,' Andrea snapped.

'Look, there's a paddleboard there, we could go and get her on that,' Aleksy said, spotting a board on the shore.

'You can't go without an instructor, or a life jacket,' Tomasz pointed out.

'But someone needs to rescue her, please, please I'm begging you,' Andrea said. I noticed she didn't suggest going herself.

'Oh goodness, I'll go,' Jonathan said. We all stared at him. 'How hard can it be?' he asked. Claire looked a little horrified. 'It's just standing, isn't it?'

'It's quite hard, actually,' Tommy said. But Jonathan wasn't listening. He was already approaching the board.

'Are you sure about this?' Claire asked, sounding terrified.

'Sure,' Jonathan lied. 'I've got to get that cat, and no one else is offering to go.' He took his shoes off, grabbing the board and the paddle and taking them into the water. I wasn't sure if I could look. I had a bad feeling about this.

'I have to rescue my love,' George said suddenly, and before I could do anything he had run up to Jonathan and leapt onto the paddleboard.

'My goodness, your kitten's on the paddleboard!' Lily exclaimed.

'Oh no,' I said to Gilbert, my panic was building. 'I have to go after him!'

'No, Alfie, stay here, he'll be alright, Jonathan will take care of him,' Gilbert said, giving me a reassuring nuzzle.

But who would take care of Jonathan, I wanted to ask.

'Oh blimey, George, you've made this even harder,' Jonathan shouted. Jonathan was in the water attempting to get on the board while George was staring out to where Chanel's boat was. We were all watching from the shore, closer to the water than I liked but I had to be as near to my boy as I could be. Of course George wasn't making it harder for Jonathan to get on the board, and I remembered how good he was on it when he went off with Tommy, so I tried to stay calm. Especially as the silly kitten seemed to like water.

'Are you sure he knows how to paddleboard?' Andrea asked. No one replied. No one needed to. It soon became clear Jonathan had no idea, as he tried to get on the board, and kept slipping off. He finally managed to get on but then fell straight off the other side, almost taking George with him. Luckily my kitten had really good balance. I felt my fur shaking with fear for both of them, but I tried to stay calm, in case I was needed. Not that I had any idea what I could do.

'Can I help him, Dad?' Aleksy asked after a while.

'Sure, you better help him get on, Aleksy,' Tomasz said, patting his shoulder. 'But don't go too deep.' It was lucky Tomasz said that, because Andrea was on the sand, sobbing in a heap, Franceska trying to comfort her and, well, we might have been here all night if Aleksy hadn't gone.

He waded out to where Jonathan was, luckily the water

was only waist-deep. He held onto the board and the paddle while Jonathan sat down. Aleksy tried to take George but George wouldn't cooperate.

'George, come to me,' Aleksy said, putting his hand out to grab him.

'Meow!' George swiped a paw at him. My goodness, he had never done that before.

'Ow, George scratched me!' Aleksy exclaimed as he held his hand away from George.

'For goodness' sake,' Jonathan said. 'If this isn't bad enough.'

'Right, Jonathan, just sit on it like you are doing and paddle either side to steer. Don't try to stand up,' Aleksy directed, rubbing his hand.

'No, no chance of that.' Jonathan looked mildly terrified as he started paddling off. The board was very wobbly and not exactly going in a straight line. I wanted to close my eyes again but, knowing George was on there, I couldn't quite tear them away. It seemed to take him a very long time to move at all, but he kept trying. By this time Aleksy had returned to shore, soaking wet, and when we all examined his hand, it was only a tiny scratch.

'He really wanted to go with Jonathan,' Aleksy said. You don't know the half of it, I thought.

I couldn't help but notice that Jonathan and George were already soaked as they made their way, in a very long-winded manner, to the boat where Chanel was. After what felt like hours, they pulled up beside the boat. Jonathan had the paddle in one hand and was reached out to hold the boat with the other. Chanel looked at George and recoiled slightly. I couldn't hear what they were saying, but I could imagine that Jonathan was saying those words that Claire said 'not in front of the children' to him about.

'Get onto the board, Chanel!' Andrea was screaming. I wanted to scream too, I wanted George back safe and sound and I could see that if Chanel didn't get onto the board soon the whole thing would capsize. Although I wasn't worried about Jonathan – he could swim – I was terrified for George who I wasn't sure could. Finally, after Andrea had screamed herself hoarse, Chanel climbed out of the boat and somehow Jonathan managed to grab her without falling off. Everyone on the shore cheered loudly.

'Go Jonathan!' Tommy shouted and Jonathan started to paddle.

After going round in circles a few times, Jonathan managed to get the board and the cats near enough to the shore for the boys to go and help.

'Hooray!' Tommy shouted as he and Aleksy ran to greet the paddleboard. Aleksy held it tight while Tommy grabbed George and Jonathan disembarked, the latter clutching a terrified Chanel.

'Thank you so much!' Andrea grabbed Chanel from Jonathan's arms and tearfully cuddled the cat. I had never seen Chanel look anything but disdainful but now she seemed shocked and shaken up. I almost felt sorry for her. Andrea wasn't letting her go although she was wet and dishevelled. 'Thank you so much again, but I ought to rush off, sorry to leave you like this but she's traumatised, and with a pedigree such as Chanel's I can't take any chances. I think I ought to call the vet.'

'Do you think we should have George checked over?' Claire said.

'No, he's just a bit wet, he's fine,' Jonathan said. 'I, on the other hand, am soaked and also a little bit unsettled from that little jaunt. I need a towel and a beer.'

'What on earth was she doing in that boat?' Franceska asked.

Yes exactly, I thought, glaring at George. Hide and seek, my tail.

'You said you thought it would be a piece of cake,' Tomasz pointed out, laughing at bedraggled Jonathan.

'Yeah, you did, mate.' Matt patted his shoulder.

'OK, so maybe it's not as easy as it looks,' Jonathan conceded. 'But now can I go and get dried off?'

'So . . .' I started. After being towel-dried in the utility room, Gilbert, George and I were alone. Well we weren't, because Lily had followed us home for some reason. 'Tell me why you thought it was alright to risk your life, George.'

'OK, so it's like this.' George grinned. I could see he was mustering all his charm. 'It was my fault that Chanel was in the boat, so I owed it to her to help rescue her. I'm good at paddleboarding after all, and did you see Jonathan, he was hopeless, he needed me.'

I wasn't sure if I had the energy to argue. George's logic was, well, George's logic.

'You were very good,' Lily said. 'I have to say I'm very impressed.'

'Sorry, I don't mean to be rude, but just who are you, Lily, and why are you here?' Gilbert asked.

'I live a few doors down. We've just moved into the village, well a while ago, but I've only recently been allowed out. It was awful being cooped up inside all this time, but anyway, I wanted to make friends as soon as I got out, and look, now I have!' Lily grinned.

She was an attractive cat, I thought, and perhaps would be company for Gilbert when we weren't here; after all she seemed quite determined and not even Gilbert seemed to be able to put her off.

'Welcome to Lynstow,' I said, trying not to sound short; I still had things to sort out with George. 'But, George, why did you scratch Aleksy? He's your friend.'

'Ah, yes I will say sorry to him, but he tried to grab me and I needed to go to save Chanel. Now she is bound to love me,' he said.

'Oh boy,' Gilbert said. 'You've got it bad. Real bad.'

'I don't really understand,' Lily said.

'It's a long story, and, honestly, you don't need to worry,' I replied. I wasn't sure how we were going to sort this one out. But as it was nearly teatime, I had other fish to fry.

We gathered on the lawn to watch the sunset. Polly and Matt had gone to the village and brought back fish and chips for everyone, including George, Gilbert and I. We were all sitting on picnic blankets, enjoying our meal.

After Gilbert had assured her she could visit again, Lily had reluctantly gone home. He seemed to find her irritating but then he'd been the same with me when we first met. I kind of liked the idea that he would have another cat friend when we were back in London – after all, it wasn't going to be Chanel, was it?

Andrea had phoned to say thank you, that Chanel was

316

alright but needed to rest. As did we all after our ordeal, I thought, sneaking a look at George. Not that you would know it looking at him – he was nibbling happily on a piece of fish. But as I thought back over the day, I was glad that it ended happily. Chanel floating off out to sea had brought us all together, yet again, and my lad, who yes had probably caused it in the first place, had proven to me how brave and good he was. Toby had shown how amazingly forgiving he could be and what a lovely boy he was. As I watched him feeding George his chips, I couldn't help but think how similar those two really were. We were lucky to have them both.

'I can't believe that George went out to sea with you,' Claire mused.

'I think he's sorry for scratching me, he gave me lots of cuddles and it's not so bad.'

'He's a crazy cat, but you know who he reminds me of?' Matt said.

'Jonathan?' Polly asked.

'No, Alfie. It's the sort of mad thing Alfie would do after all. They really are like two peas in a pod.'

'My goodness they are. We now have two cats who seem far too human at times, or maybe three, after what Gilbert did to Liam,' Franceska said.

'Well how lucky are we then?' Claire finished.

I looked at my boy, he looked at me, and I raised my whiskers, blinking at him. He blinked back. We really were two peas in a pod, if that meant what I think it did. My boy, a chip off the old block. And despite the fact that he had worried me, I wouldn't have it any other way.

'So,' Tomasz said. He was holding a bottle of beer, munching his food and looking at the sky. The sun was almost burnt orange as we watched it slowly disappear, as if it was sinking into the sea. It was one of the most breathtaking sights I had ever seen. 'Do you still want to leave here, this house, and go home?'

'No way!' Toby said. 'Please can we always come on holiday to Seabreeze Cottage?'

'Yes, I have to get better than Aleksy at paddleboarding,' Tommy agreed.

'At least you are both better than Jonathan,' Claire said, laughing but giving him an affectionate kiss on the cheek.

'Well maybe next time I'll get some lessons. I can't quite see how it can be so difficult when it looks so easy.' Jonathan scratched his head. 'I mean, it's just standing.'

'I find it easy,' George whispered to me. I nuzzled him, my infuriating, but wonderful boy.

'It's my best ever place in the whole world,' Summer said.

'Mine too,' Martha agreed. 'Well apart from the other places which are my best ever,' she added.

'And we have so many friends here, don't we?' Henry asked. 'Even the girls are our friends now.'

'We certainly do, love,' Polly said.

'I propose a toast,' Claire said, raising her glass. Everyone raised their glasses, or beakers in the case of the children. 'To Great Aunt Claire and to Seabreeze Cottage. We are going to have many years of happy holidays here, I just know it.'

'Meow!' I agreed. We certainly would.

Chapter Twenty-Two

Andrea invited us to her house for a farewell tea. We all went except for Gilbert, who cried off. He had accepted our families but he wasn't interested in the neighbours, and I didn't want to push him. I also had a sneaking suspicion he was going to see Lily. He pretended he wasn't interested in making friends, but I wasn't sure I believed him. I think he had a bit of a soft spot for her after all.

While George was sad to be leaving, he was very excited about tonight. It was his last chance to spend time with Chanel, and he was determined to make an impression. I dreaded to think what that might involve. However, I was going to be there and I wasn't going to take my eye off him, so there would be no repeat of the other day.

We all made our way next door. The children were excited, the adults far more relaxed and even I felt jubilant. The cottage was coming on a treat and the adults had decided that as they'd forgiven Andrea it was only fair they forgave Liam too, so he was back working and he was doing an amazing job now he wasn't trying to burn the place down.

Both the children's and adults' floor, as well as the en suite and main bathroom, were now complete. The builders had started work on the small living room which the adults thought would be a 'snug' for them, a sort of cosy TV room with a wood-burner and two nice sofas in, it would be a child-free space apparently although I doubted it would be cat-free. The main living room would be done after we left and would open onto the lawn and serve as a big family room. There would be a large TV in there, cleverly hidden in a cupboard, along with a DVD player and another fire. I wasn't keen on the idea of fires at first, what with Andrea's aborted plan, but then I realised they would be lovely and welcoming and cosy. The kitchen was also being refurbished after we'd left. They were going to knock through from the small dining room at the front, which we never used, to make a huge kitchen/diner, which would fit us all comfortably when we were here together. Seabreeze Cottage was soon going to finish its transformation into our family second home, a home big enough for my family – which was all of us.

'Welcome,' Andrea said. She was wearing her trademark posh-looking dress and heels, but the girls were wearing shorts and T-shirts. Summer and Martha ran up to them and begged them to play hairdressers. The boys shuffled around, until Andrea led them to a game called swing ball and let Aleksy organise a tournament.

There was a long table, which had flowers on it and looked very nice, set with plates and glasses, which the adults all sat at. For once, Andrea put Chanel down and as she sat in the shade by the house, George approached. I followed him. I needed to make sure this didn't end badly.

'When are you going?' Chanel asked. She flicked her tail angrily.

'Are you going to miss me?' George asked, raising his whiskers.

'Not at all. Look, I nearly ended up having to live at sea because of you.'

'Hey that's not fair,' I cut in. 'My kitten saved you.'

'After he followed me relentlessly and in the end after I kept asking him to leave me alone, and he wouldn't, I ran off. I hid on a boat to get away from him, and then I fell asleep and woke up in the middle of the water, so yes he may have helped save me but he also helped put me there in the first place.'

'But I was just playing with you.' George looked so innocent, and sweet.

'Chanel, George is young, and well yes he's much younger than you, but can't you see he just likes you?' I tried.

'I really do,' George added.

'Look, I'm sorry but I'm pretty much a house cat. I like my beautiful house, my beautiful owner and the children, I don't like anyone else.' She really was one mean cat.

'Don't you get lonely, and don't you want to play with us?' George asked.

'I certainly don't get lonely and I am not interested in playing with anyone,' she huffed.

'OK, fine, I get it, you don't want to be friends with us,' I cut in. 'But perhaps you could learn to be civil. After all, if our humans can all get on then the least we can do is to try too. And we will be here a lot after all, so we may as well get along.'

'OK, but now I shall go and sit on Andrea's lap. Oh, and thanks for saving me, but in future I would appreciate it if you didn't stalk me.' She glared at George.

'Has anyone ever told you what lovely eyes you have?'

Chanel hopped onto the safety of Andrea's lap so I led George to the table. He headed off to see the children who were seated at their own table so I went to curl up at Claire's feet. I could hear the conversation from there and I could also keep an eye on George who was licking ice cream off Summer's spoon. I pretended not to see that one.

'So, when will you be back?' Andrea asked.

'I'm coming down in a few weeks to supervise the last of the decorating but I think I'll probably come on my own as it will be a lot of work,' Polly said.

'So, I'll be left looking after the kids,' Matt said.

'You'll have plenty of help,' Franceska said.

'Yes and the cottage really is spectacular thanks to Polly, it's really been a working holiday for you, hasn't it?' Claire said.

'I've loved every minute and it's for all of us. Andrea, I'm not sorry that you didn't get our cottage but I am sorry that you still have problems with where to live.'

'Thank you, Polly. I mean, I really don't know what I'm going to do. My husband is saying the house has to go on the market, my solicitor is trying to sort it out, but I'm a bit lost for what we can do, and I also don't really want to accept the settlement he's offered but again, I've been in such a mess I just can't think straight.'

'But this house is enormous,' Tomasz said.

'It is and I was wondering.' Polly sipped her wine. 'I know you can't stay in the house as it is, but have you thought about turning it into apartments which you can either sell or rent out? I mean, you could do it easily, although it might take time, and your husband will probably like the idea because you'd make money.'

Andrea looked at her, as if seeing her for the first time. 'I'm not sure,' she said, but she looked as if she was thinking about it.

'That way you get the ground-floor apartment – it'll be big enough for you and the girls – and you have two others. I know it'll be a come-down but you get to stay in the village and it won't be financially crippling. I guess if you present it to your husband as a business deal he won't be able to argue. Or if you get your lawyer to argue the financial sense of it at least.'

'Would it be easy to convert?'

'You'd be surprised at how easily, listen, let me look, maybe later, but think about it.'

'It's a great idea, Pol,' Jonathan said.

'Maybe it might work . . . Polly, please do have a look, I'm not sure how it would work, but I'm open to anything. I'm desperate still.'

'Of course, I'm sure we can sort something out,' Polly replied.

'Well thank you, I really don't deserve friends like you,' Andrea said.

'Maybe not, but you need friends like us,' Claire finished.

It was dark when we left Andrea's but George and I went straight to the sand room to find Gilbert. Summer was rapidly drawing to a close. The evenings were coming in more quickly and colder, as were the early mornings. It was still nice here, but as September dawned we could feel that summer was saying its final farewells, as were we. It was nearly time for us to go.

'Are you ready?' Gilbert asked.

'Yes, we are.' We followed him out of the house.

We sat on the top of one of the sand dunes watching the moon.

'I'll miss you two, and the humans,' Gilbert said.

'We'll be back before you know it, but this has been a wonderful summer.'

'The best summer ever,' George said. I hated to point out that it was really his first proper summer too.

'Are you sure you'll be OK here alone, I mean without us?' I asked.

'Of course. The builders are still going to be around, and that lovely lady Shelley is going to look in on me. And that tabby Lily, well she's alright as far as girl cats go.'

I looked at him with suspicion. 'Wow, Gilbert, you've gone from not needing any friends or family to having a lot,' I teased.

'It's your fault, Alfie. You made me get used to it. And also by the sounds of it your families will be here a lot, so I guess we'll see loads of each other.'

'You don't fancy London then?' I was being fanciful I knew but I quite liked having Gilbert as part of our gang.

'Nah, I'm a country and beach cat. I like this.' We all looked at the moon and agreed with him, after all what was not to like. 'And who will look after the scary sheep and watch Liam?' He sounded emotional, and I felt how far we had come from the gruff cat who hadn't even wanted to tell me his name.

I loved it here, I thought, as I breathed in the sea air. I loved how the sun twinkled on the water during the day, and the moon lit up the whole sea at night. It was so beautiful, like a light show. It had been a very eventful summer, but then what did I expect? After all, my life was eventful. But we had come through it again, stronger than ever, my kitten, my families and me. And we had added to it with Gilbert.

'We'll be back before you know it,' I said. I missed Edgar Road, I missed my friends and Tiger but I would look forward to coming back, very much.

'I can't wait to come back,' George said. He stared at the moon as if hypnotised by it.

'And in the meantime, I promise I'll look after Seabreeze Cottage for you, no actually for us.'

'For us,' I replied and I couldn't have felt prouder.

Epilogue

I was champing at the bit to get out of the cat carrier, as was George who kept standing on my paws.

'Stay still,' I hissed.

'But I want to get in the house,' George replied and I couldn't argue with that. We felt the carrier being put down on the lawn, and the door opened, George almost trampling me to get out, and I followed him.

'Wow, snow!' he said to me. There was a very thin blanket of snow covering the lawn. It looked so pretty and not deep enough to make us sink into it. We both stood and looked at the house. Seabreeze Cottage was sprinkled with white and on the front door was a huge holly wreath which covered almost the entire space. The others ran on ahead and we followed them.

Jonathan unlocked the door and Claire, holding Toby and Summer's hands, headed in. She flicked on a light and as Jonathan walked in behind her, we followed. I stood aside to let George go first. I was eager to explore but I was also the parent after all. Tinsel decorated the hallway, and in the doorway was a huge bunch of mistletoe. Jonathan grabbed Claire and kissed her under it. It was a bit sloppy.

We both ran into the kitchen, which had been extended and totally re-done; with wooden surfaces, and floors, it was a proper family kitchen. After quickly admiring it, we ran through to the sand room where Gilbert was in his new cat bed, as if he'd known when we would arrive.

'Alfie, George, hello,' he said. 'I heard Shelley saying you were coming today so I've been waiting for ages.'

'Gilbert!' George nuzzled him and I followed suit.

There were snowy footprints and little piles of snow all over the sand room, which Jonathan had already re-christened the snow room.

'How are you?' I asked. 'It feels like ages since we last saw you.'

'I'm alright, it's been quite cold here, but then that's winter for you. Not sure you'll be so keen to go to the beach during the day either, it's not only cold but full of dogs, not to mention snow! I've had to find other places to hang out.'

'And is Lily still around?' I asked.

'Yes.' I was sure that if cats could blush, Gilbert would have done. 'We're going to see her tomorrow, she's looking forward to seeing you again.' He was mumbling a bit. Well this was a turn-up!

'So, she's still OK for a girl cat?' George said, raising his whiskers. Honestly, nothing got past my lad, he had a good memory at least.

'She's not too bad,' Gilbert said, casually.

'And it's nice having friends, isn't it?' I pushed.

'Well, Alfie, I blame you for that. I was happy with my own company before I met you guys and now it seems I like being around people, and cats.'

I nuzzled him, I had taught him well.

★   ★   ★

We had come to the cottage for Christmas. We'd been back once since the summer, and that was for a holiday the humans called half-term. Claire, Polly and Franceska had come down with all the children and us, and the men had joined us at the weekend. It had been a great week away, and it had been then, with the cottage looking so beautiful, that they had come up with a plan for us all to spend Christmas here. Our first Christmas together.

'Claire,' I heard Jonathan say from the kitchen. We walked in.

'Yes, darling.'

'There's an enormous Christmas tree in the living room. Do you know anything about that?' he asked.

'Yes, I asked Colin to arrange it and Andrea decorated it. Quick, kids, let's go and see.' We all went through. The tree was bigger than any I'd ever seen and it was decorated beautifully. Claire reached down and turned some lights on, it sparkled and was truly magical. The living room was fully decorated with sprigs of holly, and garlands, and fairy lights hung everywhere. Andrea had clearly wanted to make it lovely for us and I felt warm towards her. The fire had been lit too. It was such a beautiful scene, I couldn't have been happier to be here.

When we'd seen Andrea at half-term she had been very sweet and fun too, as had her children. It was as if they had all had personality transplants. She'd said she realised she was better off without her husband and her and the girls were doing really well. She'd also said she might start dating again, I just hoped not with Liam. But it was true what everyone said: before the divorce she had been nice, as had the girls, they had just been horrible when they were unhappy. I understood, I'd seen it before.

'Wow,' Toby said. 'It's the best tree I've ever seen.'

'Can I climb it, Dad?' George asked, out of earshot.

'Absolutely not,' I replied.

'But will Santa know to find us here?' Summer asked, sounding anxious.

'Yes, we've given him full instructions and when everyone else arrives I expect there will be lots of presents going under this tree,' Jonathan said, picking his daughter up.

'But Henry and me asked for the same robot this year, what if Santa only has one?' Toby chewed his lip. He had come such a long way, he was far more secure and confident, but there would always be something that made me, and George, want to protect this little boy. The vulnerable edge that could never be fully eradicated, no matter how much we loved him, but we would never stop trying.

'Oh, Santa can always get more than one, Tobe,' Claire said. 'Don't you worry.'

I saw Jonathan look at her and she nodded, he smiled. I had learnt that Santa was really Claire and Jonathan but I wasn't telling. George and the kids still believed in him and that was all that mattered.

While we were getting reacquainted with the festive cottage, Polly, Matt and the children arrived, Franceska and Tomasz, Aleksy and Tommy following soon after.

We were all together, just as it should be.

'So, our first fish and chips of the holiday,' Matt said as he and Jonathan returned from the chip shop with bags full of dinner. For all of us. George, Gilbert and I licked our lips and waited by our food bowls. We weren't disappointed.

The children dug in, as did the adults. The women had wine and the men beer. It felt as if there was a celebration going on, and I guess there was: our first night back at our holiday home.

'I have some news,' Tomasz said, suddenly.

'Oh no, nothing bad,' Claire shot, looking worried.

'No, no, all good.' He looked around the table. Then he took Franceska's hand. 'We went off to the town when we came here for the weekend, and we saw a restaurant.'

'A restaurant? Here?' Polly asked.

'Well, you know our three in London are doing well now, and I thought why not try one down here? We all love it, we spend time here and it will give me an excuse to spend more time here! So we are opening in the new year. What do you think?'

'Yay, Dad, that's amazing,' Aleksy said.

'Can we live here all the time?' Tommy asked.

'No, not quite, boys, but we can spend time here, and Polly, we were wondering if you'd design it?'

'I would love to.'

'You know, when I thought we might lose this place, when the restaurant flooded and then there was all that business with Andrea, it hit us how much it means to us. I get it, Claire, how much you love it here and now we do too,' Franceska said, and they all drank a toast.

'Shall we go to the beach?' Gilbert said when the adults were putting the children to bed. George was with us, because although he still slept with Toby he had started going to bed a little later. He was growing up, my boy. And although we were both sad not to be seeing Tiger on Christmas Day this year, we'd had a little family get-together before we left. It had been lovely; although it had been a cold day we had gone to the park, played with very cold leaves, and spent quality time together – that was what Jonathan often said, and I think it meant good times with those you loved. But Tiger understood that we needed to be with our families the way she had to be with hers so it was alright. George and I still loved her very much, she knew that, and that was all that mattered.

'It's freezing,' I replied. I thought of the fire Jonathan was lighting in the snug and how I would very much like to be in front of it.

'Please, Dad, just for a bit, it's a tradition.' George had still got a crush on Chanel but in half-term week he had become a little more in love with the beach than her, and I encouraged that. When the dogs weren't around, of course.

'OK,' I said. 'But not too long. I don't want us to get too cold.'

We went out the back and round to the front of the house. I imagined our families all snuggled up by the fire in the living room. This was a second home for us all.

We jumped on the wall. I struggled slightly, my leg was always a bit stiffer in the cold, but Gilbert helped me and thankfully George didn't notice. The sand was cold, icy and with a thin layer of snow under paw as we made our way to the top of the sand dune. The spiky grass glistened white in the moonlight, and as I sat down my bottom immediately felt cold.

'It's my favourite moon!' George squealed excitedly at the crescent-shaped moon that faced us. I liked it too, it reminded me of one of Summer's story books which pictured a man sitting on a crescent moon. Replace him with a cat and it would be perfect.

'Well I am so glad to see you and I can't wait for this Christmas,' Gilbert said. 'I mean,' he looked a bit embarrassed, his enthusiasm still confused him sometimes, 'what you've told me about the food and stuff.' Poor Gilbert had never had Christmas dinner before, so we were all excited for him. He would be overjoyed when he tried turkey, I just knew he would.

'This is going to be the best Christmas ever!' George exclaimed. I tickled him with my whiskers.

'You said that last year,' I pointed out, smiling indulgently.

'Yes, Dad and it was. This is what I have learnt about life.' He sounded so serious that Gilbert and I turned to face him. 'And I have mainly learnt it from you, and that is that every year will be the best Christmas ever if we are lucky, because that's how life works when you have people, and cats, in it that you love. It just gets better and better and better.'

I thought my heart would burst with joy, but it didn't, because it seemed, like life, it had the capacity to get better and better too.

Japan: a cat lover's heaven

I was lucky enough to go to Japan in July this year. It's a country I have always wanted to explore; the culture, history and the food fascinate me, so it was a dream come true. **The Ultimate Travel Company** – www.theultimatetravelcompany.co.uk – organised a bespoke trip.

And it was, naturally, all about the cats.

Japan is a cat lover's paradise. I could write a book about it – but I'll just share the highlights! I stayed in a cat-themed room, visited a cat temple, met the cat who works as a station master, travelled on a cat-themed train, visited the world's first cat cafe, shopped in shops dedicated to all things cat, ate at a *Hello Kitty* restaurant and visited one of Japan's cat islands.

In Tokyo, I stayed in the Park Hotel, which has a floor of local artist-themed rooms. Of course, I was in the *Lucky Cat* room . . . It was beautiful waking up to cats on the walls and ceiling every morning!

I also visited a Buddhist temple which claims the origin of **maneki-neko**, The Beckoning Cat – also known as the lucky waving cat, a true Japanese icon. The **GotoKuji Temple** just outside of Tokyo is not only beautiful but people flock there to pray for prosperity and you can buy a maneki-neko, pray holding it, and leave it in a shrine at the temple as a way of giving thanks. The legend of The Beckoning Cat dates back to the Edo period, when a feudal lord passed a poor Buddhist temple as he arrived in Edo (now Tokyo) and saw a cat beckoning him in. He went inside just as a huge storm broke. Although the monk and his faithful cat had very little they shared what food and shelter they had with the lord, who, once the storm had passed, raised funds to rebuild the temple, which became his family temple and prospered greatly. Today, people gather there to pray for the sort of prosperity that the cat brought to the temple in the first place.

Te GotoKuji temple is so beautiful and peaceful, and I love that the beckoning cat is symbolic of good fortune. You will see him everywhere in Japan in various guises, but especially outside restaurants and shops where they 'beckon' the customers in.

In Osaka, a Japanese city known as the food capital of Japan, and a bullet train ride away from Tokyo, I visited the world's first ever cat cafe, **Neko no Jikan**. The owner of this cafe opened it because of his love of cats and he breeds them. Cat cafes can now be found everywhere and have been joined by owl cafes, which are also becoming popular in Japan. I stayed in the Ritz Carlton in Osaka, and it was a gorgeous hotel; a very interesting mix of English grandeur and Japanese culture. The perfect place to relax and be pampered in after a hard day of cat-spotting.

Osaka castle, a magnificent building of historical importance in the city, is set in one of the most beautiful parks I have ever seen. There cats congregate, and a local group take it in turns to feed them, ensuring they are all healthy and well-fed. Seeing cats strolling around becomes the norm but when one of the volunteers appear, they all rush over to be fed!

There are shrines and temples aplenty in Japan, either Buddhist or Shinto, and you often find cats wandering around or sleeping there. I was worried about this as the cats are stray, but I learnt that Japanese people who can't care for their cats take them to temples and shrines (the way we would a cat shelter) as they know they will be looked after. A logic which leaves me with very mixed feelings – yes, they are looked after, but they are still strays. However, anywhere there are stray cats, there also exists a well organised group of Japanese cat lovers who watch over them, making sure they are well cared for. I also noticed that, as in Alfie, some of the cats seem to spend time together, as if in a friendly gang.

In Kyoto, an hour's train ride from Osaka, the **Fushimi Shrine** is home to many such cats; they won't show themselves when the tourists are too plentiful, but find a quiet time and a diverse range of cats will appear. This is also the case in **Enoshima**, which is known as one of Japan's cat islands, due to the number of cats you'll find there. Just over an hour from Tokyo, the **Enoshima-jinja shrine** is also home to many cats, and, also in Enoshima, you will see cats roaming the beach.

One of my final, favourite cat trips was to Kishi station (also a short ride from Osaka via Wakayama), where you get to meet **Nitama**, the cat station master. He is the second generation of cat station masters – he even has a uniform and also an apprentice who 'works' on different days. One of the most charming things about this trip is the cat-themed train you can ride on to visit him.

Cats aside, Japan is a real bucket list destination. The history, the culture, the people and the food make it an experience that you will never forget. On leaving, my thoughts were of how much I would like to return. And also where I was going to put the suitcase full of cat memorabilia that I managed to bring back with me!

For any further information contact The Ultimate Travel Company: www.theultimatetravelcompany.co.uk
020 7386 4646

They were a family in crisis.
He was a friend for life.

Read the follow-up to the smash-hit bestseller,
Alfie the Doorstep Cat.

One ordinary neighbourhood.
One extraordinary cat.

Read the *Sunday Times* bestseller and find out how it all started. The tale of one little grey cat and his journey to become a Doorstep Cat.